D0259296

No Saints
or Angels

Also by Ivan Klíma

A Ship Named Hope
My Merry Mornings
My First Loves
A Summer Affair
Love and Garbage
Judge on Trial
My Golden Trades
The Spirit of Prague
Waiting for the Dark, Waiting for the Light
The Ultimate Intimacy
Lovers for a Day

NO SAINTS
OR ANGELS

Ivan Klíma

Translated by
Gerald Turner

Granta Books
London

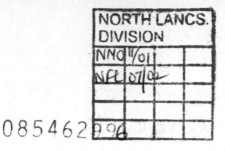
Granta Publications, 2/3 Hanover Yard, London N1 8BE

First published in Great Britain by Granta Books 2001
Published in the Czech Republic as *Ani svatí, ani andělé*
Published in the United States by Grove Atlantic, 2001

We would like to thank the Arts Council of England
for their support and assistance in this book.

Funded by:
THE
ARTS
COUNCIL
OF ENGLAND

A CIP catalogue record for this book is available from the British Library.

1 3 5 7 9 10 8 6 4 2

ISBN 1 86207 448 8

Typeset by M Rules
Printed and bound in Great Britain by
Mackays of Chatham plc

CHAPTER ONE

1

I killed my husband last night. I used a dental drill to bore a hole in his skull. I waited to see if a dove would fly out but out came a big black crow instead.

I woke up tired, or more exactly without any appetite for life. My will to live diminishes as I get older. Did I ever have a great lust for life? I'm not sure, but I certainly used to have more energy. And expectations too. And you live so long as you have something to expect.

It's Saturday. I have time to dream and grieve.

I crawl off my lonely divan. Jana and I carried its twin down to the cellar ages ago. The cellar is still full of junk belonging to my ex-husband, Karel: bright red skis, a bag of worn-out tennis balls, and a bundle of old school textbooks. I should have thrown it all out long ago, but I couldn't bring myself to. I stood a rubber plant where the other divan used to be. You can't hug a rubber plant and it won't caress you, but it won't two-time you either.

It's half past seven. I ought to spend a bit of time with my teenage daughter. She needs me. Then I must dash off to my Mum's. I promised to help her sort out Dad's things. The things don't matter, but she's all on her own and spends her time fretting. She needs to talk about Dad but has no one to talk about him with. You'd think he was a saint, the way she talks about him, but from what I remember, he only ordered her around or ignored her.

1

As my friend Lucie says, you even miss tyranny once you're used to it. And that doesn't only apply to private life.

I don't miss tyranny. I killed my ex-husband with a dental drill last night even though I feel no hatred towards him. I'm sorry for him more than anything else. He's lonelier than I am and his body is riddled with a fatal disease. But then, aren't we all being gnawed at inside? Life is sad apart from the odd moments when love turns up.

I always used to ask why I was alive. Mum and Dad would never give me a straight answer. I expect they didn't know themselves. But who does?

You have to live once you've been born. No, that's not true. You can take your life any time, like my grandfather Antonín, or my Aunt Venda, or Virginia Woolf or Marilyn Monroe. Marilyn didn't kill herself, though; they only said she did in order to cover the tracks of her killer. She apparently took fifty pills of some barbiturate or other even though a quarter of that amount would have been enough. Her murderers were thorough. I myself carry a tube of painkillers; not to kill myself with though, but in case I get a migraine. I'd be capable of taking my life, except that I hate corpses. It was always an awful strain for me in the autopsy room, and I preferred not to eat the day before.

Why should I make the people I love deal with my corpse?

They'll have to one day anyway. Who will it be? Janinka, most likely, poor thing.

I oughtn't to call her Janinka, she doesn't like it. It sounds too childish to her ears. I called my ex-husband Kajínek when I visited him recently on the oncology ward. I thought it might be a comfort to him in his pain to hear the name I used to call him years ago. But he objected, saying it was the name of a hired killer who recently got a life sentence.

We've all got life sentences, I didn't say to him.

I can feel my early-morning depression taking hold of me. I had one glass of wine too many yesterday. I won't try to count the cigarettes. Lucie maintains I don't have depressions – I'm just 'moody'.

Lucie and I got to know each other at medical school, but whereas I passed anatomy at the second attempt, she never mastered it. She dropped out and took up photography and was soon better off than those of us who stayed the course. She and I always hit it off together, most likely because we differ in almost every conceivable way. She's a tiny little thing and her legs are so thin you'd think they'd snap in a breeze. I've never known her to be sad.

What do photographers know about depression? Mind you, she advises me quite rightly to give up smoking and restrict myself to three small glasses of wine a day, though she drinks as much as she likes. I'll give everything up the day I reach fifty. It's awful to think that I'm less than five years away from that fateful day, that dreadful age. That's if I'll still be alive in four years and eleven months' time. Or tomorrow for that matter.

The best cure for depression is activity. At the surgery I have no time to be depressed. I have no time to think about myself. But today's Saturday: an open day for dreams and grief.

I peek into Jana's room and see she is peacefully asleep. Last year she still had long hair, longer than mine, and mine reaches a third of the way down my back. Now she's had it cut short and looks almost like a boy. The stud in her ear twinkles, but on the pillow alongside her head lies a rag doll by the name of Bimba that she's had since she was seven and always carries around with her. After she'd wriggled out of her jeans last night she left them lying on the floor, and her denim jacket lies in a crumpled heap on the armchair, one sleeve inside out. She hangs out with punks of both sexes because she says they don't give a damn about property or careers. The last time we went to the theatre she insisted we take the tram. She wants to do her own thing, but what does it mean to do your own thing in a world of billions of people? In the end you always end up getting attached to something or someone.

There's an open book on the chair by her bed. It's not long since she read fairy stories and she loved to hear all about foreign countries, animals and the stars. She was lovely to talk to. She always seemed to me wise for her age and to have a particular understanding of other people. She'd generally sense when I was feeling sad and why, and do her best to comfort me. Now I get the feeling she hardly notices me or simply regards me as someone who feeds and minds her. I tell myself it's because of her age, but I'm frightened for her all the same. We were watching a TV programme about drugs and I asked her whether she'd been approached by pushers on the street. 'Of course,' she answered, almost in amazement. Naturally she had told them to get lost. I told her that if I ever found out she was taking anything of the sort I'd kill her. 'Of course, Mum, and you'd feed me to the vultures!' We both laughed, although the laughter stuck in my throat.

I close her door and go into the bathroom.

For a moment I look at myself in the hostile mirror. No, the mirror's not hostile, it's dispassionately objective; it's time that's hostile.

My former and so far only husband once tried to explain to me that time is as old as the universe. I told him I didn't understand. Time couldn't be old, could it? For one thing it was a masculine word.

Time was feminine in German and Latin, and neuter in English, he told me. He was simply trying to explain that time began along with the universe. It hadn't existed before. There had been nothing at all, not even time.

I told him how awfully clever and learned he was, instead of telling him he should get a sense of humour.

I couldn't care less what happened billions of years ago and whether time began or not. I only care about my lifetime, and so far time has taken love away and given me wrinkles. It lies in wait for me on every corner. It rushes ahead and heeds none of my pleas.

It heeds no one's pleas. Time alone is fair and just.

Justice is often cruel.

Still, time has been fairly good to me. So far. My hair is not quite as thick as when I was twenty, and I have to use chemicals to stop the world seeing that I'm going grey. My golden locks – one time I wove them in a braid that reached below my waist. But I still carry myself as well as I did then. My breasts have sagged a bit but they're still large. Not that there is much point in humping them around with me any more – apart from men's enjoyment. Selfish bastards. But nothing will save me from time. They say that injections of subcutaneous fat can get rid of wrinkles round the mouth, but I don't like the idea of it. I don't have too many wrinkles yet. Just around the eyes. My former husband used to call them sky blue, but what colour is the sky? The sky is changeable and its colour depends on the place, the wind and the time of day, whereas my eyes are permanently blue, morning and night, happy or sad.

When I step out of the shower I'm shivering all over and it's not from cold. Even though it is already April, I still have the heating on in the flat. I am shivering from loneliness – what shakes me is the weeping I conceal, weeping over another day when time will simply drain away, a river without water, just a dried riverbed full of sharp stones – and I'm barefoot and naked, my dressing gown lies on the floor and no one looks at my breasts. Abandoned and uncaressed, milk will never flow from them again.

From the bedroom behind me comes a roar of what is now regarded as music and what my little girl idolizes: Nirvana or Alice in Chains or Screaming Trees, heavy metal, hard rock, grunge, I can't keep track of it any more. The time when music like that excited me is past. It's true that when the chair in the surgery happens to fall vacant, Eva dispels the quiet by tuning into some radio station, but I don't notice it. My assistant is scared of silence, like almost everyone these days. But I like peace and quiet, I yearn for a moment of silence within myself, the sort of silence in which I might hear the rush of my own blood, hear the tears roll down my cheeks, and hear the flames when they suddenly come close.

But that sort of silence is to be found only in the depths of the grave, such as in the wall of the village cemetery on the edge of Rožmitál where they buried Jan Jakub Ryba. He cut his throat when he could no longer support his seven children. His poor wife! But in that sort of silence you don't hear anything because the blood and tears have stopped and Master Ryba was never to hear again from the nearby church the words of his folkish Christmas Mass: 'Master, hey! Rise I say! Look out at the sky – splendour shines on high . . .'

For me blood, unlike tears, means life, and when I bleed from a wound in my gum I try to stop it as quickly as possible.

2

I've given my daughter her breakfast and I've reminded her she has homework to do. I'm dashing out to see Mum. Jana wants to know when I'll be home, and when I tell her I'll be back around noon, she seems happy enough.

The street is chock-a-block with cars on weekdays but it's not so hard to cross on a Saturday morning. And there's not such a stench in the air. I actually think I can smell the elderflower from the garden in front of the house.

The houses in our street are sexless, having been built at the end of the thirties. They lack any particular style. It was the time when they started building these rabbit hutches, except that in those days they were built of bricks instead of precast concrete, and most of them had five or six floors instead of thirteen. Mum used to tell me how in summer before the war people would take chairs out in front of the house and sit and chat. In those days this was the city limits and people had more time to talk. Little did they suspect that one day normal human conversation would be replaced by TV chat shows.

They weren't afraid of each other yet, I didn't tell Mum. During the war they were afraid to speak their minds because it could cost them their lives. But Mum knows that all too well from her own experience. People were afraid during the Communist years too, although Mum wasn't affected so much, thanks to Dad. What happens to people who spend their lives afraid to voice their opinions? They stop thinking, most likely. Or they get used to empty talk.

During the war Mum's life was at risk, even though she was only a little girl. Her mother – Grandma Irena, whom Mum never talked about much – was murdered in a gas chamber by the Germans. So were Grandma's parents, her brothers and sisters and her nieces. Mum didn't tell me about it until I was almost an adult. All I knew before then was that Grandma died in the war. And it was a long time before Mum told me she was Jewish. Mum wasn't sent to the camps but spent the war with her father. Even so, throughout the war she had a little suitcase packed ready with essential things just in case, as one never knew. 'They only gave my mother an hour to pack her things,' she told me.

Mum's father, Grandpa Antonín, had a furniture shop. To avoid being Aryanized, my grandfather made a show of divorcing my grandmother as soon as the Germans invaded. He saved the business – though not for long, because the Communists took it away from him. But by then it was too late to save his wife.

Mum never forgave him that trade-off and left home as soon as she was eighteen. Two years later she got married. She deliberately married a Communist, who wasn't a Jew or a Christian but believed religion was the opium of the people.

Grandpa Antonín also never forgave himself that divorce. When the Communists ordered him to leave the shop they had confiscated from him, he saw no reason to go on living. He went to the storeroom, sat down in a brand-new Thonet armchair and shot himself. But that was long before I was born.

Mum lives not far away and I can walk to her place through streets of villas. On the way I pass the villa where my favourite writer, Karel Čapek, used to live. He was a good man and a wizard with words. I stop by the fence as if hoping that his free spirit might somehow still be hovering here so many years after his death. No sign of a spirit hovering but the trees have grown up here. They must have grown since he died because they were no longer young when I first saw them. When I was born that green-fingered writer was already fifteen years dead. *My darling*, he wrote to the only real love of his life, *please learn to be happy, for God's sake. That's all I wish for you, and apart from your love you can't give me anything more beautiful than your happiness.*

That's something Karel would never have written to me, even though he claimed to love me, in the days when perhaps he really did still love me.

Why do good people die so young, while scoundrels manage to keep going for years?

Good people suffer more because they take the sufferings of others to heart. I don't know if I'm a good person, but I've had more than my share of suffering.

I wend my way through the narrow streets until I reach the street that's been known as Ruská for as long as I remember. The name has survived all regimes, unlike many other street names. Here, in a two-bedroomed flat, in an apartment house with a miniature garden in the front and one only slightly bigger at the back, I came into the world. On the other side of the street there are villas, and between them and the street there is a strip of grass with two rows of lime trees. In those days the treetops were full of the chatter of wagtails and the song of flycatchers, warblers and finches – which was drowned from time to time by the insistent blare of a siren as an ambulance sped past on its way to the nearby hospital. There is only cheap furniture in the flat, the sort made since the war, but at least it's real wood. There are no pictures on the walls. Dad used to have a coloured portrait of Lenin above the table, and Mum had a framed tinted photograph of her mother from the period when Grandma Irena was a student. In that picture Grandma apparently resembles her famous contemporary Mary Pickford, with her pronounced chin and nose. Her hair in the photo is strawberry blonde. I have never asked my mother whether my grandmother really had auburn hair, but I hope so, as I like redheads.

Mum's hair has already lost its red colour. It used to be strawberry blonde like mine, but now it has turned white. She still wears black even though it's six weeks since Dad died. Grieving should last at least a year — that's something I remember from psychology lectures. Do I feel grief? No, no more than usual. It's as if Dad didn't belong to me, as if he were part of another world. No, it was the same world, but a different time. Parents tend to live in a different time — some of them, at least. But there's no reason why they should; after all, what are twenty or thirty years? That's what my one and only husband would say. Just an insignificant moment compared to cosmic time.

'What am I going to do with all those things?' Mum laments. She opens a wardrobe stuffed with old clothes that stink of mothballs and I discover to my horror that the vile grey uniform of the People's Militia is still hanging there. He didn't even throw that away. As if he wanted the shame to survive him. *Es war, als sollte die Scham ihn überleben.* That was written by an author Dad never read. I used to read him because he was virtually banned and because he tended to be sad and lonely too. And he was scared of his father and the future. Maybe he was also scared because he was a Jew like my Grandma Irena, who died horribly in the gas chamber ten years before I was born. He would have ended up there too if he hadn't died so young. I wonder whether Grandma was scared of the future too. Was she able to imagine it? Could anyone imagine it, in fact?

'Do you think you could make use of any of it?'

'But, Mum, there's no man living at our place.'

9

'I know, but maybe you could get it altered.'

'Yes, that one in particular,' I say pointing at the uniform.

'That's all you ever see. Dad was already that way inclined. He didn't alter overnight like a lot of others . . . He had that made for our wedding,' she says indicating a black suit whose origins I've heard about a hundred times already.

'I know.'

'It's one hundred per cent wool. Wool was very hard to come by in those days.' Mum sorts through the suits and frets. She can't just throw them out, can she? But she doesn't know anyone who might need them. I sense behind it a reproach that I'm on my own. If only I'd managed to hold on to my man as she had, right up to the last, even if it meant being made a slave, then I could bring him home a caseload of old, worn-out, useless rags.

I tell her I'll help her sort the clothes and what is reusable I'll take to a charity shop or to a homeless shelter.

'And what about the uniform?' she asks. 'Do you think a museum might take it?'

'They're bound to have wagonloads of uniforms like it. And just one would be enough for posterity.' I imagine the display case: 'Uniform of the People's Militia, mailed fist of the working class. Donated from the bequest of Alois Horák.'

'So what shall we do with it?' Mum asks.

'Cut it up for rags. You should have done it long ago.'

I happened to be born at a moment when Alois Horák and others of his ilk had been put on alert. Naturally – it was the day God's little messenger finally rid the world of the Soviet tyrant. Mum told me how, when they were carrying me screaming out of the labour ward, she looked out the window and was amazed to see a black flag slowly being raised on the flagpole. Dad first came to visit Mum three days later. He was wearing his uniform, and now and then he would start crying. He asked my mother as she showed him the baby, in other words me, 'What are we going to do now? How will we live?' His desperate question had nothing to do with how he'd live now he'd become a father, but how he'd live now the tyrant was dead and he was left an orphan. It was a slight against me and it was only my third day in this world about which I suspected nothing. He was a master at slighting others or making them feel guilty.

'Kristýna! He'd never get over it.'

'Oh, yes he would,' I say, but don't add that he's dead and gone and it's time she stopped deferring to him in slavish fashion. But Mum is only using him as an excuse: she'd never destroy anything while it could still be used. The war had left its mark on her. When she had to buy herself new clothes she always felt it as an offence against her relations who died. I didn't survive it to doll myself up! is something I heard her say on countless occasions, so I always felt guilty any time I indulged in something new.

'They wrote in the papers,' Mum says suddenly, as if she'd just recalled, 'that the skinheads had a rally and were shouting Sieg Heil. And the National Security just let them.' Mum still hasn't got used to the fact that we've had a normal police force for the past nine years – or at least we call them normal.

'Don't worry, nobody's going to resurrect Hitler.'

'It's not myself I'm worried about, but the two of you. Goodness knows what they're up to.'

I stroke her hair. 'Don't worry about us. The world has changed.' Just recently she's talked about feelings of anxiety she must have had since she was small. I never suspected it because she never let on. On the contrary, she was always full of life, and worries never got her down. For years she worked in the municipal housing office in charge of maintenance. It meant she came into contact with lots of workmen and from time to time she would take me along with her. And although I tended to be miserable among strangers I liked the way she was able to have a laugh and a chat with them. And at home, too, particularly when Dad was out at some meeting, which he was almost all the time, she used to laugh at things that would have most likely irritated my father.

She takes me over to a cupboard that is full of books. 'And what about these?'

'There's no need to get rid of the books, is there? The moths aren't going to harm them.'

'His books? I'm never going to read them, am I?'

Yes, of course: books by the Soviet luminaries, their covers as boringly grey as the language they were written in; a red star above the title, symbolizing the blood shed on their account.

'Oh yes, and there are all sorts of letters and things,' Mum remembers. 'I can't bring myself to sort them out. And there are some letters from you.'

I can't recall ever writing to Dad. But I expect I did. Maybe from Pioneer camp. 'They can stay here, can't they?'

'And loads of speeches and notes.'

Dad trained as a locksmith, but he didn't repair many locks in his life. He was in charge of political indoctrination and was also a paid official, so he had to give speeches. I never heard or read any of his speeches but I can well imagine them, having heard plenty of others. They were all the same. Cold grey tedium that nevertheless managed to arouse dread because the spectre of that bloody star hovered above it.

'I've wrapped up these things for you. I thought you might like to find out something about your dad. That he wasn't as awful as you imagine.'

'Mummy, what could I possibly find out? I knew him for forty-five years. Every year on my birthday he'd light a candle in memory of a murderer he never set eyes on. And he'd buy a white carnation to put in front of the bust of him that he had on his desk. He bought me flowers about three times in my life. And of course they had to be carnations because they were sort of comradely.'

'It's ages since he did anything like that.'

'Really?' I won't tell her that it was probably because he begrudged the money for the candle and the carnation. In recent years he didn't even send me a flower. In fact he didn't even visit on my birthday; he just telephoned to wish me lots of success. I don't know what he had in mind. Whether some dazzling career in dentistry, or a splendid marriage, or first place in the competition for the most beautiful elderly woman. Nothing, most likely. For him success was happiness. There was no love lost between us. There was a time when we used to argue, though we even stopped that. But we didn't start to like each other. Lack of affection for one's father would seem to run in our family. I wouldn't say he was never right. He tried to talk me out of marrying my first and last twice-divorced husband. 'He's a man without ideals,' he warned me.

Better none than yours, I thought.

I've now discovered that people without ideals are like machines. Machines for churning out words, making money and love, degrading others and exalting themselves, machines for supporting their own egos. Dad had ideals, I'll grant him that. Maybe he really did believe that with his Party in power nobody would go hungry and justice would be established in the world. It was such a blind belief that he couldn't see all the injustices being committed around him. He himself tried to lead an honourable and even abstemious life. He had just one suit for weekdays and the famous wedding suit. When it was cold he would wear the same old beret he'd had since I was a child. He was terse with Mum, but he never left her and I don't think he was ever unfaithful to her. I don't remember ever getting a hug from him, but from time to time he would tell me stories about wise Lenin or Young Pioneers who loved their parents and their homeland. Yes, they were the phrases he'd use, but at the time I was just happy that he sat down by me and spared me a bit of his time. It was only later, after the Soviets invaded and he welcomed them as saviours not occupiers, that I became antagonistic towards everything he praised or believed in.

Almost as soon as I got into medical school – partly due, no doubt, to my class background – I started to let my hair down and sit around in pubs, drinking, smoking and having a succession of boyfriends. I did it to spite Dad, even though he never knew the whole story, and I felt a sense of satisfaction at going my own way.

'You shouldn't talk about him that way, Kristýna,' my mother scolds me. 'He never meant anything badly. Stalin, or rather the Russians, saved his life. If they'd come a day later he'd have been dead.'

'Or so he'd have you believe.'

'No, that was the way it was. He showed me photos of him taken when he got back from the camp. He looked like a skeleton. A skeleton covered in skin.'

'But that didn't stop him helping set up concentration camps here.'

'Your father never set up any concentration camp.'

'Maybe not, but his Party did.'

'Your father fought the Germans,' she said. 'That's something you should respect him for at least, seeing you know what they did to my mother.'

It's inconsiderate of me to torment her with this sort of talk. Even in the days when I tried to spite Dad by my behaviour, she was the only one I hurt. Dad would only have noticed something that affected him personally, or his career.

I sit down by Mum and take her hand. 'You must stop thinking about him all the time.'

'Who am I supposed to think about, then?'

'You've got us, haven't you?'

Us is me and Lída, my songstress sister who lives down at Tábor and only visits Mum four times a year. Of course there's also Jana, her sweet little granddaughter, who has started to grow wild recently. She sang at her grandfather's funeral – not the 'Internationale', as he'd probably have wanted, but the spiritual 'Twelve Gates to the City'. And me – tired, worn-out and empty: a vase without flowers.

I take the box containing Dad's writings and give Mum a hug and a kiss.

The box is wrapped in Christmas paper and tied with a gold ribbon. It weighs at least ten pounds.

3

It's not yet midday and I'm home again. I rushed to be in time to cook my daughter's lunch, although at her age she could and should be making lunch for her mother.

From her small bedroom comes the sound of drumming. She has a set of two drums and practises on them to the distress of the neighbours. She also strums the guitar fairly well, plays the recorder and has a nice singing voice. Since she got into grammar school she has stopped going to Scouts, but instead she sings and plays in a band called Sons of the Devil. Not long ago she invited me to come and hear them play. They were performing at a disco in a pub outside Prague. The pub was horrible and what they played depressed and disgusted me by turns. She asked me afterwards how I liked it. I didn't tell her it was the sick music of lost souls. I just praised her faultless delivery.

Where are the days when she'd skateboard innocently round the paths of the little local park with a crowd of other kids, terrifying peaceful pensioners? They don't say good things about her at school. She failed her mid-year maths exam and just scraped through in chemistry. And yet she inherited a talent for those subjects and not so long ago she was coaching her classmates. But now she's lost interest. She says she wants to concentrate on music. And to her mind all a musician needs to know is music.

I ought to ban her strumming and drumming, and her slacking. But after all I had a yen to play the violin and my teacher said I had talent, and were it not for my lost violin, or rather for Dad and his pigheadedness, I might have had a different career, instead of standing by a dentist's chair eight hours a day.

I peep into her room. She is sitting in just a nightie on her unmade bed. Her jeans still lie in a heap on the floor amidst a pile of paper – sheet music most likely. The book that was lying on the chair this morning has since fallen to the floor and on top of it lies a half-eaten slice of bread; my daughter must have gone to the trouble of making a trip to the kitchen. 'Is that all you've been doing while I've been out?'

'So what? It's Saturday, Mum.' She seems to be in a great mood. She puts down the drumsticks and announces that she has a date with Katya and Marta in the afternoon.

'With those punks?'

She nods.

'Jana, I don't like the crowd you hang around with.'

'They're great friends.'

'Great in what way?'

She shrugs and says uncertainly, 'All ways.' She doesn't say how they spend their time convincing each other that it's right to scorn school, work and people who waste their time working, particularly parents. Their parents admittedly maintain them, but apart from that they're an obstacle to them living the way they'd like to.

She prefers to change the subject. 'Do you think lunch will be ready in time?'

'Are you in a big hurry?'

'I'd like to leave by two. Or rather, I have to.'

'And homework?'

'But Mum, it's Saturday.'

'Yes, you've told me already. When do you mean to be back?'

'But I haven't gone out yet!'

And I'd be happier if you didn't go out at all, I don't tell her. Because I'd sooner have you where I can see you. 'You ought to visit your dad.'

'Sure. I'll go and see him some time.'

'You shouldn't put it off. What are you making that face for?'

'I'm amazed that you of all people should care.'

'Dad's in a bad way.'

'Things were never in a good way with him, were they?'

'I'm talking about his health. You do realize he had a difficult operation?'

'OK, I'll look in on him tomorrow maybe. And I'll steal a rose from the park for him.'

I tell her irritably to save her witticisms for something else.

'Yeah, you're right. That was tasteless of me. I'll buy him a rose or maybe I won't buy him anything, but I'll definitely go round to see him tomorrow.' And she starts to strum the guitar.

That's what she's like these days. She sits there like the Queen of Sheba and hasn't lifted a finger since morning. On the other hand she has driven the neighbours crazy with her drumming, taken the rise out of her ill father and is now hassling me to get lunch ready. On account of this selfish creature I'm run off my feet from morning till night. 'Get yourself dressed straightaway! Then after you've tidied up here you can kindly scrape the potatoes.'

She puts on an obliging or even guilty face. 'For you anything, Mummy.'

I know it's just an act, this deference and cordiality. She's just playing the embodiment of filial love so I'll leave at last and stop disturbing her indolence. She deserves a good hiding; from time to time, at least. She needs a father to keep her in line. I won't slap her. I was never able to spank her even when she was small. Now it's too late: for her father, whose only concern these days is his illness, and for her: she'll soon be sixteen and no manner of beating would set her on the right track now.

'I'll come and see to the potatoes right away,' she calls after me.

4

M y little girl made tracks precisely at two. I ought to have kept
her here and insisted she did her homework before leaving.
Of course school isn't important. Let her fail, but at least let her
know why. Why she failed or more properly what she's living for.
But then which of us knows what we're living for? If I were sure
myself I'd try to guide her, though I suspect I wouldn't manage.

Not long ago she was a good, well-behaved little girl with a
pigtail. Slim, beautiful and obliging: even my father liked her.
Once, when she had only just learnt to walk, she offered to go for
a stroll with him; he walked through the park at her side like an
obedient dog. It had rained earlier and she led him round the pud-
dles and made sure he didn't get his paws muddy.

She made a terrible job of scraping the potatoes. Half of the
peel stayed on and she left the eyes in. I served them to her just as
they were. But she doesn't even notice such trivial details.

She promised to be back by midnight. I'll wait up for her and
insist she gives me a report on how she spent the rest of the day.

She flees a home of which there's only half left. And half can be
worse than none at all.

I've driven myself for the last six years to support her and have
tried to compensate for the missing half, to somehow make up for
the fact that I wasn't able to hold on to her father. But, even so,
she used to complain from time to time and ask me where he had
gone and why he didn't come home any more. She would drown
her sorrow in tears until it got into my bloodstream and when
those tears reached my hurt they burnt like salt in a wound. When
I'd consoled her and put her to bed, her lamentations would go on
growing inside me and I would weep late into the night. There
was no one to comfort me, no one to stroke me when sleep abandoned me to my suffering.

Only once did I try to start again with another man. Why
not? I wasn't forty yet and I was sure I could still escape from the

unfortunate experience of first marriage and tear myself away from the man I'd spent twelve years with. He had the same name as my first husband and I used to call him Charles the Second, which almost had a feudal ring to it. And he had a feudal look to him, a thickset fellow with a gingery beard. Emperor Barbarossa. He struck me as loving and lovable, and I thought he might have been capable of loving Jana too. My assistant Eva introduced him to me. He wasn't of totally sound mind, my emperor, being an epileptic, but as long as he observed a regime and took regular medication he managed to avoid attacks, and I was ready to take care of his routine. We already talked about the possibility of marriage. We booked a seaside holiday – a sort of pre-honeymoon. It was only to the cold Baltic Sea but I looked forward to the sea and being alone with him – I was planning to have Mum take care of Jana. Just before we were due to leave, Eva informed me ruefully that the guy was probably being unfaithful to me. We set out on the trip together but I returned alone.

I fetch myself a bottle of Moravian red and a glass, sit down in the armchair and light a cigarette. I happen to glance up at the ceiling. At the edge, above the wall between the living room and the kitchen, there has been a large dark stain for over a year already, since they had a burst pipe in the flat upstairs. I'll have to get a painter in but I keep putting it off. I have to do everything myself and I'm scarcely able to cope with what is already on my shoulders every day.

I ought to take a look at those writings of Dad's.

I cut through the ribbon and the Christmas wrapping and open the lid. It is full of neat bundles of old exercise books, some blue, some black, one pink, twelve of them in all, a few photographs and old, yellowing newspaper cuttings. The paper gives off a musty smell. I've never seen these exercise books before; he can't have had them at home. Perhaps he kept them in one of his desk drawers. But if he had them in his office, what could he have noted in them? He couldn't have been so naïve as to think that nobody would take a peek at them.

I rummage through the little heap of cuttings. *The victorious Red Army welcomed in Prague.* 10th May 1945. How old was he? Nineteen. *We salute Marshal Stalin.* At that time he was still stuck in a German concentration camp. He hadn't yet met Mum and had no inkling that eight years later she would bear him a daughter and insist on giving her the distinctly unrevolutionary name of Kristýna. *One thing is for sure. By now you probably won't find a Czech who isn't ready to pay back evil with evil or punish the guilty and innocent alike.* In those days Mum didn't yet know how her mother died. Apparently they were expecting her any day.

When, years later, she told me what really happened, I was unable to rid myself of the image of a tiled room with pipes from which came the hiss of gas. I could hear the people gasping. If Mum had been sent with her mother, like many children were, I'd never have been born. It also occurred to me that in a world where enormous shower rooms are built just to poison people, life can never be the same again.

I open one of the exercise books: Nineteen Hundred and Fifty Eight. The date is written in copperplate, but I don't feel like leafing through it. I put it back in the box.

The time ahead of me puffs up like a dead fish on the surface of a pond. If only I had someone to look forward to, someone who'd ring the doorbell or call me up and say, 'How are you, my little dove?'

'Little dove' was what Psycho, my first boyfriend, called me. How long ago was that? More than two blinks of God's eye.

Twelve years, that's just one blink of God's eye, said my first and only husband. It was when we were bargaining over my first and his third divorce. I had just burst into tears at the thought that he wanted to leave me after twelve years – or actually fourteen, as it took us two years getting round to the wedding – after all the time I had served him, looked up to him and lain alongside him night after night.

'You've started to believe in God?' I asked in amazement.

'No, it was just a figure of speech. What I mean is our time compared to cosmic time. But cosmic time doesn't have eyes.'

God, if he existed, wouldn't have eyes either, I didn't tell him.

It's only half past two. I run some water into a bucket and go to mop the kitchen, taking my glass with me.

When I come back into the living room I switch on the cassette player. The cassette inside is Tchaikovsky's Sixth but it's too mournful for two-thirty in the afternoon so I change it for his violin concerto.

I called him Psycho because he was training to be a psychiatrist. He was very handsome – dark and with what seemed to be a permanent tan. He wore his black hair tied back in a ponytail, which looked very exotic in those days. He used to carry drugs in his pockets and willingly share them with others. He offered me grass, magic mushrooms and mescaline, but I refused them. I was afraid of drugs. I didn't mind doing myself damage, but I didn't like the idea of losing self-awareness and not being myself.

The look in his eyes made me uneasy but it also excited me. It was strange – piercing and lustful; I could be wearing a fur coat and still feel naked beneath his gaze.

Then something happened that was to happen to me several more times. The first time I hesitated – I didn't want to kill my child, but the future psychiatrist didn't want to become a father. He regarded fatherhood as an obstacle to his career, as if a career could mean more than a life. He was willing to marry me but I mustn't become a mother. He made it a condition. He persuaded me to apply for an abortion. Afterwards I didn't want to see him again.

It's odd that I didn't leave my future husband even though the same thing happened with him. I wanted him so much I even put up with that from him, but for a long time afterwards it remained an open wound (not physical – but a mental wound), and it has never really healed over since.

Yehudi is a bit on the old side for me, he must have been eighty when he made this recording, but I was capable of loving old men too; my first and only husband came into the world almost two blinks of God's eye before I did, but he never learned to play even the mouth organ, whereas this English knight was playing Mendelssohn's concerto in San Francisco at the age of seven.

At first I hated the violin. It consumed the time I could be playing with my doll. The doll was quite ordinary (blue-eyed like me) and seemed to me fairly plump – this was before the leggy Barbies came into the world. The doll was my real sister – not the live one that everybody made a fuss of and was sorry for because she was weak, sickly and short-sighted. Anyway I always wanted a brother, not a sister.

From the age of seven I had to attend violin lessons three times a week, as well as practise at home. My teacher used to praise me and once told me that I was her best pupil. So I started to consider the possibility of becoming a violinist. For a while the idea of it enchanted me as I imagined myself in a concert hall like the ones I'd seen on television. I'd be dressed in a beautiful evening gown of dark blue velvet and playing Beethoven. I'd play so wonderfully that the conductor would bow to me and kiss my hand, while from doors hidden behind curtains they would bring me baskets of flowers.

I started to practise strenuously. Even though all I had was a mediocre violin, Dad still complained it was too expensive for my 'scraping'.

My playing came to a sorry end. I left my instrument at the post office where Mum had sent me with a letter. There was a queue at the counter so I had put my violin down on a ledge by the wall. The lady in front of me – I can still recall it almost forty years on – must have had about a hundred letters to post and I was terrified of being late for school. So when I'd finally handed mine in I just grabbed my school bag and dashed out; I didn't give a thought to my violin. I rushed back about a quarter of an hour later but my violin was already gone and I arrived at school late.

At school my teacher excused me when she heard what had happened to me, but Dad never forgave me, and Mum spoke up for me in vain. He didn't beat me and didn't even scold me particularly, but he was unmoved by my despair at the loss of the violin. I had committed an unforgivable offence: someone with ambitions to be a violinist doesn't leave his instrument at the post office or on the train and on his deathbed he asks for his violin to be brought to him so that he can caress it with his eyes at least. That was the explanation I received from the father who never once caressed me. I never received another violin, and I had no more lessons.

I could have bought myself a new violin ages ago, but what good would it be to me? I've forgotten everything I knew. These days I wield a dental drill instead of a bow, and it could be that I provide as much or more satisfaction with it when I save someone's tooth or rid them of a toothache – even if I don't garner applause. Instead of flowers they tend to bring me a bottle of booze, a home-made strudel or a banknote in an envelope. One of the nurses from the hospital brings me a set of hypodermic syringes and sometimes she actually brings an ampoule of morphine or Dolsin if she needs my services. I'm sure she steals it all at work. I always refuse them but she just leaves the packet on the table in the surgery and walks out.

Yehudi has finished caressing me. I've always yearned to live with a kind and sensitive man who would know how to caress me, listen to me, protect me and not betray me. The banal dreams of TV soap heroines.

I expect such men don't exist.

And if one did, what hope would I have of meeting him? And if I met him what hope that he'd love me?

I can still hear the music inside me: the main theme from the opening Allegro. I once read about Tchaikovsky somewhere that he tried to overcome all sadness by willpower. As if it were possible to drive the sadness from one's soul. My feeling is that he increasingly expressed the despair that he tried in vain to suppress. The *Pathétique* was simply his final cry. I have an affinity for Tchaikovsky. He loved his mother, although he lost her at an early age, and had little praise for his father. He was definitely a sensitive man, and kind too, but being a woman I wouldn't stand a chance with him. Of all the various stories about his sudden death, the one I find most convincing is that he took poison.

My assistant Eva and I call suicide self-extraction, though she herself would never consider such a thing. Pulling oneself out of life. Or casting oneself out?

I married a man who was neither sensitive nor kind. At first he used to caress me but he never listened to me or protected me. And in the end he betrayed me.

I might have suspected it, or ought to have. He betrayed me exactly the same way as he betrayed his first two wives. How many women he betrayed in total I don't know and don't care any more. But I ought to have given it a thought when I first got to know him.

When someone gets used to lying it's hard for them to learn to tell the truth. And someone who manages to desert another will find it easier the second time. It's sheer vanity to think that one has the power to transform one's partner and drive out all the demons from his soul. Why should he desert me, I used to say to myself, seeing that he is old and greying and I am young and beautiful?

Because it's in man's nature. *It seemed*, wrote Virginia Woolf, *that he ruled all, apart from the fog. And yet he raged.*

Unhappy Virginia considered that if a woman wanted to be equal to men she would have to go mad or kill herself. She did both. In her fits of madness she apparently used to hear the starlings chattering in Greek. She tried to kill herself by jumping out the window; she also swallowed a hundred veronal tablets, but she was always saved. In the end she had to turn to water for help. And yet she had a fairly easy life as well as, by all reports, a kind and loving husband. People who have never known soul-rending misery can have no understanding of her grief.

I sip wine and puff away at a cigarette. Maybe I'm still beautiful. Mr Holý, one of my patients, told me I have beautiful hands and said it was a shame they had to hold a drill.

I asked him what he'd have them hold.

'Me, preferably.' He's old, as old as my ex-husband when I first met him. Except that my husband didn't have a paunch; he was a sportsman. Thanks to skiing and tennis he had the physique of a Rodin statue. When he first held me in his arms I felt a thrill I'd never before felt from a mere embrace.

He managed to live with me for twelve years, during two of which he was unfaithful to me, as far as I discovered. Maybe he was unfaithful to me for longer than that but I didn't try to find out. I was always good at netting men, but not at holding on to them; it always seemed to me that I didn't deserve their love. I was never unfaithful to him. I wanted to live in truth. And I wanted our daughter to be able to live in love.

I know that men are like that: they need to conquer. And when they do, they lose interest. But maybe I could have done with a bit more humility. I wanted to live freely even though I was married. From time to time I would dig in my heels and refuse to serve in the manner expected of me. I refused to listen to orders or good advice; I didn't do any shopping or cooking and regaled my husband with sandwiches. I was no worse then he was. What right had he to demand that I take care of him on top of all my other activities? Why couldn't I spend the evening with someone without his supervision? He was incapable of understanding this or accepting it.

The woman he left me for was expected to look after him like a mother, but she ran away from him anyway. Since they discharged him from hospital, he sits in his living room waiting to see how his body will cope now that they've removed almost his entire stomach and he has no one to stroke him or make him a cup of tea.

When I shut my eyes I can see in front of me snow-covered trees, standing like angels with their hands linked above the path. Every year we would make a trip to the mountains. I felt good there. I could breathe freely and I felt it was a joy to be alive.

I was just slightly wary of skiing. He was much better at it than I was.

'Wait for me, don't leave me behind!'

'Life doesn't wait either,' he told me when we reached the bottom. He was well developed and had beautiful arms and legs, but sometimes he was terribly ordinary: a secondary-school teacher and tennis coach who would astound his students with his *bons mots* and graceful movements.

Bach wasn't ordinary. Nor was Tchaikovsky: he was just sad when he ordered swans to dance on the shore of a lake of human tears.

Finally the phone rings. I jump up from the armchair and almost knock over a chair. A familiar female voice introduces itself and complains about a sudden toothache.

'But I have no surgery today. Have you tried taking something for the pain?'

'I did. I took two in fact and my head was all muzzy but even so I didn't get a wink of sleep last night.'

It was my husband who first sent this woman to see me. He used to recommend me to his relatives, his colleagues and his acquaintances. Maybe to his mistresses too. He left but they stayed. People leave their partners but stay faithful to their dentists. 'You should have come yesterday.'

'I hoped it would go away on its own.'

'It never goes away on its own. You'll have to go to the emergency clinic.'

'But I don't know anyone there.'

'I can't help you here. All I've got is a pair of pliers and a hand drill.'

'And would it be possible at the surgery?'

I explain that I live on the other side of Prague from my surgery, but she begs me to have pity on her because at the clinic they'd extract the tooth.

It's four o'clock in the afternoon. It's hot outside. I glance at the bottle: I've drunk half of it already. I oughtn't to drive and I don't feel like dragging myself there by metro and tram. But if I stayed here I'd just sit and feel sorry for myself.

An hour later I had treated the Saturday patient. She offered to drive me home and buy me a drink, but I didn't feel like spending any more time in her company. I told her that one of my friends lived nearby and I fancied a bit of a walk. In fact no friends of mine live around here, but if I were to take a half-hour walk in the direction of Zlíchov I would arrive at the house where my former and thus far only husband lives and is possibly convalescing.

For years after the divorce I avoided him. If he wanted to see Jana he had to come for her. We would greet each other and I would tell him when he was to bring her home. There was nothing else I needed to tell him and nothing I needed to hear from him.

But now I've nearly forgotten my pain, and what remains of it looks as if it has been outweighed by the pain that gnaws his insides.

I decided to take the riverside path. The wall on the opposite bank has been sprayed with garish graffiti. In front of me a flock of ducks rises out of the undergrowth. Several rowing eights speed by out in the current, as well as a few double kayaks.

When we first got married we used to go canoeing, mostly on the River Lužnice, but also on the Dunajec in Slovakia. We played tennis and I occasionally managed to win a set, although never a match; but I fought bravely, as if I really wanted to win. I knew that for him that was something that counted. Winning against everyone, and everything. In some ways he resembled my father, and not just because his hair was grey.

My one and only – and last – husband revered the victor. He played the hard man, but he wasn't one, for all his muscles. He was plagued with anxiety. He feared his pupils because they could denounce him; he feared the school principal who could ruin his career; but most of all he feared death. A stomach upset, a sore throat or a mole on his arm and his first thought would be the onset of cancer. Whenever he'd ask me about such symptoms there was always a note of anxiety in his voice that he was unable to hide. He expected me to brush aside his fears and reassure him – which is exactly what I did: I'd prescribe him tablets, bring him food and tea to his bedside, help him into his pyjamas . . . And no sooner was he well again than he'd be out two-timing me; me and his little girl. I don't know which of us he hurt more, but I for one lost any shred of self-confidence that I had – that's if I had any in the first place.

I really shouldn't think about him. I wasted so much time waiting on him hand and foot, and now I am free of him I waste time remembering him and thinking about him.

The house where he lives was built around the time I was born. It has five storeys; Karel has an attic flat. I took the steps up to it several times when fetching Jana. I never entered the flat, but could see through the open door a wall covered in the diplomas and pathetic medals that he had won at various second-rate tennis tournaments. They had hung in our front hall when we were still living together. He gave me up but hung on to the medals.

I stop at the street corner. I am not sure whether I want to enter. There is a phone booth around the corner. It would be enough to phone him and ask him how he is getting on and whether he needs anything.

The last time I visited him in hospital there happened to be another visitor there. It was some young man: thin and pale and with a mane of reddish hair, but with dark eyes behind small spectacles. His teeth were very white, and his lower jaw jutted slightly. He had beautiful hands with slender fingers – I noticed them right away. My ex-husband introduced him to me as one of his former pupils. I remembered his name, since it's like my daughter's. He addressed me as 'doctor' and offered to leave straightaway in order not to disturb us, but I reassured him there was nothing to disturb. So we eventually left together, and as soon as we were out of the ward he asked me whether I thought things looked bad for his old teacher. I told him truthfully that the tumour was large and had been neglected, which is always bad.

'That's awful,' he said in alarm. 'I'm terribly sorry.' He went on to add that he remembered me from the odd occasions when I'd wait for my husband with our little girl. 'We all used to envy him,' he added, and I had the impression that there was a slight rush of blood to his pale cheeks.

I didn't ask him who they 'all' were, or why they envied my husband his wife, who at the time was playing second fiddle to some slut; instead I quickly took my leave.

Oddly enough what he told me stuck in my memory and I fondly recalled it that evening before I went to sleep. And I even remember his words now, almost three weeks later, and the thought occurs to me that the young man just might happen to be visiting him now.

It's hardly likely, though.

I walk to the telephone booth, but still hesitate. The crowlike soul that flew out of his head last night frightens me. At that moment I catch sight of him: the crow. He is walking, or rather shambling, along the opposite pavement. He stoops slightly and is thin, and even on this warm day is wrapped in an overcoat. The sportsman leans on a stick. But he is still walking. He has been for a lonely walk somewhere. How I cried when he left me. Now I could only cry for him, this abandoned soul.

I don't call out to him or run after him. I watch him shamble back to the house where he lives. What duty do I owe to a man I used to live with and who is unlikely to be among the living much longer?

He occupies my thoughts too much. Somewhere deep down in my soul there is a sense of guilt that cries out that I wasn't a good enough wife to him, which is why he left me, and also maybe why he neglected his illness – he had no one to care for him. I turn away and start walking to the tram stop.

5

I'll be thirty already at the end of November. I was a Prague Spring boy. In other words I was endowed with hope, or false hopes, more likely.

My mother was a primary-school teacher. She was thirty-five when I was born. She married late although she had known Dad since she was very young. But he was jailed before they could marry. Dad had been a Scout leader and wanted to remain one even after the Scouts were banned. Mum waited nine long years for him, for which I admired her. When he came back, Dad apparently told her she was the best woman in the world, but he didn't want children. He said there was no point in bringing new slaves into the world. And then came that brief period of hope that justice would be restored. All such hopes that justice will suddenly drop from heaven are mostly false, as I fairly soon discovered. But I was glad that twenty years later Dad lived to see the end of the regime that ruined his youth. Dad died seven years ago, when enthusiasm still reigned after that long-awaited and yet sudden end of Bolshevism.

In fact the end wasn't so sudden. I remember the second half of the 1980s; they were interesting times. The regime we detested was just about to pass away. It was no longer capable of arousing enough fear, particularly among us younger people. It wasn't able to jail all its opponents or drive them out of the country. It could no longer prevent our demonstrations, even though it sent its truncheon-wielders against us and used water cannon against people it seemed to regard as worse than fire. For my part I always managed to extricate myself from such situations and I was only arrested once. But even that was an experience for me. When you're standing there defenceless against the wall of a police station with your hands above your head and they're yelling at you and you know that they have you in their power, you start to think the worst. I have to admit that like all people who find themselves in such a situation for the first time, I was afraid. I was afraid even though I knew that – unlike the time when my dad was in prison – they didn't murder people any more and in most cases they didn't even send them to prison. I knew that I risked being kicked out of university, and at the interrogation they shamelessly hinted as much, but they didn't manage to intimidate me that way. I was increasingly losing interest in the study of history – or rather the 'Marxist' version of it we were taught, which tried to formulate some firmly quantifiable and pathetically simplified laws to cover all phenomena.

And the dean actually did summon me a few days later and voiced profound disappointment that I had besmirched the good name of the faculty by my indiscreet behaviour. I was afraid he was going to ask me whether I at least regretted behaving rashly, at which I would either remain silent or say I had done nothing rash, but the dean preferred to avoid any such confrontation and dismissed me, saying that the faculty senate would deal with my case.

I waited for another summons or even a verdict in writing, but nothing happened. The *patres minorum gentium* who had been imposed on us as professors couldn't make up their minds to chuck me out, and even the regime's most dyed-in-the-wool supporters knew that its time was up. I gave up my course anyway, but I did so of my own free will.

The demonstrations weren't what held my interest most at that time. I couldn't help feeling I was part of a play and everything had already been written by someone else. History has probably always looked like that. The soldiers move according to the generals' orders, the generals move according to the emperors' or other leaders' orders. And the latter move in accordance to some invisible forces, some *Weltgeist*.

In those days what interested me most were concerts of protest songs. Some of the protest singers had admittedly been forced to leave the country; but for every singer exiled, two appeared in his place. They used to come and perform for us from all over the republic and we in turn would travel to their concerts, every one of which seemed to me like a ceremony, a promise of future freedom.

It was also a time of debates. Sometimes we'd stay up all night in the hall of residence discussing everything we thought important: politics first, followed closely by sex, but also religion and the prospects of our civilization. These didn't seem very bright, although in our corner of the world news only reached us in mutilated form.

We were all agreed that communism was a perversion, but there was less consensus on other matters. In fact it worried me that we had no ideals. We were against communism, but not so much because it was criminal as because we wanted an easier life. Different food, a car and a villa with a swimming pool – or at least a country cabin with a vegetable patch. Except that when they asked me what I proposed instead, I didn't have much idea either. I'd just say something about freedom and a fully independent judiciary, or about how we'd miss the real point of life if we only set our eyes on material goals.

And then a revolution – or what was declared a revolution – descended from on high, and there was no more time for talk about ideals. In those days we'd go from factory to factory as representatives of the striking students and I even travelled as far as Ostrava to meet the coal miners. I went there in trepidation as I'd never been in that part of the world and from what I'd heard, I expected them to arrest us before we even left the station. Goodness knows where or how we'd end up.

We weren't arrested. The city was filthy and the air almost unbreathable, but the people seemed friendly and they listened to us with interest, even applauding our speeches and our promises which, as I later realized, had little in common with reality.

I don't know how those people are doing these days. Maybe they're worse off. Maybe they're sorry they didn't send us packing and instead march in ranks on rebellious Prague.

That was something else I grasped only later: that people almost always long for a change. As soon as the mood for change prevails, they are seized by enthusiasm and the ecstatic conviction that change will suddenly lend their lives some unexpected meaning. But because they expect that change only from outside, they generally end up disillusioned.

There are also moments in history when people strive for a change within themselves, but probably the last time that happened was during the Reformation.

When the period of strikes, demonstrations and speeches came to an end, I was so enthused by politics that I decided to abandon my studies. I was attracted by the idea of becoming part of history, of being a player in the major events that I used to read about with fascination and wonder. I started to write political commentaries for the press because I realized straightaway that the press and above all television were the best places to capture people's attention, and that they were a good stepping stone into politics. My political ambitions didn't please Vlasta, my then girlfriend. She maintained that I wasn't cut out for politics, that I was still a kid who enjoyed playing games. I wasn't hard or determined enough to be a politician, by which she meant I wasn't mature enough. But most of all she was afraid I wouldn't have enough time left for her.

I didn't have anyway. As soon as it appeared it was about time we were married, it suddenly struck me that there were no really strong bonds between us, but instead there stretched an emptiness, a silent void. That began to horrify me, so we split up. I'm a

Sagittarian, so I'm not supposed to be very constant in love, but actually I've always tended to idealize the people I love, and then when I'm confronted by the reality I discover to my horror that I've built my ideal on quicksand.

When I dropped the idea of a career in journalism or politics, I toyed with establishing an agency for promoting my favourite singers. I knew a number of singers and started to make enquiries about obtaining the necessary authorization, but in the end I abandoned the project before I even got into it. I wasn't tough enough for that sort of work either, or rather I lacked an entrepreneurial spirit. But most of all I lacked the capital to get started. Mum also talked me out of going into business. I was beginning to regret dropping out of university. Perhaps I really wasn't cut out for anything better than sitting in some library or archive and rummaging through old manuscripts. What do you do with someone who can't manage to succeed at anything? But then I was offered a job in that well-known but much-maligned commission set up to uncover the crimes of the former regime. They also took into account the seven semesters I had spent doing history at university; at least it was some sort of grounding for the work I was supposed to do. So I haven't escaped my destiny after all. I do research in the archives to lay bare the methods and rules adopted by the former intelligence services and secret police in their activities at home and abroad.

It was interesting and fairly tricky work and my searches were often fruitless. It took me at least a year even to comprehend how the secret brotherhood operated and to learn how to find things that were meant to remain hidden, to locate microfiches that to all appearances had never existed.

Intuition helped me a lot in this. I would sense connections for which no evidence could be found, and occasionally this would lead me to surprising and important discoveries. I am speaking about my work, but it's impossible to divide oneself into *homo nascitur ad laborem* and *homo privatus*. I can tell when someone is concealing their emotions or thoughts, and likewise when they are feigning them. But who, sometimes, doesn't feign emotions in an effort to transcend the void that suddenly looms between them and someone they believed themselves to be on intimate terms with? It looks as if it's only possible to be genuine in a game in which you have more than one life. Or rather it is easier to achieve justice and authenticity in a game than in real life.

My researches into people's recent pasts have taught me distrust. Sometimes, for instance, I come across depressing information about singers who were inciting us to resist while at the same time informing on us. I discover similar things about people who are held in esteem or who are in posts of authority. I pass the information on to my superiors and wait for what will happen. Mostly nothing does. I expect the game being played in those cases is at a higher level and is more complex than I, who regard myself as one of the players, am able to imagine. It is at such a level that it is foolhardy of me to make ripples. One day I'll be garrotted from behind or bumped off one night on the way home. But even though the thought of it sometimes makes me shiver, I still believe I'll find some means of escape; besides I'm doing everything to avoid it happening.

As I go through the old reports of secret police agents I'm amazed how much of them is taken up by accounts of infidelities and deceptions. It's as if they were all being unfaithful to each other.

Only here did I come to realize the logic of the regime I was born into. Very soon only a few people were subjected to real violence, just enough to ensure that everyone else lived in fear and submitted to control and humiliation as the only possible form of existence.

My dad resisted and ended up in prison, where he was beaten and tortured with thirst, hunger and cold. They'd kept him in an underground bunker and didn't give him even a blanket to cover himself with, just a piece of mouldy rag. It's true that Mum defiantly waited for him, writing him letters and buoying up his spirits with her love, but at the same time she tried not to step out of line, teaching what she had to teach and voting in the sham elections. When I started to understand these things, it rankled with me. She used to say, 'You don't know the way things are in real life.' I didn't. I had no notion. It is only here that I've discovered how they were. Although Mum was an ordinary primary-school teacher, she was under the surveillance of usually two of her colleagues, and one of the neighbours used to inform on her and Dad. I discovered it in the files, in pathetic and humiliating reports in which the informers and fellow teachers shamelessly made use of what Mum's pupils unwittingly said about her.

That was how it was. So now I can understand Mum's caution.

But even though I understand it, I still cannot accept it as the only option available to people. I'm sure that like Dad I'd find the strength to resist if the worst came to the worst.

Vlasta was right in saying I wasn't cut out for politics. I'm not even cut out for the job I'm doing right now, because I can't reconcile myself to the fact that people are the way they are. I'd like to live in a different world – one in which respect is achieved by deeds and actions completely unlike the ones recognized in today's world. And so I occasionally imagine myself in impossible situations; I suddenly think I can hear distant tom-toms; I rush towards them and find myself in a hail of arrows and bullets, but I dodge my way through. I also imagine myself stretching a rope between two peaks and walking across a valley as deep as the Grand Canyon. I've only ever seen it in pictures, of course. In reality I get dizzy just looking down from a bridge.

The stars also entice me. Not that I have any longing to fly to them, but I try to understand the message they send us about our possibilities and destinies. Mum says I'm nuts and that if she didn't keep an eye on me I'd definitely come to a sorry end.

Last week, when I had a moment to spare at work, I had a look at my horoscope on the computer and discovered that I'm about to experience something that will change my life. So I've started to perceive things around me in sharper focus.

A few days later, I went to visit my old history teacher in hospital. I think he was the person who most influenced me in my life, apart from Dad. When he explained history to us he would often go to the very limits of what was still permitted at the time. I could tell. Revolutions, which were always talked about in our textbooks with wild enthusiasm, were described by him as a bloody conflict followed by terror. And the terror was either the vengeance of those who managed to suppress the revolution or the revenge of those who achieved victory thereby. That remarkable teacher managed to draw my attention not only to history but also to the stars, although not in the sense he intended. I don't know what I did to draw his attention but he showed me favour and occasionally would invite me to his study and discuss with me problems that no one else talked to me about. I had the impression that his thoughts inhabited infinite space and endless time, in other words, stellar time, which was different from the time that history described. In that way he scaled humanity and himself down to a real dimension, i.e., an infinitely tiny dimension. That struck me as wise. He maintained that this new perception of the inconceivable duration of time and the inconceivable extent of the cosmos was the most important discovery of our times. I felt he had revealed to me something fundamental about life. Most likely someone denounced him for his views, because he stopped teaching history and instead was assigned to physics and PE classes. But I don't want to talk about him. His ex-wife also came to visit him in hospital. I immediately noticed that she radiated some sad, unreconciled pain and it touched me. I wanted to console her in some way and told her how years earlier, when I had seen her waiting with her child for her husband, I had envied him her. She blushed. I think the child was a little girl. She must be at least fifteen by now. The woman's name was Kristýna, as I recall. I have a good memory for faces, quotations and dates. I couldn't estimate her age, but she seemed to me just as strikingly beautiful as she had back then.

6

I t's gone ten already. The street outside the window is falling
silent and the breeze coming through the open window is
starting to be almost cool. I've put on some Bach, but I can't pay
attention to it. I'm waiting for Jana, although I know she won't
be back before midnight. I wait for the doorbell to ring but it
doesn't, the phone to ring but it doesn't, a messenger to arrive
with good news, but he can't arrive because he hasn't even set out
yet.

I open the box of Dad's letters but then close it again. I ought
to sort out my own papers first. I always chuck all my letters,
including the ones from that anonymous lunatic – of which there
have been more and more recently – into the big cardboard box
which the vacuum cleaner came in. If I turned it upside down, I'd
find right on top letters from my old flames. I had plenty of the
latter and even more letters. I'd always look at the greeting first and
then at the last sentence. *Darling . . ., I love you, Your . . .* What
came in between seemed to me of secondary importance.

There are so many letters I haven't the strength to sort them all
out. I've taken to putting only the latest ones in the box: invita-
tions, greetings cards, death notices, letters from women friends,
threats, holiday postcards and New Year cards. There are fewer
love letters. Their number almost equals the contents of an empty
mathematical set, as my one and only husband would define it.
When I die Jana, or whoever accompanies me on my last journey,
can chuck that box into the coffin and it can be cremated along
with me.

I get up and go into the junkroom where the box stands under
all the shelves. I pick up the uppermost letter. It's one of the
poison-pen letters, of course. It's written in block capitals, which
lean to the left pathologically and are decoratively rounded at the
bottom. The greeting is not very flattering, which is appropriate,
I suppose, for this kind of correspondence:

YOU DAUGHTER OF A RED SWINE,
   YOU BLOODY REDCURRANT, YOU POISONOUS HOGWEED, I'M
COMING TO WEED YOU OUT SOON. YOU'LL BE BROUGHT TO BOOK
AT LAST. YOU'LL WEEP AS I WEEP, YOU'LL HOWL AS I'VE HOWLED
EVERY DAY OF MY LIFE. YOU WON'T FIND A BUCKET BIG ENOUGH
TO HOLD ALL YOUR TEARS.

There are a few more lines of abuse. I drop it back in the box
instead of flushing it down the toilet. I have no idea who has been
sending me these rather rude messages regularly for the past six
months. Maybe it's some mad naturalist; he enjoys regaling me
with the names of plants and animals. Maybe it's a spirit letter from
Charles the Second. Maybe it's not a spirit letter, maybe he's still
alive. Maybe he just went somewhere where nobody knows him.
I quickly reach for another letter. It's a brief note from Father
Kostka thanking me for treating him.

My dear young lady,
   The new teeth are better than the ones I chewed with all my
life, of which only a few remain. I'll say nothing about how
beautiful they are, as it would be inappropriate (particularly at my
age) . . .

I think I hear the phone ring. I drop the letter and run to catch
the good news before the telephone grows tired.
   'Hi, love.' I recognize my sister's voice. 'I've been phoning you
all afternoon there and at the surgery, but you've been nowhere
around.'
   'I must have told you a hundred times already that I don't work
on Saturdays.'
   'Really? I must have forgotten. Or maybe I didn't notice it was
Saturday. Things are in total chaos here.'
   They always are, or at least any time she thinks I might want
something from her. But I don't want anything from her.

'Mum wrote to me. She seems . . . doesn't she strike you as a bit strange?'

'We're all a bit strange.'

'OK. But some are a bit more than others. She said she's got backache and can't cut the grass. She hasn't got any grass to cut, has she?'

'No.'

'See what I mean?'

'Maybe she wanted to cut the grass in front of the flats. She needs to be doing something to keep her mind off things. Her husband died.'

'Dad, do you mean?'

'Do you know of any other one?'

'Don't you think we should get the doctor to see her?'

'A doctor won't tell us any more than I know already. And I also happen to know her. She's my mum. And she's yours too, though you wouldn't really know to listen to you.'

'My love, you're picking a quarrel again.'

'You could have spent a couple of days with her when Dad died.'

'But I explained why I couldn't. I had a tour of Austria already arranged. It'd taken a year to set up. And it was a success.'

'And what if you were to die?'

'Me?'

'You think it couldn't happen?'

'I don't see the connection.'

'I was wondering whether you'd have had to go on the tour if you happened to have died.'

'There's only one answer I can give to your impertinent questions, my love: kindly get stuffed.'

'Was there anything else you wanted, Lída, love?'

'I was wanting to know how Mum is.'

'Mum's fine – if you bear in mind what she's been through. If you want to know any more, then come and see her. That's unless there's some enormous, successful tour you simply have to take part in.'

It's nearly midnight; I'm tired. When I was young I used to be able to sit around in pubs and even make love until morning, and sometimes I'd go for a week at a stretch before collapsing and sleeping sixteen hours; and there was no waking me up. It was during one of those sessions that I was discovered by my former – then still future – husband. That's how he first saw me: drunk, dishevelled and dog-tired. He was on his way back from some tennis tournament and was thirsty. He sat down at a table where I happened to be finishing off a bottle. Who was I with, in fact? It's not important. The pub was packed and the only free seat was at our table.

He was a good-looker, that future husband of mine, that's one thing I managed to register and also that he seemed to fancy me. He looked at me and asked, 'Are you all right?'

That was the first sentence he said to me: 'Are you all right?'

I told him I was OK, but it wasn't true. I had a heavy head, puffy eyes and an upset stomach.

'I'll see you home.' That was his second sentence. It wasn't a question or a request, it was a statement, and I meekly got up and left. And for the next twelve years I would meekly get up and go in whichever direction he pointed. It wasn't always a bad direction to take. He obeyed some kind of rules that required him to take care of himself, perform all his duties, do morning exercises, have a good breakfast and go to bed early. The rules even included reading some books so as to keep abreast of the times. I had no rules, although I did read books and listen to music, but he forced me to adopt his. He forced me to exchange my life of freedom for what he called a decent life. I owed that to him. I owed it to him that I didn't burn myself out. We loved each other. Why do I speak for him? I loved him. For the first time in ages I was crazy about someone. I longed to be with him and I was even jealous of his wife, that poor soul he betrayed on my account; except that he would go back to her and most likely lay alongside her, although he told me they hadn't slept together for ages.

How pathetic our stories are when we look back on them half a blink of God's eye later. No, they're also full of avalanches, lions and lionesses in full pursuit, us swaying along suspended bars, scaling rocks and bungee-jumping from a bridge, all to the accompaniment of the organ of the little Church of the Exaltation of the Holy Cross.

'This is Rožmitál, the place where I was born. It was also the birthplace of Jan Jakub Ryba. Can you hear that choir? I used to sing in it: *Master, hey! Rise I say! Look out at the sky – splendour shines on high* . . .

'Look, Jana, that's the house where I was born! And this is where I went to school. What are you smirking for?'

'Because you went to school too, Daddy! You must have been teensy-weensy!'

The sky is bare. There are stars above the avenue of oak trees and so much music that it drowns out everything and for a while I can't hear the rush of my blood or the murmur of my tears.

The phone again.

Twelve-fifteen.

'It's me, Mum.'

'Jana, you should have been home long ago. Where are you calling from?'

'Mum, there aren't any more trams, or rather there are only night trams.'

'I expect so. But that's why you were supposed to be home by midnight.'

'But I didn't notice the time . . .'

'That's your fault. And you haven't told me where you're calling from.'

'From Katya's, of course.'

'Take the next night tram and come home.'

'Mum, there's loads of horrible drunks outside, and junkies

too. Katya says I should sleep here. It'll be easier to get home in the morning.'

'Jana, you're coming home right now.'

'There's no point, Mummy, really. It'll take me two hours if I go now. In the morning I'll be home in a jiffy.'

I can hear voices in the background. The voices of some men or other come down the phone line.

'OK, I'll come and fetch you.'

'I couldn't let you do that, Mum. And anyway I bet you've had something to drink.'

'Don't concern yourself about me. Tell me Katya's exact address.'

'No, really, Mum. The cops'll stop you and breathalyse you.'

'Tell me Katya's address right away! Or do I have to look it up in the phone book?'

'I'll come home then, if you're going to make such a fuss.' And that's it. She's hung up. She'll graciously come home. She's still on her way, though goodness knows from where.

7

There wasn't a tram for half an hour. Mum was going to leap up and down and yell at me again, but me and Ruda couldn't afford a taxi; we were completely broke. Anyway we wouldn't have taken one even if we had some money left. We'd sooner try to get a joint. But I didn't want any more today. I'm spaced out enough as it is. When Mum eventually cottons on, there's going to be hell to pay. But that's her fault. She still hasn't realized that I'm not her little girl any more running around like a trained monkey.

Ruda made me go up to the park because he wanted a bit more snogging, but I'd had enough and made faces until he lost the urge. As we were walking past some parked cars he bent over and pulled the valve out of the tyre on some Ford. The tyre hissed and went flat. We laughed. I know he did it for me, 'cos I can't stand cars, even though I ride in Mum's banger sometimes. I have to.

Ruda isn't much of a talker, he prefers action. That's what's great about him. Once, about a year ago, we were flat broke like now and he says, 'If we want to shoot, we'll have to find some loot.' And he takes us down to some old flats in Vršovice, saying he knows of a flat where the people are always away. I was really scared and told him I'd sooner stay outside. But he says, 'Don't be daft. You're not even fifteen. They can't do anything to you.' So we go right to the top of the building and there's this big wide door. Ruda had a piece of rusty old iron under his coat and used it to break open the door. Katya had to stay in the passage and keep watch. We went inside and Ruda blocked the door with the iron bar. I was still really scared about being in someone else's flat and afraid I'd get nabbed and sent to approved school. Ruda yells at me that I'm paranoid but I couldn't really hear him, and I couldn't see anything around me either, except for two stupid angels hanging on the wall with golden wings growing right out of their heads. Ruda pulled them off the wall and stuffed one of them in his rucksack. He wrapped the other one in some rag or other and shoved it in my arms for me to carry. But I just couldn't because my arms and legs were shaking like a jelly and I started to cry. So Ruda grabbed the other one too and shoved me out the door. It wouldn't close any more so we rushed down the stairs and I could hear the door creaking and banging. It was so loud they must have heard it in the street. It was horrendous.

Ruda didn't talk to me for eighty years after that.

Two cops had just got out of their tank.

Ruda spotted them first and beat it. I don't blame him. He's done approved school and a year inside; you never know what they'll do when they nab someone who's done time. They didn't look more than twenty. 'Another virgin in chains,' one of them says to me and asks for my ID.

I pretended I couldn't find it and asked him to explain what I'd done. I told them that while they were wasting time with me, someone round the corner was pinching a car or knocking off some old lady.

'Shut your trap!' said the one who had stood and watched so far. 'Or you'll be sorry!'

So at last I pulled out my ID and the one of them who could possibly read thumbed through it and then looked in some list or other. 'You're not even fifteen.' He couldn't even do his sums. 'How come you're not at home?'

'I'm a year older,' I pointed out to him, 'and I'm outside because we've got a flood at home.'

'What have you got?'

'No, really. The bedroom's flooded. It's only just drying out.'

The only reply he could think of was to tell me to shut my trap again. They handed back my ID but they didn't say thank you. They just told me to clear off.

'I'm waiting for a tram,' I said. 'That's allowed, isn't it?'

They didn't give a fuck about the fact that some old wino was throwing his guts up just behind me and they moved off with the refined gait of two thoroughbred stallions. What a laugh! Dumbos. Horrendous. But at least they helped pass the time and I was still really spaced out, high as a kite. But I knew I'd start to come down, and then I usually feel bad. Mum will have to notice it one day. I bet she's waiting for me. She couldn't do me a favour and spare me her carping. I'll have to pretend I hung around at Katya's. If she only knew! If ever she suspected where I'm sleeping when I say I'm at Katya's. If ever she found out about Ruda she'd be in shock for at least a year.

'I'll end up killing you one of these days,' she's told me at least a thousand times. But she won't kill me. She's more likely to do herself harm, from what I know of her. She suffers from downers and she's always pissed off or tired because she spends all her time drilling in people's gobs and she's got no real enjoyment in the world. Sometimes she goes spare and yells at me and when she gets over it she tells me I'm all she has. I'm sorry for her, but it's not my fault that Dad did a runner on her and now I'm all she's got. Anyway there's no reason for her to stay on her own. Any time we go out somewhere together, such as to the theatre, there are guys eyeing her all the time. Actually she's quite pretty, particularly when she's smiling or when she's singing.

A fifty-seven at last. The wino behind me had another quick spew and we climbed aboard. In the tram I caught sight of Foxie and her Fox. They were totally smashed. Foxie was sitting on his lap and wobbling her green-tinted head around like a resuscitated mummy. I had something going with the Fox last year too, but only about three times, because I found him boring. Now he just nodded to me and invited me to some bender they were on their way to.

'Now?'

'Yeah. No sweat. There's this guy there that's really big and shares it round.'

'That's great, really great.'

'Coming with us, then?'

'I'm not sure. How far is it?'

'It's no problem, we'll take you there.'

'I'm not sure. I promised Mum . . .'

'Don't be a lemon; she's asleep long ago.'

'No she isn't. Really, she's waiting for me.'

'So what? She'll get over it.'

'Yeah, I know.' I can't stand it when people talk like that about my mum. I was coming down and I started to get a headache. I was heading for a downer and really needed a top-up. 'It's a fact. She's really dependent on me,' I say finally.

But I don't think they even noticed me. They were now totally smashed. Foxie's head just wobbled around as if it was badly wired on.

I shut my eyes for a moment too and it felt as if I was flying. It was really great because I didn't need any wings. I'd just launch myself, spread my arms and soar up like a balloon. There were clouds below me like whipped cream. Really, it was just fantastic, floating and flying wherever I liked.

Then I had to open my eyes again and change trams. I said ciao to those two, but they weren't going to let anyone disturb their trip.

When I got off the tram here it was half past one. I started to feel really cold and a bit scared. Actually I was really scared that I'd meet some devil or werewolf, or see some vampire swaying from a lamppost.

I've often seen them hanging there, though I knew I was only imagining it.

CHAPTER TWO

1

Today it was announced that we have a 25 per cent ozone deficit above our heads and I was summoned to my daughter's school. The school is less than fifteen minutes' walk away. Some of the teachers and the principal herself are among my patients. Jana's class teacher isn't one of them, but fortunately she doesn't teach maths or chemistry. She teaches Czech. According to Jana she's known as 'the nun'. This lady in rather old-fashioned black clothes must be even older than I am. She has long hair, completely white, and a fine complexion, undamaged by smoking and possibly untouched by kisses. She really does have the spinstery complexion of a nun. She gazes at me with mournfully reproachful eyes. 'I'm worried about Jana.'

'I know, so am I.'

'My colleagues complain about her. She has stopped studying and her marks have dropped in all subjects. In English and maths as much as two grades, in fact. And my experience with her is similar.'

I nod. I ought to say something in my own and Jana's defence. Or at least explain that I don't have enough time or energy, what with my patients and my elderly mother. That my daughter is pubertal and enjoys loafing around at night and singing morbid songs. I can ban her from those but I can't make her want to study. 'Do you think there is any chance of improving things at the last moment?'

'Well, it's getting very close to the final call, so she'd have to get a move on,' she says with the sort of gravity employed when talking about an operation on a hopeless case. 'And then there are all her absences,' she says, continuing her indictment. 'Is she really ill so often these days?'

I flinch. 'What do you mean?'

She takes out the class register and reads to me from it. Over the past two months, once absent for three days, then for two days, three times for one day, and classes missed twice, either maths or chemistry. 'The excuse notes are all from you, Mrs Pilná. As you are in the medical profession I didn't ask for any other confirmation. But I'd simply like to reassure myself that Jana is really so sickly.'

A marvellous word, 'sickly'. Perfect for a language teacher with the appearance of a nun. I won't tell her that Jana is as fit as a fiddle. I wonder whether I ought to support Jana and her forged excuse notes and then give the minx a good hiding when she gets home, a whack on her bare backside for each signature she forged. 'She suffers from migraines,' I say hesitantly. 'She takes after me. And she also had the flu.'

'But those illnesses don't account for why she's so much weaker in all her subjects.'

I agree.

'Have you not noticed anything suspicious about her behaviour?'

I ask her what she means.

She tells me that there are twelve children in the school who are known to be taking drugs. One third-year boy is receiving treatment in the mental hospital at Bohnice. She says it is hard to say how many others there might be.

'That's dreadful,' I say. 'But I've not noticed anything.'

'They are past masters at concealing it,' she says, clearly unconvinced. 'That's something they are good at learning and the more they have to conceal the more resourceful they become.'

She goes on to quote statistics that I know anyway. 'You see, Mrs Pilná, dealers nowadays stand waiting right outside the school gates.' She points towards the window, beyond which no one is to be seen. 'But there is nothing we can do. After all, we live in a free country and the pavement is a public area. Selling drugs is an apparently normal business activity. And often they don't even sell them; they let the children have free samples. Children are curious and they like to appear grown-up. Or rather, as bad as grown-ups.'

'I'm sure that Jana . . .' I shake my head, trying to convince myself. 'She loafs around, I know, but she would be scared of drugs.'

'I hope so,' says her class teacher. I can't tell whether the tone in her voice is severe or conciliatory. 'Her father is a teacher and an athlete.'

'Her father's ill at present,' I say. 'Very ill. He has neither the time nor the energy for her. Besides, you are aware that . . .'

Of course she's aware. Almost half the kids in her class are in the same boat. But fathers can exercise some influence, even when they live elsewhere. The teacher talks for a while about how parents pay insufficient attention to their children: at the age when they are at greatest risk children spend their time either in some gang or in front of the TV, where they gawp at serials about heroes who could only appeal to people in a trance or a drug-induced state.

That was how my dad used to speak. She hasn't yet got round to complaining that young people lack an ideal, a great goal for all to strive for. Except that my father's words were full of bitterness and imbued with the idea that the human herd has to be driven along a single road to a single destination, chosen for it by those who know where paradise is to unfold. The teacher is speaking about a problem she actually has to deal with, and her words fill me with alarm.

I simply say, although there is little point, that Jana doesn't watch television and actually disdains those who waste their time on it. Then I make the usual parental promise that I will talk to her. As if I didn't spend my time talking to her about the same thing.

'Please do. Together we'll come up with something, you'll see. After all, she's a clever and gifted girl,' she says in conclusion, although she really thinks she's a little brat. And she's right.

I leave the school building and all of a sudden I feel almost too tired to walk home. Maybe it's on account of that hole in the ozone layer, or maybe it's all too much for me. I spend eight hours a day in the dental surgery, half an hour to work and the same home, and the trip by dismal metro and packed bus is enough to sap all one's strength and undermine one's mental resolve. Not to mention what I have to do at home to keep us going. And if I give Jana a chore to do, the way she does it means I have to do it again after her.

There was a time when I used to read something or listen to music. These days I no longer do that for pleasure but from fear of leading an animal existence. Not long ago I fell asleep at a concert, and on the odd occasions I read a novel, by the time I get to the end I can't remember how the thing started.

For God's sake, why is everything up to me now?

I drag myself as far as the little square in front of Čapek's villa. I can't resist sitting down on the low perimeter wall. No one notices me, apart from a dog in the house opposite who starts to bark. *So I'm well, but just a bit pooped*, my writer wrote to his dear Olga.

Not many people read Čapek these days. He's not an American writer.

As I approach our house I notice the familiar figure of the thin young man with the red hair: Jan, I can't remember the rest of his name, that ex-student of my one and only husband. But his Christian name is like our daughter's. What is he doing here? He can't be waiting for me, surely.

Now he has noticed me and is walking to meet me.

But I have no time for him. I need to talk to my unruly daughter and discover how she's been spending her time while playing truant.

The young man makes a slight bow and apologizes for waylaying me: he simply wanted to ask how his old teacher was. He rang the bell of our flat but no one was home, so he decided to wait for a while.

'There was no one in?' I ask foolishly.

No one, he repeats.

I tell him that I don't know how my ex-husband is; I haven't spoken to him since the time I visited him in hospital. I offer to give the young man Karel's phone number, but he has it already. He doesn't want to ask him directly, only to know his actual state of health.

His interest surprises me. But it's true that my ex-husband was capable of arousing people's admiration – and even love, as I myself discovered to my cost.

I am standing with this young fellow out here on the pavement, though I have no reason to. Then he says, 'The thing is that I wanted to see you again.'

I don't say, Well, you're seeing me. I don't know how to reply. But I don't intend to stand here on the pavement with him, and for the time being it's inappropriate for me to invite him in. I notice the words 'for the time being' form themselves in my mind.

'If you happen to have a few moments to spare, I noticed there was a bistro round the corner. Maybe I could invite you for a drink . . .

'I've been thinking of you ever since,' he adds.

2

My darling daughter turned up in time for supper. A new chain around her waist – new, that is, for her; otherwise it's covered in bits of rust. Goodness knows what animal she stole it from. A new hole in her jeans at knee level. Black platforms, the highest she could buy. For a long time I held out against those dreadful clodhoppers, refusing the demagogic pressure that all the girls have them now, but in the end I gave in and gave her the two thousand crowns – mostly, I expect, because when I was her age my father didn't even allow me jeans and I wasn't permitted to use lipstick. My approved footwear was fit for an elderly collective farmer. And she's even worse off than I was. She has lost half her home because I wasn't able to hold on to it for her. Let her have some enjoyment at least, I tell myself, although I know full well that no manner of rags, clodhoppers or chains will make up for her loss. And it would be wrong if they did.

'Jana, where have you been for so long?'

'At Dad's, haven't I?'

'You went to see your dad? Why didn't you let me know?'

'It was your idea, wasn't it?'

'You went to see him dolled up like that?'

'Of course.'

'What did he say about your platforms?'

'He made me take them off.'

'And you spent the whole afternoon at your dad's?'

'I went and did some shopping for him.'

'That was good of you. How is he?'

'But you know anyway, Mum. He's got awfully thin and his hands shake. I told him I'd make him some pancakes. And he said, Go ahead. And then he only managed to eat one of them. And instead of those endless lectures he always used to give me, he just sat and looked at me without saying anything.'

My daughter sits and tells me about it while munching the bread and cheese I put in front of her. It doesn't look as if her father's suffering has spoilt her appetite.

And now to change the subject: 'I was in school today,' I announce.

'Jesus Christ.'

'Not only are you about to flunk your leaving exam, but you play truant and forge my signature.'

'Did you drop me in it?'

I say nothing.

'Mum, you're a gem. But when I wrote those excuse notes, I used the proper terminology. I found the Latin names in your manual.'

For God's sake, she's proud of what a great forger she is. 'That's going to stop. I'll call the school at least once a week to make sure you're there. And if you're off traipsing around somewhere, I'll call the police and have them find you. Where do you hang out, in fact, when you're not in school?'

'It's hard to say, Mum. When it's lovely out, it really is an awful bore to sit in class.'

'So where do you sit instead?'

'In a park, for instance.'

'A park?'

'Yeah. Gröbe Gardens or Rieger Park.'

'And the pub?'

'Hardly ever.'

'Who with?'

'What do you mean?' she says, playing for time.

'You hardly sit in a pub on your own!'

'I was only twice in a pub.'

'Or three times.'

She looks at me and shrugs. 'Mum, I really don't keep count. It's not important, is it?'

'Don't try telling me what's important. What do you drink there?'

'I dunno. Cola.'

'Jana. Don't lie to me, at least.'

'No, honestly, Mum!'

'You haven't told me yet who you loaf about with.'

'I don't loaf about!'

'So what is it you're doing, then?'

Most likely she's about to explain to me that it's life, or tell me what life isn't about, but she stops herself in time and just shrugs.

'Well, do you mind telling me who you sit around with?'

'It depends.'

'Are they all girls or are there boys too?'

'Girls mostly.'

'But boys too.'

'Very, very rarely.'

'Older?'

'How am I supposed to know? They're all thick, anyway.'

'Why do you hang around with them then?'

'It's them who come creeping after us.'

'What do you smoke?'

'How do you mean?'

'I'm asking you what you smoke.'

'But we don't smoke.'

'Don't lie to me, Jana.'

'Well, I've had a drag now and then. But then you smoke too. And how. Dad's always going on about you getting kippered lungs.'

'There's a difference between us. Between me and you, I mean.'

'I'm not saying anything, am I? But Dad never smoked.'

'Don't go dragging your dad into this. Have you tried grass?'

'What grass?'

'Jana, don't try it on me. If you'd said no, I might have believed you, but I'm hardly going to believe you've never heard of it.'

'Oh right, you mean hash.' She hesitates.

'How many times?'

'But Mum, cannabis is less dangerous than your fags.'

'Jana, stop lecturing me all the time and stand up!'

She stands up.

'Take off your T-shirt and come here.'

She adopts a hurt expression, but takes off her T-shirt and stands in front of me. She doesn't wear a bra. She has my breasts, but they are still firm, like two bells.

'Show me your arms.' I examine them as best I can. Her skin is smooth, clean and fresh, without any traces of injections. Thank God. 'Jana,' I say, 'what makes you do these things?'

'I don't do anything bad, do I?'

'No, you do nothing at all.'

'School's boring.'

'And what isn't?'

'I dunno. Sitting in the park with the girls.'

'But you can't spend all your time sitting in the park.'

'I don't know, really.'

'Each of us has certain duties. And you're supposed to be study-ing. Enough to scrape through, at least.'

She shakes her head. 'But there's just no point in it.'

'In what?'

'In anything,' she says. 'But you know, anyway.'

'What do I know?'

'Grandpa died and look at the state Dad's in. What's the point of it?'

'Grandpa was old and your dad neglected a tumour.'

'I don't want to be old. And I don't want to get a tumour.'

'Nor do any of us. Well, how do you see your life, then?' I ask her – I who, at her age, had no wish to live at all.

3

I wake up feeling that I must have shouted something. But the dream wasn't about my daughter. It was my father who appeared to me. He was clinging on to my ex-husband and yelling at me: What have you done? You've driven him out. You're a rotten daughter and a lousy wife.

I got a fright because he'd no business to be there; he was dead; he'd died, was burnt in a furnace, descended into hell and on the third day he didn't rise from the dead; but now he stood before me, untouched by the flames, my accuser, and meanwhile that hypocrite my ex-husband had a smirk on his face. I reached out as if to push my accuser back into the flames and started to scream in horror.

I stare into the darkness and shiver all over. I shudder again and again from fear. I get up and go into the kitchen, where I pour myself half a glass of wine. I fill the rest of the glass with water and return to the bedroom. I leave the light on. I'm afraid of the dark.

When I was a little girl – how old could I have been? scarcely five or six – my parents used to send me to Lipová to spend the summer at Grannie Marie's. Usually I'd spend the whole of September there too. I adored my grandmother. She rode horses and sang me songs. On Saturdays she baked *kolaches* and bread. She made her own noodles too. And she also liked a smoke.

At that time Aunt Venda still occupied a little room in the cottage. She had long, unkempt grey hair. She spent the whole time sewing away on a Minerva treadle sewing machine. She wasn't allowed to smoke, because she couldn't be trusted with matches. She used to make up for it by drinking beer from first thing in the morning. It seemed to me that my aunt never left her room; Grannie would bring her beer and food. When I visited Auntie, she'd smile at me, displaying her crooked yellowy incisors, and say something I usually couldn't make out. But I did manage to understand that she couldn't go outside because she was just a receptacle, a vessel in which a fire was constantly smouldering. All it needed was a slight breeze or for the sun to shine on her, and she would burst into flame. It would happen anyway one day.

And doesn't the fire burn you, Auntie? I would ask her.

Oh it does, sweetheart. It gives me a terrible pain here, she'd say, indicating her breasts, neck and head.

And then one day it really did happen. I was playing out in the yard when the door of Auntie's room suddenly burst open unexpectedly and in the door frame there appeared a flaming figure that started to run towards me. For a moment I couldn't understand anything and had the feeling that a fairytale apparition was coming to get me, but then I recognized my aunt.

'I'm burning,' she shouted. 'I set myself alight!'

Her clothes were on fire and it seemed to me that smoke was coming out of her head. Terror rooted me to the spot as I watched the approach of that fiery vision. Then Auntie started to scream horribly and cry for help, and I ran away. Grannie rushed out of the house and when she saw what was happening, she snatched a sack that was hanging from a beam by the door and dashed over to Auntie with it.

She managed to douse the flames, but she couldn't save my aunt. They took her to hospital, where she died a few days later. I wanted to go and visit her, but they told me I couldn't any more because Auntie was gone. She was gone because she didn't want to be here any more. Auntie had burnt up and was gone and I cried.

That was my first encounter with death, and it was a haunting experience. That image of a burning figure has never left my memory, even though I have seen lots of other frightful pictures and photos of famine, murders and wars – there have been so many of them since then that I can hardly keep count, and apparently one soldier in five was still a child.

I've noticed that almost everyone I know was marked by at least one such shocking experience in their childhood. My husband's best friend froze to death in the mountains. When Lída was small, two cars crashed in front of her eyes and they had to cut the dead out of the wreckage with oxyacetylene torches. Not to mention Mum. Admittedly she didn't see what happened to her mother and her aunts and cousins, but the thought of what was done to them must have marked her for life.

While I was still at Lipová that time I started to wonder about the strange phenomenon that one moment someone could be there and the very next they could be gone, and it seemed to me so sad that everything, absolutely everything, had to come to an end, including me. There was no escape. Death was the supreme ruler, and if he called you, you had to go and you never came back.

It was odd that they depicted that ruler as an old woman or a skeleton with a scythe.

But Grannie consoled me and sang me a song about death, from which I understood that death wasn't wicked. It wasn't a skeleton or even an old woman, it was a little girl like me. I can still recall the words of that song, though I don't sing it any more:

> *There once was an old woman*
> *And she had just one son.*
> *And he lay sick and dying*
> *For cool water he was crying.*
> *There was no one to go to the well*
> *So his old mother she went herself.*
> *On the way she met a young child*
> *A messenger from God so mild.*
> *I'm coming to fetch his dear soul*
> *To Paradise, his heavenly home.*

From that I understood that death wasn't a stranger who comes between two people. A little girl or a little boy was sent by someone to carry the soul up to heaven, where life was more beautiful than on earth.

I didn't know what a soul was – I'd only heard of the sole of a shoe. When I asked them, they couldn't explain it.

When I was at Grannie's I could run around outside with the children, but quite often something would get into me and I wouldn't feel like seeing anyone. Behind the cottage in the far corner of the garden by the fence there grew an enormous walnut tree with a hollow trunk. There was just enough room for someone my size. I'd find refuge there in my own little house, where

I'd spend hours on end. What did I do there? I can't remember. I used to take my rag doll – my sister – along with me and a teddy bear. He was actually my first husband, though I don't count him any more. He was utterly reliable and had big, brown glass eyes. We'd all crouch down in that little cave full of the scent of wood and resin. Mist ahead of us, mist behind us. I would draw it like a curtain. No one could see us or hear us, only we could hear the horse whinnying in the stable and the ducks quacking in the yard.

One day after lunch they took the horse off to the slaughter-house, the ducks had their throats slit, the doctor banned Grannie from smoking, we ate shop-bought noodles and the walnut tree breathed its last, falling asleep from old age. What happened to my teddy-bear husband? He disappeared somewhere. He's not here any more. That's the way it is with husbands: the day comes when they disappear and they're not around any more.

I light a cigarette. The first time I smoked I was two years younger than my daughter is now. I committed the crime in the little park just behind the school. I was seen, of course – by my civic studies teacher, a wrinkled old maid. She immediately denounced me to Dad. He gave me a hiding, walloping me until I perjured myself by swearing that that was the last time, that I'd never smoke again. But at that very moment I vowed to myself that I would smoke, drink and go out with boys just to spite him. Even if he beat me black and blue. I'd just be more careful and more cunning. What sort of an attitude is that, what sort of a tem-perament: being certain I know the truth and therefore have the right to judge others, take decisions for them, and ban anything I object to and don't agree with? That was how he tried to subju-gate me, that's how he and his ilk tried to enslave the whole of mankind. Without people like that, no tyrant would manage to rule for even a minute. Anyway I didn't manage to stand up to him the way my mother had stood up to her father. I didn't leave home as a way of showing my contempt for everything he stood for. All I managed to do was to harm myself and assert my right to harm myself irreparably if I felt like it.

Mum managed to stand up to her father, but it's as if that entirely exhausted any rebelliousness in her and she was no longer capable of standing up to her own husband. She even put up with his slaps round the face. Well, I did manage to stand up to my husband and his infidelity, for all the good it did me.

I know I won't get to sleep. By my bed there's a book that I've started reading and under it a few magazines, but instead I get up and open the door to the bedroom where my daughter lies sound asleep. She is uncovered and her nightdress has ridden up so that she lies there almost naked. She's not a little girl any more, she's a woman. Her bottom has broadened and her thighs have fattened; I'll have to keep an eye on what she eats: what liquids and solids she ingests, what she smokes and where she goes when she's out. All the care I've taken to stop her eating sugary things and whenever I gave in and let her have something, she had to brush her teeth straightaway. I've kept an eye on her teeth and she's totally free of caries, but what about the parts that aren't visible when you open your mouth to speak or smile?

I'd never want to act the policeman with her, the way my father did with me. It wouldn't be any use anyway. When they want to keep someone under surveillance, a squad of policemen are often not enough. What am I to tell her? How am I to convince her to change her ways? What did I neglect? Didn't I give her enough love, or, on the contrary, was I too kind?

After all, we got on well together. Often we'd be left on our own together, even before we were abandoned for good. Her father would be off at some tennis tournament – or at least so he said – and we would play with the Barbie dolls. We actually had three of them: one white, one black and one with almond eyes. And I used to tell a long story in episodes about a princess who was clever and brave. She could slay dragons that had defeated namby-pamby princes and outwit anyone who tried to deceive her. She loved travel, climbing up hill and down dale, and she had a tame killer whale who carried her on its back through the warm seas.

And whenever my little girl was ill, I would always wake up a few seconds before she awoke and started to demand my assistance or at least my presence.

Then we were left to ourselves, and every summer I would stubbornly take her to the seaside. We didn't catch sight of any killer whales, but spent our time in needlessly expensive hotels. I was equally stubborn about sending her to the mountains every winter. She had the very best in skis, boots and bindings. In that way I spoiled her and went without things myself so that she shouldn't have the feeling that she was denied something just because I wasn't able to hold on to her father. It's not long since we used to spend nice evenings together. We'd sit together in my room because it has the most space and play guitar and sing spirituals or songs from my younger days.

I lean over her and stroke her hair. The little-girl woman sighs and out of her sleep she brushes away my hand as if brushing away a midge.

I go back into my own room. The box with Dad's writings is still standing by the wardrobe.

Lucie once confided to me that whenever she picks up an encyclopaedia or book on photographers, she first looks to see if there's a mention of her. I don't look for myself in encyclopaedias. People need a dentist to repair their teeth, they don't need to idolize or read about them. But I'll check, at least, how my own father welcomed me into the world and how he spoke about me.

Before I reach that illustrious day, I have to wade through the Great Events of those times. I pause for a moment at one of the most spectacular show trials, in which the revolutionaries were true to their predecessors and started to murder each other. *Our own comrades betrayed us! It's not surprising that almost all of them were foreigners, Zionists, Jews in other words. That's how they repay our people's trust in them!*

I wonder what he told Mum. And I wonder what Mum thought about it and whether she dared say anything out loud. Maybe her mind was more on me, who was already in her tummy by then. What idea could she have had of the world I would be born into?

I go on leafing through the exercise book. Yes, of course, here's the well-retouched face of the Generalissimo staring at me out of the page, framed in black. No pockmarks, but no kindly smile either: it wouldn't be appropriate at a moment made for mourning. Just below it a brief note. *I convened a special remembrance meeting in the assembly shop. I said: One of the greatest geniuses of mankind is dead, a thinker, philosopher, military leader, revolutionary, saviour of our lives and liberator of our peoples, a man whose heart held enough love for all people. A giant acclaimed by poets the world over. I stressed that we would remain true to his legacy. At one moment I was overcome with emotion and couldn't continue my oration. I noticed that the people listening were moved too and the women were crying. Comrade V-ová came to see me after the meeting and was sobbing. Then she said: I thought he'd never die, that the Soviet doctors wouldn't let him die. I told her: Even he was mortal, but his achievements will last for ever.*

My father, a fool. At least he didn't make grammatical mistakes. He had no education, but he was a pedant. No mention of me, of course. I turn the page. A mention at last: *I have a daughter. I haven't seen her yet. The comrades suggested a celebration, but I refused. How could I celebrate at a moment when the entire progressive world is in mourning. It would be a human and a political mistake.* I simply made a political mistake. It's not the done thing to come into the world at a moment when the vassals are groaning in pain at the loss of a tyrant.

Today's paper reports that the Soviet Union has the H-bomb too. Great news for all fighters for world peace!

I close the exercise book in disgust.

When I mentioned to the young man who invited me for a glass of wine the other day that I was born on the day of the

Soviet dictator's death, he declared almost triumphantly that it was a fateful coincidence. Fateful coincidence with what? – I didn't ask him.

I now know that he's called Jan Myšák. His pals mostly call him Myšák or Mickey Mouse. He strikes me as shy and a bit childish. He probably has a hang-up about not completing his studies. I expect that's why he stressed more than once how important his job is. Apparently he's not allowed to say much about it because it has to do with uncovering those who collaborated with the State Security during the previous regime.

He tried to tell me at breakneck speed all the main things about himself. He lives with his mum but claims that he refuses her attentions. I expect he's only kidding himself; he referred to her several times in passing: 'my mother thinks . . . my mother says . . . my mother doesn't like . . .'

He also told me he regularly takes part in some kind of complicated parlour games, in which people play historical or imaginary characters: kings, jesters and so on, but also monsters, elves or aliens. As if he was ashamed about still playing games, he explained that he took part in them in order to forget what he encountered every day when reading the reports of police informers.

Then he talked about my ex-husband, who was apparently the one who aroused his interest in history, and why he started to study it at university.

I don't have much interest in history. Descriptions of battles and famous victories horrified me. I used to imagine the soldiers who were left lying dead on foreign fields and the anticipation of those they left behind. Women watching out for men who could never return, children who grew up without hearing a man's voice.

Soldiers mostly didn't have children yet, he pointed out. They used to recruit single men.

Even so, someone was waiting for those who were butchered, I said. And in the most recent major wars they recruited everyone whether they were twenty or fifty. When my beloved Karel Čapek wrote *The Mother* before the last world war, he tried to see history through a woman's eyes. In the end he was unsuccessful, because he had her send her fifth and last surviving son to the war. That's something I'd never do. I told Jan I'd refuse to accept the laws of a man's world that demand bloodshed and tears.

He said he understood me and admitted that the world of men is essentially cruel. He couldn't imagine a woman devoting herself to wiping out entire nations, races or social classes as the dictators over the last century had done. Then he started to talk about revolutions, not omitting one of my one and only husband's lessons about the tyrants who changed the fate of Russia and set about changing the fate of the world.

He spoke with passion, but I couldn't concentrate on what he was saying: I was taken by his eyes. It's unusual to find a redhead with large, dark eyes. I don't ever recall loving anyone with eyes like that. I used to be attracted by blue or slate-grey eyes, like my first and only husband's, although his gaze was cold. But that young fellow looked at me almost imploringly.

I sat with him longer than was wise. I allowed him to order me three glasses of wine, even though he himself only drank some of that sweet muck that ruins teeth and health.

I worked out that he was almost fifteen years younger than me.

What lunacy am I being tempted into? It reminds me of some lines of Yesenin's that I once found moving:

> *Not sorry, not calling, not crying,*
> *All will pass like smoke of white apple trees*
> *Seized with the gold of autumn,*
> *I will no longer be young.*

He was twenty-six when he wrote that.

What about me, then? What sort of delusions are these? That lad who looked at me so imploringly could easily go out with my Jana.

Something makes me start. I put the lid back on the box and

quietly go back to the bedroom where my daughter is still lying exactly as I left her a moment ago, her bare bottom thrust in my direction. I switch on her table lamp and shine the light towards her. I lean over her and like a detective I search that smooth skin, unmarked by time. All I lack is a magnifying glass. And sure enough, I find it, a tiny red spot, maybe left by a syringe. *They are past masters at concealing it. That's something they are good at learning and the more they have to conceal the more resourceful they become.* Perhaps she was bitten by a midge. Midges sometimes come in the window. Maybe she scratched herself. Best not to think about it. Best not to look. I'll tackle her about it tomorrow.

I go back to bed.

Please God, say it's not true.

I try to think which of my former colleagues might advise me.

It's nonsense. It's that nun in the guise of a Czech teacher who put the idea in my head. My daughter's hardly going to do anything as stupid as that.

That's just the point: she is my daughter. Her forebears include a crazy grandmother and great-grandparents who committed suicide: more cases of suicide in the family than is healthy. On top of that a depressive mother that no man could put up with, even when she knelt before him and hugged his legs.

You're so beautiful, so beautiful, said that fifteen-years-younger ex-pupil of my ex-husband, and gazed at me as if about to declare his love.

I ought to go and see my ex-husband. Tell him that our daughter, the only thing we'll have in common as long as we're alive, smokes cannabis and possibly does worse things than that. Maybe it won't interest him any more. His daughter never did interest him very much. He didn't just leave me, he left her too.

Please God, let all this I'm going through be just a dream.

No, not everything, after all, something has to remain part of my life. But there's so little that I'd like to retain as part of my actual waking life.

4

I oversleep. The alarm clock doesn't even wake me. And then Jana is standing over me, repaying me my nocturnal visit. 'Mummy, aren't you going to the surgery today?'

I leap out of bed. I have a splitting headache. I've no idea when I fell asleep. 'I've made you breakfast, Mum.' And sure enough, there's a cup of coffee on the table and she has even buttered some bread. She plants a kiss on my cheek; she's sprayed herself again with my Chanel, which I save for only very special occasions, and she's eager to be gone.

I delay her. 'Jana, tell me: was it only the grass?'

'Mum, what's got into you again?'

'Answer me. Did you inject anything?'

'Mum, you must have been dreaming – either that or you're paranoid.'

'Yes or no?'

'Of course not! I'm not some stupid junkie, am I?' She swears that she's not lying. She looks the picture of health and full of energy, and I want to believe that she's perfectly all right and I'm just anxiety-prone.

I arrive at the surgery twenty minutes late.

Eva helps me into my white coat. I thank her and ask her to make me a strong coffee.

Eva and I have been together for eleven years already. We understand each other without the need for words. I don't have to tell her what to mix for me. If she's not sure, she asks. We're together every weekday and sometimes we even spend weekends together. When she married she became the owner of a little cabin on a rock above the Vltava just outside Prague. I don't own anything of the sort, and yet whenever I get out of town it's an enormous relief and my cares fall away.

So Jana and I sometimes take her up on her invitation and it strikes me that my daughter gets on better with Eva than with me.

Eva sometimes takes her to Mass at the village church. I don't join them. I only went to church or read the Bible to spite Dad. I didn't care whether the church was Protestant or Catholic. I even wandered into a synagogue once when I was in London; but none of it had any effect on my soul. But I think it does Jana good to make herself kneel before something from time to time.

Thanks to Eva, my patients include Father Kostka, who now sits in the chair waiting for me. At the time my father first donned militia uniform, Father Kostka was sent to Leopoldov Prison, so I feel guilty in front of him. But he doesn't know about it. He addresses me as 'young lady', and when he is unable to speak, he smiles at me with his eyes, at least. I ought to ask him what he would advise a non-Christian mother to do or say in order to help her sixteen-year-old offspring come to terms with life and find some meaning in it. I wonder what he'd say?

But at this moment Father Kostka has to clench his jaws and the waiting room is still full of people. I'll ask him next time.

'You're a bit down in the mouth today, Mrs Pilná,' he says as he gets up from the chair.

I don't tell him that I have little reason to be cheerful, but simply say that I slept badly. 'The nurse will fix you a new appointment.' I quickly finish my coffee.

But while she is leafing through the diary, Eva remarks, 'I couldn't make it on Sunday. What was your sermon about, Father?'

'You know me, nurse. I only have one theme.'

'Yes, I know. Love.'

'This time it was more about humility and reconciliation.'

'You really are a bit odd today,' Eva said when we were alone for a second.

'I'll tell you all about it when we get a moment.'

That moment doesn't arrive until lunch time.

'Don't get into a state over a bit of grass,' Eva said after listening to me. 'They almost all try it these days.'

I swallow my greasy goulash soup and would like to nod in agreement that nothing's wrong. She can talk. I bet her boys wouldn't do anything like that. 'And what about her truancy?'

'Did you like going to school?'

'I went, though.'

'Those were different times. Besides, your dad was a tartar.'

They were different times and my father behaved like a tartar. These are better times, or there's more freedom at least; my daughter's father isn't a tartar, he's just missing, he just went else-where.

Eva believes in something. There has to be something that transcends mankind, she says, or there'd be no sense to life. And that's how she brings up her boys. The trouble is I haven't man-aged to give my little girl any belief because I myself am not sure that life has any meaning.

As I'm coming out of the surgery at the end of the afternoon that young man, who is fifteen years my junior and thinks I'm beautiful, is standing there waiting for me. He is holding a bunch of flowers. He can't seriously be intending to offer me five white roses. Who has he mistaken me for?

5

When I was a little boy I had a terrific urge to go to Africa and take part in a snake hunt. I'd read about a snake hunter in South Africa who was bitten by a black mamba, whose bite is supposed to kill you within five minutes. But that hunter was carrying a syringe with serum. He injected himself and man-aged to drive to hospital, where he still had the strength to ask them to put him on an artificial lung. Then he became paralysed. He was aware of everything and could hear everything, but was unable to show it. For six days he listened to the doctors talking about him and discussing whether he'd survive. He did survive. I longed to experience something of the sort. I wanted to own a black mamba, except that a black mamba is very big: an adult can grow to four metres in length and we only had a small flat. Besides, where would I find a mamba?

But I did manage to make a terrarium and got a beautiful red-horned snake to put in it, as well as a rattlesnake, *Sistrurus catenatum*, that I used to catch frogs for. People regard the snake as a symbol of evil and cunning. It's not true. It's people who are cunning; a snake simply has to feed itself. When it's not hungry or doesn't feel threatened, it is harmless.

But Mum couldn't stand snakes or frogs and one day she declared it was either her or those 'monsters'. So I had to sell them. I don't have any snakes, but I still live with Mum.

These days I satisfy my thirst for adventure partly at work and partly in hero games. In those games you can have African war drums playing if you want to. Each player has a number of lives, so one can be a bit more reckless than in real life.

I met my last girlfriend, Věra, at one of those games. She played to perfection a rich girl captured by terrorists. She wasn't afraid of being killed or mistreated and she flirted fantastically with the nobody being played by me. We started going out together last autumn. We could have had a child together, which would definitely have pleased my mum, but Věra didn't want a child until she'd finished college, and I wasn't particularly keen either. We split up a month ago.

I think I hurt her when I suggested we break it off. She wanted to know what I had against her.

What could I tell her? That it annoys me how little she knows about life, that she knows nothing about what happened in the past, that she has no understanding of what's going on nowadays, and has no idea of the sort of life she'd like to live. Nothing terrifies or bothers her, but nothing excites her either. She just flirts with life.

I didn't find anything particularly wrong with her, nothing that could be put into words, nothing she would be able to understand. I simply realized once again that I was confronted by a void, that I was simply incapable of completing something that others would have completed. Or could it be, on the contrary, that I was able to put a speedy end to a relationship that would have ended anyway?

That dizzy sense of standing above a void meant that I am still single. On more than one occasion, the moment has loomed ominously that I might change my status and I'd probably never hear my war drums again, let alone set off in search of them, but suddenly they would start thundering so loud I'd have to run away. I'm a born tightrope walker who's scared of the wire, unless it's placed on the ground. That's an exaggeration. My present job, which has already become a routine for me, might be considered by many to be like balancing on a wire above the Grand Canyon. Maybe I really am dodging bullets and arrows and just can't hear their whistling; I simply refuse to believe it. I know facts that could ruin the careers of many people, so it wouldn't be surprising if one of them tried to cut my wire. Then when they find me with a broken neck, many people will heave sighs of relief and almost no one will shed a tear. I prefer not to talk to Mum about my work. I pretend to her and maybe to myself too that all I do is rummage in various insignificant documents about who attended what meeting and how many people took part in some stupid demonstration. I don't let on to anyone that I make copies of documents that one day, I suspect, and probably quite soon, some powerful individual is going to attempt to destroy for good. Not even good-natured tubby Jiří from the radio, who is my faithful companion in the hero games, has any idea what's on the diskettes that I'm storing at his place. Luckily my immediate superior Ondřej is doing the same thing; I know that for sure, and I assume the others are too. If they cut one of our wires it won't do them any good; the others will simply publish everything. That's how we protect ourselves.

Mum sometimes makes pointed remarks about her contemporaries who already have grandchildren. The way she sees it, grandchildren are a source of great pleasure.

I'd love to give my mother some pleasure; she hasn't had much of it in her life. First of all she waited almost nine years for Dad and when he was released they didn't have a flat or any money. She spent her whole life in jobs that required abject obedience. I can't tell how much it took out of her, but her position filled her with bitterness.

I tended to be sorry for my mother, but I idolized my father. He embodied for me courage and integrity. He was forced to work in the uranium mines for five years, and when he was finally released from the camp the only job he was allowed to take was as a warehouseman, even though he had studied maths and spoke five languages. That's how things were in those days. But he didn't complain. He maintained that they had already ruined enough of his life, so why should he ruin it even more by fretting?

When I was small he used to read me stories from the *Tales of Old Bohemia* and later he helped me with maths, Latin and English. He also taught me woodcraft: how to make fire without matches, how to distinguish different animal tracks and, of course, how to put up a tent and not leave the tiniest bit of litter behind in the countryside. He would also tell me about the Red Indians and he carved me a beautiful totem, which I still have hanging above my bed. He also made me a little tom-tom and taught me how to play it.

Once I was quarrelling with a boy of my age – I must have been nine or ten at the time – and the boy hurled at me, 'Anyway, your dad's an old lag!' We had a fight over it, but that accusation stuck in my memory. It's true that Mum told me Dad was totally innocent and in fact he was a hero, but what if she was just saying it? And what if people around me didn't know?

Dad seldom talked about the camp, although on a couple of occasions he told me how cruelly he had been treated at interrogations. He only mentioned one of his torturers. He went by the name of Rubáš, but no one knew what his real name was. This man was particularly cruel; he would wake my father up night after night, and while he was interrogating him he would beat my father on the hands, the soles of his feet and his back when he refused to divulge anything about his friends. He ordered Dad to be put in a punishment cell where it was close to freezing, and instead of a blanket he was given a stinking mouldy rag. 'Just so you know what you're worth,' was his reply when my father complained.

I wanted to know what had happened to the ruffian, but Dad had no idea. They all disappeared, he told me, and he definitely had no desire to meet them. But I imagined tracking the brute down one day. I would watch out for him on one of his walks and then tie him up, chloroform him and carry him back to Dad on my back, the way Bivoj brought home the wild boar in the legend. Then let Dad do with him what he liked.

I could tell Dad all my secrets as I knew he'd never try to interfere in my life.

When he was dying I used to sit with him at the hospital. The day before he died he said, 'Don't worry, I'll fight it.' He didn't moan although he was in pain and wanted to go on living. When it was all over I cried like a little boy, although I was almost twenty-three.

The moment I accepted the job at our Institute I thought about him. I'm sure he'd have been pleased that I want to do something about restoring justice to its rightful place in the world. I still had the same plan: to find those who landed him in prison and the ones who interrogated and tortured him. I'd imagine the moment when I'd perhaps stand face to face with them and demand that they explain and defend their behaviour.

It wasn't at all easy to fulfil that resolution. I wasn't the one who chose the individual cases I worked on – they were assigned to me. And the further one looked back into the past the more difficult it was to look for information; and even when I turned up names in our files it didn't mean I would find the people they belonged to. It was as if they had disappeared from the face of the earth, or it was that the threads of their lives had been severed again and again. And even when I managed to retie some of them or root out new addresses and places of employment, I would discover that the thread had been severed for good, years before. And instead of meeting the scoundrel face to face, I'd find myself in a graveyard.

On the contrary, it was Mum who made demands on my life, particularly after Dad died, and I've resisted them. Only rarely have we spoken together about matters of importance. I didn't even tell her about breaking up with Věra, even though they knew each other and Mum was already sizing her up as a future daughter-in-law. I haven't even told her about my new love; I expect it would alarm her.

I find it impossible to say what attracts me to Kristýna. It's probably something subconscious. It's as if she reminded me of some encounter in the distant past, so distant, in fact, that it may not even have taken place in my present life. But it was an encounter that must have made an indelible impression on me.

We're poles apart in terms of age, profession and personality. She's educated – a dentist with an adolescent daughter – and she told me she suffers from depression. She warned me that she is insufferable when she's down. She smokes. She enjoys wine. I drink wine only rarely and I've never even tried smoking, probably on account of Dad.

I bring her roses.

'You're crazy,' she said the last time. 'Why should you offer me flowers?'

We were sitting in the wine bar again. We're still in the phase when we share important details about our lives. She told me about her father, who was a Party busybody whose activity she despised, and about her sister, who is a professional singer: apparently she predicted Kristýna would die by her own hand. She also spoke without anger about her ex-husband, whom I esteem and she loved; I think she still loves him, although she won't admit it. I was also struck by her date of birth.

The thing is, I'm more and more convinced that the position of the planets is important for our lives, but I'm also beginning to penetrate the mystery that numbers have for us. When she mentioned that she was born on the day Stalin died, it struck me as an odd or even fateful coincidence.

The Soviet despot seems to me like some dreadful Titan: not one born from the blood of Uranus, but one constantly being reborn from the blood of his murdered victims. Although he died long before I was born, I am constantly being reminded of the crimes of some and the paltriness of others as I encounter them daily in the files I deal with. I'm convinced that his death reopened for part of mankind a door that was firmly locked against human dignity, tolerance, justice and compassion. To be born on the day of his death meant entering the world on one of the most momentous days of the twentieth century.

Kristýna also told me that her grandmother and all her relatives on that side of the family died in the gas chambers and that she was unable to reconcile herself with the fact that there were people who could poison others in their thousands, even babies and infants. I thought she would burst into tears as she was speaking about it; I could see she was crying inside over those murders of long ago and over the atrocities committed against her relations.

Was it possible to live in such a world? She had nothing to expect from life: she really expected nothing. From the way she assured me of this I sensed that, on the contrary, she still lives in expectation, she teeters on the borderline between expectation and despair. If despair prevails she could well put an end to herself. I think she is one of those who would not fear to take that step.

But she is afraid of me. She is afraid to come closer. We fear each other and yet we also attract one another.

But we have to live, I told her, in order to make discoveries, for instance. To share them with others and pass them on. We have to strive so that justice doesn't disappear from the earth, or at least so that love should govern our lives.

'That's not a matter of at least,' she objected. 'But which of us is capable of it?'

She was expecting me to say that I could, that maybe together we both could, but I didn't, because she was right: I don't know anybody who could.

She has sunshiny hair almost down to her waist; it gives her a little-girl look, but her gaze is sad. She has the bearing of a queen. I find her sadness arousing. I longed to touch her, to caress, at least, those hands that radiated tenderness, but at the same time the thought seemed to me sinfully improper, as if it would mean crossing some barrier, breaking some taboo, whose violation would provoke divine retribution.

We drank a whole bottle of wine together, although I had only one glass. As we were saying goodbye she hesitated for a moment. I realized that she was waiting to see whether I might suggest we met again, or that she herself was about to make a similar suggestion. But we suppressed our urges and said nothing. I expect it would be more sensible never to see each other again.

6

He is lying next to me, naked. His skin is smooth, clean and fresh like Jana's. I wasn't the one who invited him home. I didn't seduce him; he asked me to pay him a call; he was alone at home as his mother was out of town.

He led me to his small room. Two of the walls are lined with bookshelves. Amidst the books an old couch, wide enough for one, maybe wide enough for two to make love, but not wide enough for two to sleep on. He has no pictures. Above the bed there hangs an American Indian totem, a little painted drum and a mandolin. A computer stands on a small battered table. Alongside the windows there are two black loudspeakers. The window looks out on a yard; I noticed that even though the curtains are drawn.

He promised to show me some old prints. He promised me Beethoven, Chopin and Tchaikovsky and kept telling me I was the most beautiful and interesting woman he'd ever met. I didn't say I knew he had other intentions apart from showing me old prints. I didn't say that although his mother is out of town I'm also a mother, that he was simply looking at the world through some sort of hallucinatory spectacles. All I said was, 'Don't be silly, you can't mean it when you say I'm beautiful.'

He can't mean it seriously, but here he is lying next to me, caressing my breasts. He has long fingers; he could weave spells with them, not just play the mandolin or leaf through documents. His tongue is slightly rough and damp. When we were making love a moment ago he was patient and tender. Dear God, how long is it since a man was patient and tender with me? When was the last time I met a fellow who'd care about what I feel? He told me that he had only ever gone out with younger girls. He didn't add that he also wanted to try it for once with a woman who was old enough to be his mother. He just said, 'I want you to feel good with me.'

'I do feel good with you.' My toyboy put on some music but then forgot to change the CD.

'You're special,' he said.

'Special in what way?'

'As a person.'

'How can you know?'

'It's not a matter of knowing. I feel it. The way I feel you're often sad.'

'I'm not sad now.'

'Yes you are, even now.'

'Yes, maybe I am.'

'Why?'

'Because I feel good with you. Because I know it's only for a moment.' I don't say: I know you'll leave me.

'It won't be just for a moment.'

'Everything is just for a moment. We are all of us here only for a moment.' I don't say that according to my husband we're only here for two blinks of God's eye, then the sea of cosmic time closes over us and we can't even hear its murmur.

'I'd like to spend a lifetime with you.'

'Mine or yours?'

'Ours.'

'But I'll die before you. I'm old.'

He tries to convince me that I'm not old, and anyway none of us knows when we'll die. He then asks me a surprising question: 'Are you in love with anyone?'

'Yes: with you, of course.'

'With someone else, I mean.'

'How can you ask me like that? I wouldn't be here with you otherwise, would I?'

'Forgive me. But you were in love?'

'That's ages ago.'

'Your husband . . .'

'Don't talk about him now.'

He goes on caressing me. I rest my head on his chest. It's covered in almost invisibly fine blond hairs – my husband's was covered in a thick, dark growth. I used to tell him he was like a chimpanzee. He hurt me. People mostly hurt those nearest to them, and I fear that this boy will hurt me too one day. I wish I could tell him so, beg him not to hurt me!

I feel like crying. 'Look at me.'

'But I am looking at you.'

'Why don't you say anything to me?'

'I don't want to say the things people always say.'

'But I want to hear them.'

'It's lovely to be with you.'

'You don't regret it?'

I want him to say he loves me, that my age doesn't bother him, that he really doesn't find me old. But his thoughts are elsewhere; he's thinking about how to make love to me again. But it's time I went. It's starting to get dark outside and I have a daughter at home. That's if she's at home and didn't make herself scarce when she discovered her mother was enjoying herself somewhere. He asks, 'What do you fear most in life?'

'Betrayal,' I say; I don't have to think twice.

'No, I meant whether you fear something in particular.'

'Fire, I expect,' I said.

'That's because you're a Pisces.'

'I saw someone on fire,' I tell him. 'It was my aunt. She set herself alight. But I don't want to think about it now. I'd just like to light a cigarette. May I?'

He gets up and runs naked to fetch me an ashtray. At that moment he reminds me of my first love of long ago: the same narrow shoulders. I was in love with Psycho in those days, madly. I wonder if anything like that will ever happen to me again.

He returns. This household does not own such a thing as an ashtray, so he thrusts some kind of saucer at me instead. He asks whether I'm thirsty.

He has narrow wrists; in fact his arms are almost girlish, like my daughter's. Suddenly I see her arm and also the syringe, the needle she punctures it with; my little girl is out gallivanting somewhere while I selfishly lie here having a smoke in a strange bedroom on a strange couch.

'A penny for your thoughts,' he says.

'I have to go.'

'Don't go yet.'

'I have to, my daughter's waiting for me.' I gather up my clothes and make for the bathroom, which is also unfamiliar. There is nothing here of mine; I don't even know which is the hot tap.

'I'll bring you a clean towel,' he calls after me. Then he opens the door a chink and puts a towel into my outstretched hand. I'm glad he didn't have it here ready; he wasn't sure I'd ever come in here.

I have a quick shower and get dressed. I put on a bit of eye make-up. Heavens, what am I doing here?

The roses he bought me are standing in a vase. This time they are red. I take them with me.

He sees me to the metro station. He wants to descend to the depths with me but I tell him he'd better not.

OK, he'll be waiting for me again tomorrow.

'But I've got a long surgery tomorrow.'

'I know.'

'How could you know?'

'I read it on the surgery door.'

'Don't come, I have to be at home in the evening. Because of my daughter.'

'You weren't home this evening.'

'That's the point.'

'And what if I went home with you?'

I can't bring this boy home, can I? Unless I said, Jana, I've brought you a new friend: his name is Jan; he's going to give you some coaching. In what? Everything. The trouble is it's too late for coaching.

He doesn't ask me why I don't want to invite him. He'll wait for me the day after tomorrow, then. He gives me a hug and a quick kiss.

'Thank you,' I say.

'For what?'

'For everything. And these roses.'

On the steps I turn and look back: he's still standing and waving me goodbye. Why didn't I make up my mind to stay there till morning? I could have called Jana; I could have told her I'd be coming a bit later and sent her to bed. No, next time, maybe. It'll be better next time: if there'll be a next time.

81

I tremble at the thought I might never see him again. It will all end one day; the question is how many days are left before it does. If we didn't anticipate the end how could we value what we still have left?

I unlock the street door and check my mailbox. One letter from goodness knows who, the Journal of the Stomatological Association and – the handwriting gives it away – a letter from my anonymous correspondent. I ought to tear it up and chuck it in the dustbin. But the dustbin is in front of the house and I don't feel like going out again. This time Mr Anon doesn't call me names, he just issues threats. He warns me not to venture outdoors in the evening because the Hour of Reckoning is Nigh.

I venture out, nevertheless, in order to open the stinking dustbin, tear up the letter and toss the pieces into the rotting garbage.

7

I had to go and see Dad and make him those pancakes, seeing I'd blabbed about them to Mum. That was a fantastic performance. I really managed to tug her heartstrings. The thought of me taking care of my poor ailing dad, who left us in the shit. I haven't been to see him for at least a month. The last time was in hospital with Mum.

It took me a long time to find some clobber to put on, 'cos when I'm visiting Dad I have to wear something that wouldn't be an affront to decent people. The trouble is I didn't have anything that wouldn't make Dad go spare. If I put on some ordinary Levis he'd start going on about the cost of them and telling me not to buy things like that when I'm not earning and he has to pay maintenance for me. But my old jeans had three ginormous holes in them and I was afraid he wouldn't survive the shock. In the end I got out an old dress I made myself when I was about twelve. It was impossibly crude and the colour of dog shit, in fact it looked like an upside-down trash can without a bottom, but it wouldn't be an affront to decent people.

Dad was the last person I fancied seeing.

I never liked visiting him even when I was forced to every week, which was something they dreamt up at some stupid court or other. Dad was fairly OK when he was living with us. I remember him calling me Jankie-pankie and bringing me Mole colouring books. And he'd tell me how we'd fly to Mars in a rocket ship. I thought he was talking about the chocolate bar. Why not if the moon can be made of cheese?

Dad said he learnt tidiness when he was doing military service. And he was really proud of being better at folding his blankets and clothes than any of the other cretins. He'd really knock me out when he demonstrated to me how to stack clothes.

And he used to take me to the planetarium and the observatory. He had some pals there. Stars were his big thing. Most of all he wanted to shock me with Saturn's rings, the moons around Jupiter, the black holes and the Big Bang. He loved the Big Bang 'cos that's how everything is supposed to have started. He used to tell me how in the beginning all there was was a tiny little marble, smaller than a tomato but ever so heavy 'cos it contained all the stars we can see and even those we can't. A real pain. And that poor guy believed it and I bet he even told those morons in his school about it. And they'd have to repeat it after him: the stars we can see and even those we can't. That was his favourite: repeat after me. Repeat after me: I am not to laugh at the teachers! Repeat after me: before dinner well-mannered people wash their hands! Repeat after me: only louts fail to greet older people! And I used to repeat it otherwise I'd immediately get a clout and ever since then I've hated washing my hands and now and again I shout to some poor old pensioner: Ciao! or Hi!

Mum didn't have to repeat things after him, but even so she was more scared of Dad than I was. If she was a quarter of an hour late with lunch on a Sunday, Dad would look at his watch and say the time out loud. 'It's five past twelve . . . it's ten past twelve' and on and on. And Mum would apologize and be full of excuses, such as the meat was tough, instead of telling him to get lost or go to the pub.

Dad also explained to me that everything we can see, as well as what we can't see, just happened. It wasn't created by some god, 'cos he'd have to be so big he wouldn't fit into heaven and he'd have to be so incredibly old that he wouldn't be even able to survive it himself. I didn't understand that bit anyway. Sometimes I used to go to church with Mum's Eva. I quite enjoyed it, especially the singing and the saints with their eyes rolled upwards as if they'd been chewing loads of dope or had seen something that totally knocked them out. Maybe they were looking at the tiny little marble that made the Big Bang. And also I didn't understand why angels needed to have wings like geese or swans, when they could fly just like that, like when I dream about flying; that's why they're angels, after all. There was also a ginger-haired server I fancied.

Whenever we went out for the day, Dad always used to be testing our knowledge of flowers and trees and songbirds, not to mention the battles that were fought in that particular spot. That's a pasqueflower, that's an alpine currant, that's a cinquefoil and that's a wood warbler. Can you hear it singing tweet-tweet? Well I certainly couldn't hear it, but Mum made an effort and said, 'Oh, yes, tweet-tweet. You're great, Karel. How do you manage to remember all those things?' And I think she might have really meant it. And he believed her, 'cos the next thing he said was, 'Well you had to memorize the human anatomy.' Horrendous.

Mum was really nuts about him. I realized that, and even though he looked old enough to be her father she must have really loved him 'cos she still thinks about him all the time even though she pretends she couldn't give a toss about him. She really takes it to heart that he's in such a bad way.

Then when I was at least in third year they started to fight like total loonies. They'd always shut themselves in the bedroom or the kitchen and yell at each other as if I couldn't hear. At first I thought it was because of me, because Dad thought I was disobedient, untidy and lazy and that I would come to a sticky end, but then Dad stopped coming home in time for dinner and soon he didn't come home at all; and Mum would sit with the TV on and cry her eyes out, even when *Camera Capers* was on. I'd wake up sometimes in the night and she'd be sitting in the kitchen reading or just staring at the wall and I realized they'd probably get divorced.

Dad moved in with some bird who worked in a bank. She was tall and lanky and totally flat-chested. She had really ugly teeth, a bit like a vampire; perhaps she was one, 'cos Dad became really ill and whenever she said anything to me it was obvious that she was totally brain-dead. I don't know what Dad saw in her; maybe he just ran away from me because I started to get bolshie. And he also caught me with a ciggie, but they were already getting divorced by then anyway.

Dad has the sort of eyes that put fear into people. He can stand and look at someone for ages without blinking. I never knew why he stared like that. I just knew he wasn't pleased with me and that I'd done something wrong and I could expect some punishment. He was a real genius at dreaming up punishments. If I didn't finish my lunch, for instance, Mum would have to cook me the same thing for the rest of the week. One time I didn't want to wear this vile flowery frock that Grandma must have found on a rubbish tip somewhere or dug out of Auntie Lída's things. Mum split on me so Dad gave me a good hiding and then I had to wear that frock to school every day until I managed to pour some tomato soup with noodles down the front of it in the school canteen.

When he left us, he wasn't able to punish me any more. I expect he didn't feel like it any more; he wasn't bothered, he was already soppy about his beanpole. He just kept on trying to explain that it wasn't his fault but Mum's 'cos she hadn't looked after him properly and was always having those black moods of hers that he just couldn't cope with. And on top of that she smoked. He told me he needed a bit of peace, fresh air and some enjoyment out of life. And at least a hint of attention. We both needed it, he explained, but my mother would often leave us in the lurch and go off with some pals after surgery instead of coming home. Apparently he used to have to cook me something for dinner at the last minute, but I was too young to remember, according to him. He said Mum had no sense of order and he couldn't understand how someone like that could repair people's teeth properly. Apart from that their interests were completely different. Mum didn't even enjoy tennis or skiing – surely I must have noticed how she was like an elephant on skis – and she wasn't interested in history. He's told me loads of times that it wasn't a home but a place of weeping and wailing. 'Her hysteria even started to rub off on me and you were being affected too. In fact you're going to spend your life trying to recover from it.'

At first I used to try to say something interesting. I even told him I missed him. But then I realized he'd been really vile to Mum and me and I'd try to do a bunk as soon as I could. That beanpole left him last year too. It struck me he might come back to us, but he didn't.

So now he's been ill. Mum reckons he's in a bad way. He doesn't stare as much as he used to, but he still scares me. That's why I dolled myself up like Pippie Longstocking and didn't put any eyeliner round my puffy eyes. I was so sober I almost staggered climbing the stairs up to his flat; I was chewing some mint gum so he wouldn't know I'd had a last ciggie in front of the house.

I hadn't bought him any roses or even stolen any for him in the park. Why should I?

'Hi, Dad,' I said when he opened the door. 'I've come to make you pancakes.'

CHAPTER THREE

1

I won't be with my daughter this evening anyway. Lucie called me this afternoon to say she's just back from the other side of the globe and wants to see me.

I call Jana, who is surprisingly at home, and mention warily that I'll be home a bit later this evening. She wants to know where I'm going but I don't go into details; I simply tell her to get on with her maths homework and warn her that I'll test her when I come in.

I have a rendezvous with Lucie at a wine restaurant just below the Castle. It's an expensive place, but Lady Bountiful is treating me. She's tanned because she's spent almost a month in California and seen the Pacific Ocean, which I'll never see. She says it's so cold that in those hot regions a cloud of mist rises from the surface and covers the sea and the shore. She takes a box of photographs out of the shoulder bag she always carries. They really do show houses and even the Golden Gate Bridge emerging in fairytale fashion out of the mist. The suspension cables of the bridge glisten with drops of condensed water like the threads of some monstrous spider's web. My friend has also been in the desert and warmed herself up at the hottest spot on the planet; she has brought back for her own benefit and mine pictures of coloured rocks and flowers that brighten the dunes for a single day and then perish in the heat. There are also photos of giant cacti, but they are from the botanical gardens at Berkeley, which I'll never see either.

I ask her what sort of a time she has had.

Fantastic. It's a fantastic country for a short stay, because of the entertainment. That's something that people there definitely worship more than what they go to church for, and entertainers have the best-paid jobs.

That's something I know without having to travel halfway round the world. I don't have to look too far, for that matter: my sister sings a couple of tear-jerkers a month and she's a rich woman compared to me, whose only job is to help rid people of pain.

'What about your poison-penfriend?' Lucie recalls.

'Mr Anonymous is about the only one who is at all faithful to me.'

Lucie wants to know if I suspect anyone in particular. I ought to be careful, she warns me, and report the letters to the police. And I should definitely carry Mace.

I don't intend to report it to the police. They'd just waste my time with typing up some statement. There's no chance they'll go looking for an unknown person who hasn't even attacked me yet. And I don't think I'd be likely to spray poison in someone's eyes.

I ask her whether she was on her own all the time. This is the question my friend has been waiting for. She pulls out a few photos showing her in a luxury convertible with some swarthy fellow with black curly hair, a Latin mostly likely. He's holding her round the waist, flashing his pearl-white teeth and displaying his biceps. He must be at least two divine blinks younger than her. But I'm sure that that didn't bother her. She has lots of other photos in the box. These don't feature the dark Romeo; instead they show skeletons with dark skin stretched over them, children with large eyes and swollen bellies who reach out for a hand holding a bowl with some kind of soup.

'Those are from Rwanda. They must have got mixed up with these,' she explains. She takes back the photos and stuffs them back in her bag. 'And how about you?' she asks.

In my mind's eye I immediately see a small book-filled room, a young man who brings me roses running naked and barefoot for an ashtray after making tender love to me. I could mention him. I'd enjoy talking about him; but Lucie would certainly want to hear all the juicy details, of course. That was what we always used to talk about, and we'd make fun of the fellows who play the he-man and when it comes to displaying their virility they wilt, and all that's left of their pride is a little worm. But I don't feel like going into details; I'm ashamed that I succumbed and that my feelings are still getting the better of me.

I say nothing and she says, 'You wait, when that Indian-summer romance hits you.' And she goes on to tell me about the young dark fellow's sensuality. I listen to her and think of my own young man, who doesn't have biceps or curly black hair, but who loves me perhaps more than for just a short stay. He promised he'd be waiting for me tomorrow. Where will we go? I can hardly invite him home. Most likely we'll find a wine bar somewhere. And then what? We could go somewhere to a park – Petřín or Šarka, if it's fine. Twenty years ago I thought nothing of making love in the parks and woods around Prague. In those days I didn't stop to think whether it would be fine or not, but made love in the rain and even the snow. Interestingly enough, the snow didn't feel cold; my back was scorching, in fact. These days I'd be worried about my ovaries and kidneys. And I no longer feel like making love somewhere on grass covered in dog shit or having the feeling that someone's getting turned on by peeping at us from the bushes. We could go to my surgery, of course, and make love in the dentist's chair or on the bench in the waiting room.

The wine we are drinking is nice and heavy. It goes to my head and drives out all my worries.

I notice a man gesturing at me from the far corner of the restaurant. A familiar face that I'm unable to place – he's almost entirely bald, with just a bit of greying stubble at the sides. It could be one of my patients. Then the fellow stands up and walks tipsily over to our table. 'Hello, Kristýna! You haven't changed in the least.'

I can't address him by name or tell him he hasn't changed either, as I don't recognize him. I simply say hello.

'I won't disturb you,' he promises. 'I simply wanted to say hello to my great love of long ago.'

'It's impolite to tell a lady that something was long ago,' Lucie chides him.

'No, it really was long ago,' I say, remembering now the man who first forced me to have an abortion. He's lost his black pigtail, as well as the rest of his hair, but on the other hand he's made a career for himself. I occasionally read something about him. He's a drugs specialist dealing with young people. But since the time he drove me to take an innocent life I've lost all interest in him.

He tells me once more that I'm still beautiful, even more beautiful than then, in fact. He moves a chair over to our table and, as was his wont, starts to undress me with his eyes, while announcing that he works at the ministry and lectures on the new anti-drugs legislation. He is against making drug possession a criminal offence; he's a liberal and wants to influence the young through education. As he blabbers on, my 'educationalist' strips me bare with his eyes.

'Do you have any children?' I interrupt him.

He nods. 'Why do you ask?'

The prat. He asks me why I ask. Some other girl didn't let him force her to go before the board, so he became a father.

'I've got two boys,' he declares, almost proudly. 'How about you?'

'I've a daughter,' I tell him. 'I could have had two, but the criminal who fathered the first didn't want me to have her.'

Offended, he gets up, says he had no intention of disturbing us and staggers off. But my mood is ruined anyway.

'Men, they're all disgusting,' Lucie says in a show of solidarity. 'Spiders and men. Except that spiders are harmless.'

It is almost midnight when I emerge from the metro. I'm dreadful, abandoning my little girl again. I almost break into a run.

At the corner of our street a man emerges from the dim entrance to a block of flats and stands in my path, thrusting an arm towards me as if to throttle me. I freeze. 'Give us ten crowns, missus. I've got nowhere to sleep.' He is staggering so much he has to hold on to the wall. He's either drunk or high, but surprisingly I feel a sense of relief. This isn't my anonymous letter-writer wanting to kill me, but just some homeless bloke. I take out my purse and tip all my loose change into his palm.

He closes his palm and staggers off without a word of thanks.

When I reach the door of our block and try to unlock it, my hands are shaking and I'm unable to get the key into the lock. I fancy I can hear footsteps behind me and even someone breathing wheezily, but when I turn round there is no one there.

The flat is already dark and silent. I lock the door behind me and put on the safety chain, something I never do otherwise.

I open the door of Jana's room and hear noisy breathing. There's an odd smell: a mixture of joss sticks, eau de cologne and insect repellent. I don't know since when my daughter has been a fan of joss sticks, but that sweet, penetrating scent is more likely intended to cover some other smell. I'm familiar with that trick. I used to use it when I smoked a cigarette at home and didn't have time to ventilate the room and get rid of the smell before Dad got home. I feel like giving my daughter a good shake and asking her what she was up to here and what she was trying to conceal. But she'd only deny everything. There is a sheet of paper with writing on it lying on the table. I read the first sentence: 'A triangle is the plane figure formed by connecting three points not in a straight line by straight line segments.' It's not a message for me. Or maybe it is: see what a lousy mother you are; I sat here working diligently while you were living it up in a pub.

That's something Dad forgot in that dream of mine. A rotten daughter, a lousy wife and a useless mother.

2

I fell asleep quickly, but my ex-husband wormed his way into my dream again. We were travelling together to some mountains where our accommodation was a wooden chalet. We were still young and had Jana with us, but we left her in the chalet and set off up a narrow track cut out of the rocks. At a certain moment we had to hold on to big loops of rope that hung above our heads in order to cross a ravine. I was afraid as I passed from one loop to another because the ropes were rotten. And then one of the loops broke and I was suspended above the chasm, only holding on by my right hand. I called to my husband for help. I called to him by name, but he had disappeared; he was no longer with me and I watched in horror as the screws that held the end of the rope gradually worked themselves loose from the rock. I kept on screaming, while thinking about Jana and wondering what would happen to her, who would take care of her when I plunged into the abyss.

It's four in the morning and it's still dark outside. My nightdress is soaked in sweat and my throat is dry.

I get up and go barefoot into the kitchen. The fridge is humming as I enter; it also judders; I ought to put a wedge under one side. There are lots of things I ought to do – things to repair and see to, but at this moment I just take out a bottle of wine and mix myself a spritzer.

When, at last, will my husband stop deserting me and disappearing just as I'm suspended above a chasm?

I go back to bed and try to think of something positive. Once when I was depressed I asked my husband what was the point of human life.

He looked at me in amazement, as if my question was evidence of my inferiority, but then he consented to reply. Fundamentally speaking we don't actually have any life, because the duration of our lives is so brief in comparison with cosmic time that in fact it is unrecordable. And what can't be recorded virtually does not exist.

An interesting answer to my question. We live as if we actually didn't exist. If God did create this Universe, he knows nothing about us, only we think we know about him. We are too small to be measured and so we can do harm. We can also kill – which we do a lot, or at least men all over the world do.

But people want to leave something behind them. When my dad was young I'm sure he believed he was helping to plant a new Garden of Eden, though he forgot that the soil that life grows from is love. But his head gardener preached hatred and so instead of creating a garden Dad helped pave an execution yard. He never admitted it, but towards the end he must have had an inkling of how woefully wrong he had been. And he didn't build a house or even plant a tree that would yield something; he didn't have the time and it wasn't in his nature. But from time to time he would bring home some useless objects; I don't know where he came by them, most likely during confiscations he took part in. He brought home a box of angling flies even though he never went fishing. He brought books in languages he didn't understand and gave Mum a box stuffed with reels of grey thread. The thread was still there when he died. There is so much of it that if we tied all the lengths end to end I expect they'd stretch round the Equator.

What will I leave behind? Plenty of bridges, fillings and dentures, of course. And in fact, ever since I've been able to order any materials I please, they've been top-quality bridges, fillings and dentures. Also a daughter that I've not been very good at bringing up. But what can possibly remain after the tenth or even the hundredth blink of God's eye, when all the words are forgotten and there's no one left to remember what I looked like? Who then will look at the crumbling photos, if any remain somewhere?

Maybe deeds of love leave some trace behind – or at least their repercussions do. Maybe someone, some higher justice, is counting by how many drops one manages to lower the level of pain in the world. That's one thing I've managed – in people's mouths, at least. Pain in the soul I can't do anything about, not even my own.

The darkness outside is disappearing. I glance out of the window. The streets are still empty; the metal bodies of the cars are damp. A lonely drunk staggers along the opposite pavement; it could be the one I gave that handful of change to.

I take out the box with Dad's notebooks and leaf through them. I'm looking to see if he didn't leave me some message after all.

But most of the entries are boringly inane: just a mass of words, clichés and references to everyday activities – what he ate, saw to or said in speeches. He bought himself new boots. He went to a football match. He had the wireless repaired. He was at the dentist's! He chaired a meeting at the Red Glow co-operative. There were only occasional references to people. Just as well, maybe.

But he did meet with his friend, Comrade P., with whom he spent two years in a concentration camp, and they reminisced together. *The last days were the worst. There was no more food. They didn't even issue any bread. But the executions still went on and the SS went on organizing transports. We remembered how during those days we would look up at the sky, which by then was controlled by the Allies, but what good was it to us seeing that the Germans still ruled on the ground. And the hunger was awful. We'd already eaten the last of the bread and apart from water there was nothing to swallow. We no longer had the strength to get up out of our bunks and all we could think about was food and whether the Soviets would reach us before we were wiped out. We could also hear the thud of artillery shells coming nearer. They were already quite close.*

I imagine that young man: my dad, in blue-and-white-striped camp clothes lying in some hideous barrack-room, emaciated and hungry, waiting. He knows that the next moments will decide whether he'll live or die. Like a patient on an operating table. Before he falls asleep a patient has the hope that he has entrusted himself to people who want to save him. Dad was lying on a plank bed and his only source of hope was the thud of shells that would scare me to death.

Then the Soviets arrived, the windscreens of their trucks bearing photographs of Stalin, the Great Leader, and hammers and sickles. They came to the rescue, gave bread, smoked fish, a soup called *shchi* and vodka. They brought salvation and a vision, and it was as if that determined how things were to be for years to come. For him, for me, for my country and for the whole world.

I informed Comrade P. that Ilse Koch, that SS monster, has died. The fiend of Buchenwald, who collected gloves and book covers made from the skin of our comrades who were tortured to death, and who even had lampshades made of it, had hanged herself with her bedclothes a few days ago in her prison cell. A small satisfaction, at least, for all those she tortured. You see, a moment ago I was doing men an injustice: women commit murder too.

I recall Dad telling me about that pervert. In his eyes she was an SS monster. But the monster was only able to behave the way she did because a monstrous system had divided people into humans and subhumans. Subhumans could be jailed, tortured and poisoned – without trial and without mercy. How many monsters did similar things here in later years with Dad's approval or at least his tacit consent. How many people were tortured to death? They didn't make lampshades out of human skin, but lampshades weren't the essential issue.

What went through Ilse's mind when she was making a noose out of her bedclothes? Had she understood something about herself or did she simply have a sense of emptiness and of the hopelessness of her fate?

We all have a sense of hopelessness from time to time but we are not strong-minded enough.

I get up and look in on Jana. She's asleep, of course. I return to my own bedroom and Dad's notebooks. It crosses my mind to see whether he noted how I had broken what he considered a valuable vase. How old was I then? I wasn't going to school yet, so I could have been five, or at most six years old.

It was a big vase and I found it beautiful. It was indigo blue and there was the figure of a nymph etched into the side of it. I never saw a single flower in the vase. It stood on the dresser and the nymph smiled at me from above and lured me to her. I stood a chair up against the dresser and looked at the room through the glass of the vase and saw how it turned dark like the evening sky.

Once, when I was alone at home, I got the idea of putting some water in the vase and seeing whether the water would be blue too.

I took down that beautiful glass object and held it firmly in my arms, the way Mummy held me when I cried or when a strange dog pestered me in the street. It was odd how the glass didn't feel cold, but instead gave out a warmth – a blue warmth, most likely.

I reached the kitchen and turned on the hot tap. The vase slowly filled and the water in it really was blue and gave off steam. Then there was an odd sound that I'd never heard before: the sound of glass cracking. The vase broke in two in my arms. I can still recall the terror I felt as I tried – in vain, of course – to put the vase back together again.

First Dad interrogated me. Why had I taken the vase down? What was I intending to do with it? Why had I put hot water in it? Was I aware of the damage I'd done?

Then he gave me a good hiding. I screamed and promised to buy him a new vase when I was big; I'd buy him two beautiful vases.

When I started to earn money of my own I actually did do the rounds of a few antique shops until I eventually found a vase of a similar colour, at least, to the one I'd broken long before. But it had the image of a flying bird etched into its side, instead of a nymph.

I gave Dad the vase as a Christmas present. I got a ticking off. 'You're crazy. What am I supposed to do with a vase? Have you ever seen me buying flowers?' He'd long ago forgotten about the broken vase. It hadn't interested him and he hadn't regretted it; he had just thought it right to let me know what a dreadful thing I'd done.

I leaf through the notebooks from the end of the fifties and am unable to find any reference to the vase. Either there isn't one, or I missed it. On the other hand I notice that some female Comrade V.V. crops up repeatedly in his notes. It's probably the same person who is later referred to as W. *Saw V. Talked to V. about flowers for International Women's Day . . . We went to see* Ballad of a Soldier. *W. cried . . . Repaired W.'s sewing machine.* No more details. He was careful. He was well aware that what he wrote down could be used against him. Even so, I feel as if I'm prying as I read it. I ought to put the notebooks back in the box. Dad's dead; why do I need to know about his secrets and his sins?

Eventually I drop off to sleep for a while.

3

Outside, it's a fine May morning; it looks as if everything has burst into bloom. I rejoice in the scents that waft into my room from the nearby gardens. But I expect hayfever sufferers are desperate; my daughter also was complaining of sore eyes when she woke up this morning.

She's back at school. She took a maths test and got an E again. I asked her if she realized she'd fail. She said she did.

She wouldn't be earning her living from maths!

I asked her to kindly tell me what she'd be earning her living from. She didn't think she'd be living off me for the rest of her life, did she?

I wasn't to worry, she'd get by somehow. And probably a lot better than I had!

She's insolent, but what can I say in reply, seeing how badly I've coped with my own life? I tried to explain to her that if she didn't manage to pass her leaving exam, at least, the best she could hope from life was to be a shop assistant or a hairdresser.

She told me defiantly that she'd happily train to be a hairdresser. It was her life, and it wasn't for me to worry about.

When I was sitting in the metro, two girls of Jana's age were standing opposite me. They struck me as being clean inside and out: no war paint, no rings in their noses or even their ears. Why can't mine look like them?

I'm tired from lack of sleep. Luckily I've only a short surgery today and when it's fine, like today, people don't feel like going to the dentist and I can have a doze from time to time in the X-ray room.

I can't go home after work anyway; I have to go to the stone-mason's to order an inscription for the gravestone and buy an urn for Dad's ashes. Then I have to arrange at the cemetery office for their interment. All the beneficiaries have been summoned to the notary public next week so that he can share among us what Dad left. It's a pointless operation as all that remained are a few old clothes – including his People's Militia uniform – a bed and a box of his writings. As well as a portrait of Lenin, the great leader of the proletariat. My sister has to attend at the notary's too. Even though she won't deal with anything else, she'll be there to see the urn buried, so long as I sort everything out first.

Once, when my sister was sixteen, she came home from somewhere in an odd state. Nowadays I'd say she was high, but drugs were a rarity at that time, so she was probably just drunk. She donned the long, lacy dress she wore to dance classes and put on my Cream record with that long, impeccable drum solo. It was really sultry music and I'd made love to it several times. If *I'd* put the record on, Dad would definitely have protested, as it hadn't been vetted as politically correct. But he let my sister do what she liked because she was so frail and sickly. So she put on that sultry music and started squirming to it. It wasn't a dance, more of an ecstatic trance in which she started to prophesy our futures, including the way we'd all die. Dad would die of cancer and Mum from a painless stroke. I was supposed to die by my own hand.

'How?' I asked in astonishment.

'By your own hand,' she repeated. 'That's all I know. But it will be bloodless. I see you lying there pale and beautiful, as if covered in hoarfrost. Maybe you're frozen. But you're lying on something green. Maybe it's a lawn or maybe just a carpet.'

'And what about you?' It struck me. 'You won't say anything about yourself?'

'I don't know. Prophetesses aren't able to prophesy about themselves. Maybe I'll never die.' She laughed.

Our parents were dumbfounded and said nothing. I told her she was drunk and embarrassing, but stopped short of telling her she was callous to everyone but herself.

Dad died of lung cancer. Mum's still alive but the doctors are hard-pressed to keep her blood pressure slightly above normal. My sister, as she imagines, will never die and while I've considered suicide – self-extraction – on a couple of occasions, I've never had the determination to go through with it.

I don't feel like going to the stonemason's, the cemetery office or the notary. I hate dealing with officials, with anyone, in fact, who sits at a counter or behind a typewriter. Men should deal with arrangements: they're not reduced to tears by churlish petty bureaucrats. The most that women should take care of is shopping; but I'm a defective woman, I don't even like shopping. I hate supermarkets, where they offer me an alternative lifestyle full of junk and try to convince me with the help of sickly music that it's all I need for happiness. I dash through shops, toss the absolute minimum of things I need into a basket, and then flee. I choose shoes from window displays and either they suit me or I leave. The same goes for clothes. When they lure me with hundreds of garish outfits I have the feeling I'm looking at rows of people hanging from gallows. They hang there headless, as if their heads have been removed so as not to get in the way, because heads are totally out of place in that particular world.. Those gallows give me the horrors, and as usual I make myself scarce.

I don't have a husband; possibly I have a lover. When he last called, he asked me how I was fixed at the end of the week. I told him I'd probably be devoting myself to my daughter. He told me excitedly that he would be going to Brno to attend a seminar and was just finishing the paper he would deliver.

I asked him what it was about.

He said it was an attempt to explain how and why people subordinated themselves to criminals. He is proud to be delivering a paper. It bothers him that he didn't complete university and sometimes it strikes me that it's one reason he's attracted to me: being able to make love to a doctor. As if it particularly matters how many years one spends acquiring knowledge, which is mostly pointless.

Before the end of surgery I call home, but there is no reply. Where has she got to now, that creature who is fawning and stubborn by turns and is almost certainly pulling the wool over my eyes? I'm a gullible fool; it's obvious to everyone, and everyone eventually takes me for a ride. But there's no one I can complain to. We're each of us engineers of our own fate – to a certain extent, at least.

The stonemason's is just by the entrance to the cemetery. The lady behind the counter has an Art Nouveau look, which suits her line of business. She is also good-natured but with a gravity appropriate for dealing with the recently bereaved. She makes a computer record of Dad's name and the details to be inscribed on the headstone. Then she takes a deposit from me and prints me a receipt.

While I'm there I ask about urns and she shows me the five different types they offer, which differ more in price than in appearance. As if it matters what an urn looks like when it's going to be buried in the ground. I choose the cheapest, which is expensive anyway. I don't know what urns used to cost in the past, but the price is bound to have gone up, like everything else, from the cradle to the grave. People now have to pay for dental treatment. If you have the talent and the determination you can now make enough to afford several urns at the end of your dental career.

'Would you also be interested in a lamp or a vase?'

I'm not interested in a lamp – but what about a vase? I recall the incident from my childhood and how I promised my father I'd buy him two vases; I have only half-fulfilled that promise. And one should keep one's promises, even belatedly.

I take a look at the heavy stone and metal vessels on display. They also have ordinary ceramic vases, the lady at the computer explains, but the massive ones are preferable. The lighter ones can easily fall over in the wind or be knocked over by birds. Thieves are also more likely to steal the ceramic and metal ones. The best thing is to put everything on a chain and padlock, but they don't sell chains here.

I don't know whether any of the vases resembles the one I broke. I've forgotten its shape; I can only recall its colour.

'Do you have a blue one?'

She brings me a vase that is more amethyst than blue, but the colour doesn't matter. Not even the brightest blue will please Dad now. I buy the amethyst vase and thereby fulfil a long-standing promise. A foolish promise and a foolish purchase.

I phone home but again there is no reply. There is a bus terminal nearby; one of those buses could take me to the part of town where my former and now terminally ill husband still lives.

Half an hour later I ring his doorbell. It takes a while before I hear the sound of shuffling footsteps.

The door opens and my nostrils are assailed by the stench of unaired rooms, sweat and urine.

He looks at me, my former, only and last husband, as if he doesn't recognize me. 'It's you, is it?'

101

'I can go away again if it's not convenient.'

'No, no, I'm glad you've come.' He is visibly moved. He's wearing the dark-blue dressing gown I bought him for Christmas years ago. In those days he still had broad shoulders and muscles; every morning he used to exercise with a chest-expander and go for a run around the walls of the New Jewish Cemetery. Now the dressing grown hangs on him like on a scarecrow. His hair has thinned and is matted into dirty grey tufts. He follows my gaze and says, 'Sorry, I look dreadful.'

The voice whose clear tones used to excite me with their colour and warmth is now thick and lifeless.

'No, you look better than at the hospital.'

He asks me to sit down and he shuffles to the dresser. I notice that the large pendulum clock that hangs alongside the dresser, one of the few things he asked to take from our joint household, has stopped. It shows precisely midday or midnight. I am surprised. He always made sure it kept the right time.

He registers my gaze. 'I stopped it. Its ticking got on my nerves.' He opens the dresser and takes out a bottle of cheap red wine. 'Someone brought me this, but I'm not allowed to drink. I'll open it for you.'

I shake my head. I don't feel like drinking in front of him. 'Have you had supper?'

'I haven't had lunch yet,' he says. 'I've no appetite and I've nothing to eat.'

'Would you like me to cook you something?' I go into the kitchen and open the fridge. There is nothing in it apart from a cube of processed cheese, a roll that has gone hard, and a few raw, shrivelled potatoes.

'I'll get you something from the shop.'

'Stay here. I don't feel like anything anyway.'

I sit down opposite him. 'How do you feel?'

He just shrugs. 'They've given me some tablets, but they make me feel rotten. What about Jana?' he asks.

'She told me she'd been to see you and made you some pan-cakes.'

'Did she?' He seems surprised. 'Oh, yes, that's right. She was here,' he recalls. 'She's turned into a real beauty.'

I tell him that the beauty will probably fail her exams, that she plays truant and hangs about with a bad crowd, and that she probably smokes cannabis.

He gazes at me wearily and then asks, 'What are you going to do about it?'

Yes – what will I do about it? For a moment the old bitterness wells up in me. That's what he'd always ask. Whenever our little girl ran a temperature, when he selfishly got me pregnant but definitely had no wish to be a father, when our flat was burgled one time, whenever there was a burst pipe in the upstairs neighbour's bathroom, he would ask me the same question: 'What are you going to do about it?' Not what he was going to do, or we were going to do. A modern man, I realized at the time. Latching on to a woman and clinging to her: a little boy at his mummy's breast, who stays there until he grows tired of it and fancies being suckled elsewhere.

I realized it too late, unfortunately.

No, I mustn't be callous. Whatever he was like before, he now sits here on this chair a poor, abandoned human being who suffers and fears the end. How could it have occurred to me to seek his advice or even expect any sign of interest?

I tell him I don't know what I'll do with our adolescent. I'll seek advice from someone who is better informed.

'Drugs. We didn't have that sort of thing when I was still teaching,' he says. 'Apart from smoking in the toilets. But you oughtn't to smoke. Not at home, anyway. You set a poor example.'

Whereas he always set a good example. He didn't smoke, he didn't drink, he did morning exercises, brushed his teeth and he took his shoes off when he came in. All he did was find a mistress and demonstrate to our little girl that deception and desertion are part of life. 'How do you spend your day?' I ask, in order to switch the conversation back to the only person who still interests him.

'I sit here like this. Sometimes I read for a while. But what's the point? So most of the time I just sit here and wait and listen.'

'Do you listen to music?'

He shakes his head.

'What do you listen to?'

'The murmur of the universe. At night, when the street is free of cars, I can hear time rolling through motionless space. It's not nice. That's one reason why I stopped winding the clock. It was too much of a reminder of how time never stops rolling onwards.'

I don't know whether he is really recounting his own experience or trying to play on my emotions, or whether he is simply repeating something he read somewhere. 'Don't you sleep at night?'

'I sleep on and off, whether it's day or night.' Without looking at me he says, 'I'm scared of falling asleep. It's stupid because I won't escape the moment anyway; but I'd like to be awake.'

Father Kostka mentioned humility and reconciliation at the surgery the other day. I ought to have asked him what he had in mind. Maybe I could have said something comforting to give courage to my ex-husband, who maybe believes that he will outwit death, or even overcome it if he doesn't let it surprise him in his sleep.

'Don't think about it,' I say and it strikes me that it's not really the best way to finish my visit. So I ask him, 'Do you remember when I last visited you in hospital? There was a young man with you; you introduced him to me.'

'I don't recall.'

'You told me it was a former student of yours.'

'Oh, yes, now I remember. Why do you mention it?'

'He called me and asked how you were.'

'That was nice of him.'

'He seems like a nice person,' I say, trying to make my voice sound as disinterested as possible.

'Why not? Young people tend to be less spoiled. Some of them, at least. He was a quiet young fellow, a trifle erratic, but he was interested in history and the stars. We talked together about time. He once let on to me that he was interested in astrology and I tried to explain to him that it was obscurantism.'

'Maybe it isn't,' I countered in his defence.

'I know you believe in it too. I tried to explain to him that it was pseudo-science. I'm sorry to see that you as a doctor attach any importance to such heresies, but I'm hardly going to convince you now.'

'I'm glad you don't intend to convince me,' I say, and as I bid him goodbye I tell him I hope he'll get well soon.

But being a doctor, I don't fool myself that he'll ever get well.

4

Saturday morning. It was a hot night and I slept badly. I've been sleeping worse and worse lately. And yet I'm tired. I'm so tired that in the evening I collapse into insensibility. But no sooner do I overcome that deathly torpor than I'm awake again and trying in vain to get back to sleep. I am too weary to fall asleep; everything aches, my body, my back and my legs, as well as my thoughts. I need a rest. I need a seaside holiday.

The sea enthralled me from the very first moment I set eyes on it.

Water is my element.

Virginia Woolf loved water too. *There one might have sat clock round lost in thought. Thought – to call it by a prouder name than it deserved – had let its line down into the stream. It swayed, minute after minute, hither and thither among the reflections and the weeds . . .* she wrote. And she also ended her own life in water. The river was called the Ouse.

Nadya, the wife of the Soviet tyrant, shot herself. They say that outside the room where they found her, a rose lay on the floor; it had just fallen from her hair.

Four years ago I went to the seaside with Charles the Second. We had a room booked in a pension and the sea was just beyond some low dunes. Our room was small and clean, with fresh flowers on the table and painted flowers on the walls. We lay down side by side and even made love. His treatment of me was as always kindly and loving, but I was obsessed with the thought that the way he treated me was the way he must have treated some other woman just a few days before, that he had no difficulty in declaring his love to two different women. When, one evening, he started to talk about our future and about how we'd get married, I finally broached the subject. But I did so in the hope that he would deny everything, that he'd tell me I was crazy and that he loved only me.

But instead he said, 'Eva's been spilling the beans, I see.'

I told him it didn't matter who told me.

He hung his head and without looking at me asked me if I wanted to know the details.

That was something I really didn't want.

He asked me if I could forgive him.

I told him I could forgive him, but I didn't want to live with him.

He remained motionless for a moment, then got up and left the room. From the place where I sat I could see him climbing the dune. The sea was rough and a ban on bathing had been in force since that morning. Charles the Second was an epileptic and he hadn't taken his tablets yet that day. I don't know whether he reached the sea. Had it been a few years earlier, I might have thought he had simply taken the opportunity to stay in the West. But for the past five years there had no longer been any need to flee to freedom, he could only be fleeing from me. But why should he flee from me, seeing that I'd just told him I didn't want him? He could also have been fleeing from his conscience, from despair or from loneliness. Or he was drawn by the sea and death. That's something I'd have understanding for. Whenever I've stood alone on some isolated spot overlooking the sea I have imagined myself swimming further and further from the shore until I don't have the strength to return. I found the thought of sinking to the bottom both terrifying and enticing. But anyway I know it won't be water that kills me, because I'm a Piscean. If I'm to perish or choose my own death, it will be a fiery one.

It's strange how they didn't find even his clothes on the shore. For a long time afterwards I had qualms about whether I'd been too severe with him. But then in the same way that he disappeared without trace, all traces of him started to disappear from my memory. It's possible that he's still alive and he just disappeared to spite me for rejecting him.

It looks as if Dad not only went out with V.V. alias W. but also had a child by her. *W. refused to apply to the medical board or even see my friend Dr H. She got angry and told me she wasn't a rabbit. We had a row but she didn't change her mind.* V.V. then left town and found a job in Chrudim. She virtually disappeared from Dad's life but not from the world. Years later he complained in his notebook that the regular monthly allowance he had to pay her *to keep alive something that oughtn't to have been* was draining him.

He always spoke about that child as 'it', so I can't tell whether it was a son or his third daughter.

I suddenly realized I might have another sibling – a half-brother or half-sister. It stunned me and I was staggered at the thought that something like that could happen without any of us suspecting: either Mum, my sister, or me. The deception that Dad practised on us all! And I stupidly believed that at least towards us he acted honourably.

I go and take a shower. I let it run full blast: maybe I'll manage to wash away all that nastiness, my fatigue and my sins real and imagined.

I find my daughter in the kitchen already dressed and already having had her breakfast.

'Are you planning to go somewhere?'

'We're going to an anti-racism demo on Old Town Square.'

I ask her who the 'we' consists of and she reels off a string of names that mean nothing to me.

I commend her concern for the fate of her fellow citizens but voice my doubt that they would be demonstrating so early in the morning.

No, the demonstration is planned for the afternoon but they have to make preparations and discuss a plan of action because there is likely to be an attack by the skinheads.

I imagine my little girl being beaten up by some enraged shaven-headed lout, but I quell my anxiety and refrain from asking her to stay home.

'What time are you intending to come home?'

She hesitates for a moment. 'I was thinking I might spend the night at Katya's cottage.'

'You said you were going to a demonstration.'

'Yeah, we are, but afterwards I'd . . .'

'Afterwards you come home.'

'But Mum, it's so nice out. You can't really want me to moon around in Prague when the weather's so great.'

'I don't want you spending the night goodness knows where with goodness knows who.'

'But I told you I'll just be with Katya at her cottage.'

'And who else?'

'Her mum will be there too.'

'And no one else?'

'It's only a tiny cottage. Really teeny-weeny.'

'And you'll be going there with Katya's mum?'

'Of course. We're hardly going to kick her out.'

'And what about study?'

'But Mum, I can't study in this heat!'

'Whereas you could when it was cold.'

'Yeah, I did slack, I agree,' she concedes, 'but it's too late now anyway; I'll never catch up.'

'It's only too late when you're dead.'

'But the marks are already in. Really.'

I don't want to be a restrictive or repressive parent. I had enough of Dad's restrictions at home and I don't think I've got over them yet. But what will become of this child if I don't manage to arouse any sense of responsibility in her?

'You're not hiding anything from me?'

'Mummy . . . !'

'Don't try to butter me up; I want an answer.'

'I'm not hiding anything from you.'

'Will you call me after the demonstration and tell me how you got on with the skinheads?'

'Of course. If the skins don't do me over I'll call you from the first phone box.'

'And if I let you go to Katya's, you're to be back by tomorrow afternoon at the latest.'

Instead of making promises she won't keep anyway, she flings her arms round my neck and tells me I'm a fantastic mother. Then she loads herself down with chains and rings of various kinds, daubs herself with war paint and makes her exit from the flat, and before she reaches the front door she has already forgotten about it and her mother.

The remains of the day now leer at me.

I water the rubber plant and remove two yellow leaves. I load the washing machine and give the windowledges above the radiators a wipe. I ought to cook something, but I don't enjoy cooking for myself alone. For a moment I consider going over to my ex-husband's and cooking him something at least, but I can't make up my mind to do it. I'm a lazy Samaritan. I call Mum to ask how she is. We talk for a while and Mum tells me her dreams. I listen to her patiently, knowing that these days dreams are increasingly what affect her the most, now that life has little excitement or comfort to offer.

'What about Jana?' Mum wants to know.

I tell her she has gone to demonstrate against racism.

'And you let her go? She could get hurt.'

I try to explain to her that it is necessary to protest against evil, but I fail to convince her.

'It's no business of children,' she tells me. 'At least you should have gone with her.'

Maybe she's right, but the thought of festooning myself with chains and going to yell slogans makes me smile.

I switch on the news at midday to learn that the police have broken up a gang of traffickers, that strike action is planned by lorry drivers, teachers and state employees, that eight people have died from the heat, although I don't catch where, and that a locomotive caught fire on some railway line. No mention of any anti-racist demonstration. They either didn't know about it or they have no interest. They'd only be interested if there were violent clashes. Maybe there isn't any anti-racist demonstration today, and my daughter just made it up as a way of getting out of the house as soon as possible.

I can't help thinking she has deceived me.

People tell lies: Dad lied to us, my ex-husband lied to me, my long-lost lover lied to me. Why should my daughter be any better?

She didn't hesitate to forge my signature at school and even boasted about how well she did it. And I'd like so much to trust her, to trust everyone, or those people, at least, that matter to me.

I make myself a cheese roll and pour myself a glass of wine. I finish my lunch in five minutes and then make a dash for the metro.

It is boiling on Old Town Square. Tourists cluster around an ice-cream trolley. In front of the astronomical clock a crowd waits in the scorching heat for the apostles, who make their appearance come rain or shine. There is no one to ask where the anti-racist demonstration will take place. If it were to take place here it would be drowned in waves of Coca-Cola and lost amidst the crowds of pagans, as tourists are described by my Mickey Myšák who has gone swanning off to Brno and left me at the mercy of the pagans.

There are too many people. Apparently there'll soon be six billion of us, I recently read.

While I was still at university I managed to visit London – thanks, no doubt, to Dad's unimpeachable political record. That was the first time I became aware of masses of people, a universe full of human beings whom I'll never know, never speak to and never understand. Ever since then I've been afraid of those masses, especially when I see people bunched together so tightly that they touch shoulders.

I can go and sit down on the steps by the Hus memorial and wait. I can go home and wait and wait – what for, who for, in fact?

We await salvation, which has departed from us. A line of verse crosses my mind, goodness knows where from, the Bible maybe. Perhaps I heard it some Sunday when I was attending church to spite my father.

The narrow lanes of the Old Town offer some shade at least and to my surprise I find an empty telephone booth.

I insert the phone card and hesitate before dialling the number.

A woman answers the phone. She's not particularly old by the sound of her voice; but then why should she be? His mother needn't be much older than I am, and my voice hasn't aged – or at least so I tell myself.

I overcome the temptation to hang up without saying anything; I introduce myself and ask after her son, my lover.

'Hold the line, please, Miss. I'll call him.'

It is stiflingly hot in the phone booth and his 'Miss' is bathed in sweat.

'It's me, Kristýna.'

'I recognize your voice, of course.'

'You haven't left yet?' I ask stupidly.

'No, I'm leaving in an hour.'

'What will you be doing in the meantime?'

'I was making a few more notes.'

A moment's silence and then he asks, 'And what are you doing?'

'Walking around Prague.' And I'm miserable – I don't say.

'I thought you said you'd be with your daughter.'

'She's out. She told me she was going to some demonstration and then to some cottage with a girlfriend.'

'And you're home alone?'

'I'm not at home. I'm walking around Prague. I went to have a look at that demonstration but I couldn't find her. The place is so crowded it's impossible to find anybody, not even a demonstration.'

'Do you think we could meet for a short while?'

'But you'll be leaving soon.'

'Where are you now?'

I tell him truthfully that I'm in a phone booth.

He wants to know where I'll go after I hang up, but I don't know.

'So try and help me to find you.'

'You won't have time anyway.'

'But I won't go to the seminar if I've got a chance to be with you.'

I'm touched by his words. I'm touched that he gives me precedence over something that's bound to be important for his career. For a moment I'm unable to speak, then I simply say, 'You're crazy. You'll only regret it if you stay here.'

We talk it over for a bit longer, then we agree to meet in an hour in front of the National Theatre. I hang up.

My hair is matted and my blouse is sodden with sweat. I didn't really put on any make-up. I'm wearing the old threadbare skirt I wear at home. I rushed out without changing into something else. How did it ever occur to me to make a date with him look-ing like this? He's bound to be fed up that he didn't go on my account. Maybe he's already regretting it.

I'd make a bad violinist because my hand would shake when I performed, even though it's usually firm. I used to get butterflies when I started going out with my first and only husband. Before every date I'd be terrified he wouldn't turn up. I was afraid, even though I was still a beauty – or so fellows told me, and Karel assured me too. I was terrified of falling out of favour, as if it were my job to be anxious and fearful for our love. I never entirely rid myself of that fear, even though I knew I was stronger.

If I make a dash to the metro I'll still have time to get home, have a shower and change. I can take a taxi back. On the other hand I could phone my lover back and tell him to go to his sem-inar instead. Or I could invite him straight home.

5

According to my horoscope, Pluto is crossing the Sun – a fatal aspect that foretells a major upheaval in my life. It looks as if my work for the Institute is heading in that direction. That's unless the upheaval concerns my private life. Most likely it concerns my entire life.

There are too many people who feel threatened by the things I uncover. I'm not trying to say I'm particularly important. Thousands of others could do the work I've been doing. Anyone who took this work seriously and tried to discover the truth of what happened, instead of covering up the tracks, would be con-sidered a threat. The previous director, who tried to prevent others blocking our work, was given the boot, with all honours. Now it's our turn and there won't be any honours.

On several occasions I have noticed that I was being tailed; mostly after I'd arranged a meeting with someone who could supply interesting information. It was impossible to say whether I was being tailed by the former operatives or the present ones. Maybe it was the present ones after consulting the former ones.

They never stopped me. If I happened to have a rendezvous in a pub or a café they'd try to sit as close as possible to me. I made their work harder by choosing a place where all the adjacent tables were full. I don't know what listening equipment they used, but four years of reading about their activity has taught me that if they are determined to listen in to what I say, I'd have a hard job eluding them.

Nobody says anything to my face. Sometimes I get worried that I'm becoming paranoid.

The people whose reports I study are either dead or act as if they had nothing to do with that activity. And when they admit it, they insist that they never harmed anyone. And what about those for whom the reports were written? They've disappeared; the waters have closed over them; they have all been spirited away to some unknown destination. But occasionally a miracle occurs and the waters open once more – as happened just a few days ago. Ondřej came to ask me whether I'd ever come across a Captain Hádek in the files.

Ondřej is my immediate superior, but we're friends more than colleagues. We share a number of interests. We both like games. Ondřej is great at computer games and he's an excellent chess player, so we nicknamed him Alekhine. He's never kept snakes, but he has two tortoises at home. Maybe he's more of a realist than me. He scoffs at my belief in horoscopes. In his opinion, what can't be proved doesn't exist – that's probably the best approach in our line of work.

I couldn't recall any Hádek. In what connection might his name have arisen?

He explained that this man had been in charge of interrogating a number of Scout leaders, maybe even my dad. My friend and superior had managed to discover from one witness that the captain – who was apparently promoted to Major afterwards – is still alive. His real name is Rukavička.

That name seized my attention. The first two letters made me think of the guy called Rubáš who dealt with Dad.

'He's really still alive?'

'He lives in some retirement home just outside Prague.' Ondřej shows me the place on the map that hangs on the wall of our office. Naturally the former interrogator is very old now – over eighty. But Dad's interrogator operated under a different name.

That was possible, of course, Ondřej said. The files from Dad's trial have all disappeared. Ondřej told me he'd try to question Rukavička–Hádek as soon as possible. I could attend too, if I liked.

That reminder of Dad's fate provoked my return to a project I'd previously put to one side. About a month before, I'd been invited to a seminar in Brno, where they wanted me to talk about the beginnings of Communist terror in this country. The seminar was to be attended by several well-known historians, as well as some politicians, so it would be an opportunity for me to say something about our work and voice my own opinions. At the same time I feared I wouldn't pass muster. That was why I hadn't written a single line so far.

So that very day I got down to it and continued writing my contribution every evening for the rest of that week.

I wanted to talk in more general terms, not simply to report on what emerged from my daily study of the files.

In the twentieth century, unlike in the previous one, so many people were murdered behind the front lines that you'd think mankind must have suddenly gone berserk. But the innocent have always been murdered. According to the Bible story, the Israelites slew the inhabitants of Ai in the field and in the wilderness to which they had pursued them. 'For Joshua did not draw back the hand that held out his javelin until he had destroyed all who lived in Ai,' it says in the book of the same name.

That's how things were and still are. Unlike animals, people think and feel, so they are aware of their victims' anxiety when they kill them. They are aware of their own desire to live and preserve their stock, and they can guess that those they kill have the same desires. In order to kill without remorse or fellow feeling but instead with a sense of a job well done, it is necessary to regard the victim as one of the damned, a lesser being, or as a lethal and treacherous foe. By destroying him and his descendants, the killers are serving the rest of mankind and protecting the faith or the great goals they espouse.

Why was it in the twentieth century that theories emerged about the damned that had to be wiped out in their millions and why did they receive massive support?

An explanation can be found in moral decay, or rather the decline of religion. During the almost two millennia that Christianity exercised a spiritual influence there was much cruelty of course. At the time of its supreme power, the Church demanded total obedience and discipline and cruelly punished apostasy, but gradually it established limits. The trouble is that in the twentieth century Christianity responded to the questions people were asking with diffidence or perplexity, and that must inevitably have affected their faith. They either lost it or it assumed nightmarish forms that had little in common with the original belief in Jesus as the Son of God, the Messiah. And the belief in a miracle that happened, or in a God who was concerned for the world, gradually dissipated.

But the majority of people needed to believe. They wanted saints to revere. They needed a God and rituals. The time was therefore ripe for latter-day, barbaric pagan religions which the great nonreligious movements started to revive. The Nazis and the Communists alike presented their leaders as gods, whose images must be present at every celebration, of which they invented untold numbers. Party congresses, secular holidays, anniversaries of their own victories, elections and even show trials with death sentences were all transformed into ritual celebrations intended to fire the emotions of the faithful and stun and numb their reason.

These new faiths also demanded obedience and discipline, but they were devoid of mercy and did not establish any inviolable limits. They revived human sacrifice in proportions without precedent in human history.

Of course it would be possible to find economic and historical reasons for what happened. Consternation at the massacres of the First World War, anxiety due to the uncertainties associated with the industrial epoch, a longing for a better organization of society. Nevertheless, for people to become an enormous, unthinking and obedient mass ready to do anything their leaders ordered, it needed a boundless belief in something that seemed superhuman and redemptive. Its prophets knew that every new belief needs to define itself in terms of those who reject it, who are then declared damned. It was necessary to kill kulaks, Jews or counter-revolutionaries, shoot priests, behead kings, poison infants and execute more and more victims in order to validate the new religions.

It was only when I'd touched on the spiritual basis of terror that it seemed to me appropriate to give an account of what happened here and explain why so many members of the intellectual elite – poets, lawyers, journalists or academics – willingly supported the Communist terror. Finally in my contribution I would deal with what the seminar organizers no doubt particularly expected from me: the efforts to trace the ringleaders of the terror campaigns and bring them before our none-too-willing courts for judgement.

On Saturday I was packed and ready to leave for the bus when Kristýna called and I detected even more sadness in her voice than usual. So I said something that immediately flabbergasted me. I promised her I'd cancel my trip and come and meet her. What made me do it? Was it love for her or my subconscious fear that I wouldn't make the grade when confronted by all those experts?

6

I wake up. I'm lying in my own room on my own divan, but someone is breathing quietly at my side and someone else's hand is lying on my thigh. You're here with me, little boy. You said such lovely things to me as we were making love and when we were falling asleep.

It's a long time since anyone said 'my love' to me or called me their little girl, after all it's ages since I was a little girl; no one has touched me or stroked me until I fell asleep. I've been neglected.

The divan is too narrow and I'm afraid to move lest I wake him. I could get up and go and sleep in Jana's room but I don't want to leave him.

I wonder where my daughter is sleeping. I oughtn't to have let her go; I ought to keep an eye on her at night, at least. She promised to call me, but she didn't. Unless she called when I was wandering around Prague. I know she's beyond my control now. She needs a father. Maybe this young man next to me might help play that role, but I'm afraid to bother him with it, and also I can't be sure how my daughter would take it. Maybe she'd accept him as a pal or flirt with him, or maybe she'd refuse to have anything to do with him.

If I hadn't let Jana go, he wouldn't be lying alongside me now.

The yellowish light of the street lamp shines in the window. I raise myself slightly and study his face. It's peaceful and somehow childlike. It seems guileless to me, which is odd for someone in his line of activity. Maybe I'm projecting my own feelings, my own hopes, on to him. I have no son. Maybe I could have had one, or more than one, but I allowed them to be aborted. Maybe one of them would have looked like him.

I'll never have a son now – I'm too old. My lover could still have lots of sons or daughters, but not with me. He must realize that. I ought to ask him if he wants to have children, but what could he reply? If he said yes it will be tantamount to telling me he'd have to find another woman. Maybe he doesn't hanker after children. My first and only husband didn't want a child. It was I who eventually persuaded him, no longer wanting to destroy the life that he had engendered in me.

There must have been a time when men longed to have heirs to whom they could pass on their land, their business or their estate – these days most of them don't have anything to pass on.

I'll ask my young man anyway.

I feel love for him and make believe that he loves me too. He lavishes more care on me than all the men I've ever known. He gave me an enormous rainbow shell that made a sound when he blew into it. A shell because I'm a Pisces. I happened to mention that I'd broken my sunglasses and he brought me a new pair the very next day. Admittedly they don't suit me, but I wear them anyway because they're from him. He brought me back a silk scarf from some official trip; it is sky blue and there is a skein of flying geese woven into each corner.

'Where are they flying to?' I asked him.

'To freedom.'

'Do you think one can fly to freedom?'

'People can't, only geese can.'

'If you were a goose, where would you fly to?'

'To you, of course!'

I love him for all of that. But at the same time I can't understand why he should love me – there is nothing unusual about me: an ageing woman who messes around in people's mouths, who has an almost adult daughter and suffers from early-morning depressions that she exorcizes with nicotine and a glass of wine. What have I to offer him? Maybe I resemble his mother or correspond to some other subconscious notion of his. Feelings are kindled in people without their being able to explain why and these feelings fizzle out just as inexplicably.

I search for an explanation and persuade myself that the lad next to me is different from other men – less selfish: kind and

IVAN KLÍMA

accommodating. But even if he's like that, nothing will efface the fact that one day, maybe tomorrow, maybe in a month's time, maybe in a year, his feelings will fizzle out. What will he do then?

He'll leave, of course.

And if he didn't we'd only have a hard time, both of us. My beloved Karel Čapek wrote a novel about a woman who has a young lover. It's a tragic story that ends in a senseless murder. How will my story end?

Jan stirs and opens his eyes, which are completely dark in the gloom. 'You're not asleep?' he asks.

'I woke up and started to think about my worries.'

'What worries do you have?'

I was thinking about how you'll leave me one day, I don't tell him. 'Jana's playing up. She doesn't study properly, she plays truant, and she smokes marijuana.'

'You've never even shown her to me.'

'She doesn't know about you.'

'Are you ashamed of me?'

'You know I'm not.'

'I could maybe help you with her. Although I don't have any experience of marijuana.' He snuggles up to me for a moment. Then he realizes how little space he has left me and offers to sleep on the floor.

I tell him I want him to stay by me and it occurs to him that we could shift Jana's bed in here.

'Now, in the middle of the night?'

'I only ever shift beds in the middle of the night.'

At two o'clock in the morning we carry in Jana's divan. The two divans standing here side by side after such a long time are reminiscent of a marriage bed.

'That's given me a thirst,' he says. A half-empty bottle of wine stands on the table. But he doesn't want wine. He didn't even have any with me during the evening. Instead he goes to the kitchen to run himself a glass of the vile liquid from the tap.

120

'You're not hungry?' I ask him.

'I'm always hungry, because I almost never have time to have a proper meal.' And he adds that it seems to him like a waste of time to bother with food. I now know, at least, why he's so slim.

I offer to butter him some bread, but he says he'd like to make some soup. So at two-fifteen in the morning I start to cook. He insists on cooking the potato soup himself. All I need to do is prepare the necessary ingredients.

I'm not accustomed to someone cooking for me at any hour of the day or night. I'm not used to sitting and simply looking on. 'Why are you so nice?'

'I'm not nice at all. When we get together to play hero games, I generally choose the role of the villain.'

'But there's no way you can tell what you're really like.'

'So why do you ask?'

We are eating the soup and he is telling me how in some game, whose rules are a mystery to me, he played a Chinese cook who was supposed to poison his emperor.

'And did you poison him?'

'Of course I did. I had high levels of skill and intelligence.'

'You haven't mixed anything into my soup, have you?'

'Why else do you think I cooked it?'

'So that's why you stayed in Prague. You don't mind too much that you weren't able to deliver your paper?'

'At three in the morning, the only thing I mind is that it will soon be dawn.'

His reply disappoints me a little. He notices and says, 'I'll find an opportunity; give it some time,' thus consoling himself too.

When at last we lie down on our widened bed, he takes me in his arms. He caresses me again and says more tender things to me.

My little boy. What are you doing here with me at three in the morning? 'Don't go,' I whisper. 'Stay in me. You don't have to leave; I won't have any more children anyway.'

121

Silence. Lovemaking is over. 'You don't mind that I can't have children any more?'

He doesn't reply. Instead he says he loves me.

'But I asked you a question.'

'I answered you.'

'That wasn't an answer.'

'If you love someone, you love them just as they are.'

'And you'd like to have children?' I don't ask whether he'd like to have children with me.

'I don't know,' he says. 'I think my mother's the one who wants them. But it's not important.'

I oughtn't to have broached the subject. I don't want some other woman getting involved in what there is between us.

'Your mother called me Miss,' I recall.

'Mum thinks all the women who call me are Misses.'

'Do lots of Misses call you?'

'It depends what you mean by lots.'

'In this particular case, lots is more than one.'

'Well lots, then.'

'I should have known.' I laugh while, outside, dawn is breaking. I laugh while jealousy and sadness well up inside me.

He lays his head on my breasts. After making love he wants to sleep.

'And when they ask for you, your mother replies, Hold the line, please, I'll call him.' Because they're to her liking: they're young and she wants grandchildren, I don't add.

'What else is she supposed to say?'

'She's only supposed to say it when I call. She's to tell the others not to bother you.'

'I'll put her straight.' He laughs because he can't take my words seriously. Even I can't, although I wish that she'd do precisely that.

'Have you told her about me yet?'

'No, I don't talk to her about such things. I don't want her interfering in my life.'

'What's she like?' I ask.

'What do you think? She's a teacher. At her age, she had to learn how to deal with computers. But she's great, she coped with it.'

'Has she ever interfered in your life?'

'She's tried. She's my mother. What mothers don't try to?'

It crosses my mind that I've not told my mother about him either. Except that he hasn't because he's most likely ashamed of me, an ageing divorcee, whereas I haven't because I'm ashamed of myself.

7

We were lying on the grass chewing the fat. Everyone was chewing the fat but I was fed up that Katya isn't here. She's the only one who's really ace. We did everything together: we went to the flicks, borrowed each other's CDs, we went shopping together for threads and ornaments, preferably the same so we could be like two sisters. But when we were together at her cottage last weekend she came home as high as a kite. Her dad could tell she was high and gave her such a belting she couldn't go to school the next day. She told him it was a violation of human rights and that she'd totally clear out, but her dad put her nose out of joint by saying they'd totally kick her out if she tried the stuff again. And now she's not allowed to go anywhere, only to school and back, and when we're going home there's always someone from her family: her older brother, her mum, her dad or even her wrinkly grandma waiting for her at the school gates. A real bummer.

Sometimes Ruda is really ace, but sometimes he couldn't give a fuck about me. I really like the fact he's got a nose like Bono, or even a yard longer, and not a pug nose like mine. And also he's got really big, strong hands.

He just noticed I was pissed off and so he jacked me up with something, I didn't even ask what it was but it was stronger than usual, probably a mixture of piko and smack, but I started to feel great. I felt like a fuck but I also didn't feel like moving. I stared at the sky where horses cantered and flamingos were flying. It was an ace trip.

Someone next to me said that the filth were coming, but I couldn't give a shit; I don't feel like getting up. Let them come. I didn't have any stolen goods, not even a gram, or even a needle.

Now I could see them too, the whole pig pack. They had two Alsatians on leads specially trained to deal with us. They were already yelling that we were scum on the drinking water that ought to be strained out and chucked in the Vltava, that happens to have been flowing here for at least a thousand years, or since the time that followed the Big Bang.

'Hey, we'd better split,' Ruda said. 'They look really mean today.'

So I got up. Not far away there was a deserted cottage that we used to creep into through broken windows in the yard. To get into the yard you had to climb over a wall that was all gnawed by mice, rats or the teeth of time.

Half an hour later we were all back together again. There were about nine of us. I couldn't tell for sure. I was so wrecked I couldn't tell them apart. I didn't even know whether the ones I could see were really here. Fortunately it didn't matter, nothing mattered. I couldn't care about school or Mum; I promised to call her but I didn't and I felt completely free.

The cottage was cold even now in the summer. The floor was made of stones of some kind. The walls were piss-sodden. There was just an iron bedstead and some wrecked cupboards to lie on. There used to be blankets but some tramps took them away last winter. There's just a pile of old Yellow Pages in one corner. Last time we slept here the cold was so dire that Katya and I covered ourselves with the Yellow Pages. They were heavy but they gave some warmth. And there was hardly any oxygen. Ruda said oxygen is poison. The straights who go to the mountains to breathe fresh air for their health don't realize there's less oxygen there because there's less oxygen the higher you go. But down here we are poisoned and if we didn't smoke from time to time we'd be goners.

I didn't even know how many girls there were and how many boys.

It was already dark. Someone lit a candle, but it hardly burnt. It was like being in the mountains, because fire, I knew from Dad, needs oxygen, and shadows leapt about the battered walls, and beetles as big as rabbits crawled over them.

Ruda snuggled up to me and wanted a fuck. Why not, it didn't matter. The cupboard creaked under us. I heard myself say, 'Be careful,' and he told me not to worry, it was made of good timber. That really freaked me out.

I'm made from good timber too. I don't creak but I take it. If he waters me maybe I'll grow leaves, maybe I'll flower. I imagined the colours of my flowers. I like orange like marigolds. Ruda had rolled off me but some other kid in a biker's jacket was groping me. He smelt strange and scratched me with his bristly chin. Hey, fuck off, you stink!

I pushed him off the cupboard but he'd already managed to come in me.

Someone started to play a guitar and sing some crappy song about love.

I already knew something about love. I figured it out when Dad pissed off with that beanpole of his. And loads of blokes taught me about love; I don't know how many because I don't know whether the ones that jumped on me were real or not. Maybe I only imagined it all. But I didn't imagine Ruda; he was the first one who offered me hash. That was ages ago, absolute aeons, two years ago at least, but maybe it was twenty years because I was already dreadfully old, wasn't I? at least a hundred years old. I was just beginning to feel moss growing on me.

A sewer rat was watching me from the corner by the door that goes nowhere. Who are you staring at, you creep? He was as big as a small dog and had eyes like a cat. Maybe it was a cat got up as a mouse. Tom dressed up as Jerry, or vice versa.

Maybe I was only imagining it all: the moss, the mouse, the people here and this vile hole where everything stinks.

But I felt fantastic. I really liked the people here because they were like me and I was like them. We couldn't give a fuck about anything so we were still able to laugh. We were almost always laughing, especially after grass. Someone said, 'Hey it's Wednesday,' and it was Saturday and we were in stitches. I really liked laughing. It was hard to laugh at home. Mum had her downers and was always miserable over Dad totally doing the dirty on her and being alone – only having me, as she said, and that couldn't be enough because sometimes she didn't even have me, like now. I lay there and I felt better than at home and one day I'll stay here totally and the moss will grow all over me and I won't know about anything. And maybe I'll go off somewhere or fly away.

That creep kept on singing about love, as if it existed.

Maybe it does, but it was hiking in the mountains so it didn't get poisoned.

I used to go hiking in the mountains with Mum and Dad, and when my legs ached, Dad would give me a piggyback and Mum would walk behind us and every few minutes she'd say, 'Isn't she too heavy for you? I'll take her for a while.' And Mum would also sing:

> *'Don't you worry Jana*
> *That there's nothing left to eat*
> *We'll kill ourselves a juicy midge*
> *And cut it up for meat.'*

I didn't want to stay here totally, I'd like to go hiking in the mountains.

Maybe I ought to let Mum know I'd like to go hiking in the mountains. With her and Dad.

Dad can hardly climb the stairs and he wouldn't go with Mum even if he could.

There were two sewer rats now. What are you staring at, you creeps?

When Ruda first gave me some grass I was really curious and I was also a bit afraid of what it would do, but it hardly did anything. I didn't know how to drag on it yet and anyway he only gave me a couple of puffs and kept asking me, 'What do you feel? Are you high yet?'

When I got home I was in total dread that Mum would be able to tell, but she wasn't able to tell anything; she happened to be dreadfully tired and miserable; she had a downer and a headache and was pissed off because I didn't do the washing-up.

How could I do the washing-up on a day like that? I wanted to really enjoy being happy and you can't be happy doing the washing-up.

Ruda crept up on to me again, if it was him, and started to touch me up. I didn't care; it turned me on.

Now I'd like to be hiking in the mountains, but not with you, you creep.

CHAPTER FOUR

1

Dad acquired the burial plot years ago; it lies in a remote corner of Olšany Cemetery. His forebears remained in the country graveyard at Lipová; they have more light and flowers there, and a bell rings over them every day. They include Auntie Venda who burned to death and Grannie Marie. The ashes of my other grandmother were most likely washed away in the river Vistula or were tipped into some mass grave; her name, at least, is inscribed among thousands of others on a wall of the Pinkas synagogue in Prague. When I first saw it there, I found it strange, even unbelievable that my mother's mother should have died that way, and I almost felt guilty about my own untroubled existence and the fact that no one was out to kill me.

At the foot of the grave there is a gaping small hole ready to take the urn and next to it a little heap of earth like a fresh molehill.

His nearest relatives have come: Mum, my sister Lída, Jana and I. We are waiting for the undertakers to arrive with the urn. Mum is wiping tears from her eyes, Jana is evidently bored and staring into the distance with a faraway expression. A gypsy funeral is taking place at the other end of the path and we can hear the sound of dance tunes intended to accompany the soul of the deceased to a happier and brighter world.

'He could have still been here with us; after all he wasn't all that old,' Mum laments.

I refrain from pointing out that Dad was just a few weeks short of seventy-six, which is more than the average longevity of men in this country, nor do I say that how a man lives matters more than how long.

My sister can't restrain herself, however: 'He'd have had to smoke less and keep off the pork fat, the streaky bacon and the cheap smoked meats. I never saw him touch vegetables, apart from a bit of cabbage if it came with the goose or the roast pork.'

Mum senses a personal reproach, as she is the one who fed Dad all his life, and her sobs grow louder.

But now two fellows in shiny black suits emerge from one of the side paths. They are how I imagine the two court bailiffs in *The Trial*, whose author lies in the adjacent Jewish cemetery. All that's missing is the knife. Instead, one of them is cradling in his arms the urn with the ashes while the other carries a garden trowel in place of a knife. They arrive at our grave, bow to us, and for a moment they both stand in feigned solemnity of mourning.

Then the first of them leans over the cavity and places the urn in it. The other man offers us the trowel and we sprinkle a bit of soil into the shallow hole, the pebbles rattling off the lid of the urn.

It is all so brief, there's no time for even a flicker of God's eyelid. Nobody sings anything, nobody plays anything; all we can hear are the strains of a passionate *csardas* from the gypsy burial. Just recently I saw on television some old woman in Moscow defiantly brandishing above her head a portrait of the tyrant who died on the day I was born. Maybe it would gratify Dad if I held a portrait like that now over his grave. But I don't have one and I'd never take it in my hands anyway. I'd happily play the violin for Dad, even the 'March of the Fallen Revolutionaries', if he'd have let me continue learning the instrument.

The two men finish their job and come up to us to express their condolences and wait expectantly for a tip. They get a hundred-crown note each and depart from us at a dignified pace while we remain standing there for a little while longer. I don't know what's going through Mum's head, or my sister's. Mum has no inkling of Dad's infidelities and will never learn about them now. Maybe she is recalling some nice moments; there must have been some. Maybe she's thinking of the loneliness that will accompany her for the rest of her days.

Dad died at home. He was racked with pain during the final days. A doctor visited him from the clinic and gave him some injection that didn't do much to relieve the pain. I didn't ask what they gave him; most of the time I wasn't around. I myself had a few ampoules of morphine that the thieving ward sister had brought me. I'd never used them but I could have injected them into Dad, all of them in one go even, and thus shortened his suffering. I could have done it; he was already under sentence of death anyway, but I didn't. I couldn't make up my mind to shorten his life and play Dr Death. I had no right to, had I? Or was I just making excuses? To do something like that you have to feel either great love or bitter hatred – I didn't feel either. I didn't have enough compassion for someone who had never shown much pity to others. Subconsciously I told myself that each of us has to put up with our fate right to the end, and that there was even some kind of justice in it, which we oughtn't to interfere with.

'Aren't we going yet?' Jana asked.

We took Mum home and I let my daughter go off to a girl-friend's. My dear sister, who once prophesied my death at my own hand, decided to come back to my place for a chat.

Before we climb the stairs to the flat I check my mailbox and take out the only envelope it contains; by the writing I can tell immediately it's another anonymous letter. I quickly slip it into my handbag before my sister has a chance to ask who's writing to me.

I make a few open sandwiches but Lída refuses them; she's found a new belief: healthy eating. She doesn't touch smoked meats or even cheese. She's not allowed tomatoes because they are toxic like potatoes and she refuses to eat peppers because they contain too much zinc or some dangerous metal or other, besides which they could be genetically modified. Thanks to her diet she has managed to rid her body of all toxins and noxious fluids; she has got rid of all her pains and lost her excess weight, and her eyes and voice have improved.

I pour myself a glass of wine and she takes out of her handbag a little bottle with some elixir or other.

I have neither wheat berries nor fermented vegetables. All I can offer is some rye bread which at her request I sprinkle with parsley and chives.

'You ought to adopt a healthier lifestyle too,' she tells me and heaves a deep sigh. Surprisingly she refrains from saying, as on previous occasions, that my flat is unbearably smoky, but even so she annoys me with her condescending self-assurance: she knows, as our father did, just what is right and healthy – for herself and the rest of humanity.

For a while she tells me all about her successful concerts and then offers to reimburse me all the funeral expenses.

'We'll go halves,' I say. Then for a while we say nothing: two sisters who have nothing to say to each other.

I recall Dad's diaries. When I was looking through them, I tell her, I discovered that Dad had a mistress.

My sister is not taken aback by the news but simply takes it in her stride. 'There's nothing odd in that: all blokes have mistresses. He wasn't the US President, so he could risk it.'

I tell her that he apparently had a child with his mistress. When I was last looking through his diaries I came across a death notice from ten years ago announcing the death of a certain Veronika Veselá. It was signed by just one person: her son, Václav Alois Veselý, and bore his address.

'You mean to say that the one who died was Dad's bit on the side? And this Václav bloke is something like our half-brother?'

'She gave him his second name after Dad.'

'So what? We didn't know anything about him – for how many years?'

I tell her he must be about two years older than her.

'We didn't know anything about him for forty years,' she calculates quickly, 'so why should we bother about him now. There wasn't any inheritance anyway. We haven't cheated him out of anything, so he's got nothing to fight with us over.'

'But it's not just a question of the inheritance.' Doesn't she find it strange that there's someone with the same father as ours who has been walking the earth for all this time without our knowing anything about him?

'That's typical of Dad. He was well trained in keeping mum about all sorts of highly secret matters. And where does this new relative of ours live?' she asks, suddenly curious after all.

'In Karlín. It must be somewhere near the river, to judge by the name of the street.'

'I might be singing at the theatre in Karlín, if things work out.'

'Mum has never suspected anything,' I say, ignoring the important news that she will be singing in Prague.

'Or perhaps she didn't want to. It would be better for her that way.'

'No, more likely she believed all his guff about a new morality.'

For a while we argue about what Mum believed in and what Dad did. And then my sister comments that every woman prefers to shut her eyes rather than see what is really going on. I was the one who had behaved stupidly.

'What's that supposed to mean?'

'You found out that Karel was betraying you and couldn't think of anything better to do than divorce him. What good did it do you? You were left on your own.'

I refrain from saying that I was left on my own because I wouldn't let myself be made a slave. Nor do I tell her that you have to act according to your feelings and do what you feel is right, and not what is most convenient. 'You're on your own too.'

'That's neither here nor there. I always have some bloke or other and I'm not saddled with a daughter.'

'You've always got to be different. And as for Jana, I'm glad I have her.'

'By the way, I don't like the look of that girl of yours,' she says.

'Maybe she doesn't care whether you like the look of her or not.'

'There's something strange about her eyes,' she continues. 'I noticed it there at the cemetery. People normally have one kind eye and one unkind one, but she doesn't.'

'Both your eyes are unkind,' I tell her, 'and I don't think you're not normal.'

'My left eye's kinder than the right one,' she assures me, 'but we're not talking about me. Her eyes aren't kind or unkind, they're elsewhere, and that's something you, as her mother, should notice.'

'What are you trying to say?'

'That girl of yours is on drugs,' she declares. 'I'd stake my life on it.'

'Jana is not on drugs,' I yell. 'You're trying to find a way to harm us!'

'Kristýna,' she says, putting her hand on my shoulder, 'I've never wanted to do you any harm. You're the one who always did yourself harm, by brooding on everything. But that dead expression and the dilated pupils is something I know only too well.' She checks herself and then explains: 'Two of the guys in the band were injecting piko and one was on heroin. If you ignore it, it'll be the worse for your daughter. It's no skin off my nose.'

'I know it's no skin off your nose. You never could give a damn about us.' I don't go on to tell her that her diet may have cleared the toxins out of her body, but they stayed in her mind.

When my sister leaves I remember the anonymous letter and take my tormentor's latest message out of my handbag.

He tells me that he follows my every step and the moment is at hand when the gates of hell will close behind me.

2

Jan would like us to see each other every day. See each other and make love. He wants me to act his age. But I'm not twenty any more. When I get home from the surgery in the evening I'm aching all over: my legs, my back, my arms and my mind. But even if I felt like going to see him, I'm the mother of an adolescent girl that I'm very worried about.

Even though my sister never wastes an opportunity to tell me something unpleasant, I'm unable to get her warning out of my mind.

I watch Jana's eyes. Does she have a fixed stare? Are her pupils dilated? Maybe I ought to check her all over each evening and look for track marks, but I'm ashamed to because it would be degrading for both of us.

'Jana, where have you been all afternoon?'

'In the park, of course.'

'What do you go there for, all the time?'

'Nothing. There are cool people there.'

'What do you get up to there?'

'Mum, there's no point in you interrogating me all the time. You won't ever understand anyway.'

She acts more and more defiantly, convinced that her life is her own business; it's nothing to do with me how she spends her time, what she'll become or how she enjoys herself. Whenever I ask her straight out if she's shooting up she adopts a hurt expression: how could something so vile occur to me?

Jan called me twice today inviting me to some club or other where they play those hero games.

I didn't tell him that I'm already of an age when people don't usually have either the time or the inclination to play at heroes or even cowards. I asked him how long such games go on for and he told me that they often last several weeks.

'Nonstop?'

'With breaks,' he laughed. 'But they mostly go on till at least midnight.'

I'll persuade Mum to come and stay the night. Not so long ago I used to ask her to babysit more often but now I get the feeling that it bothers her to leave her flat. But she loves her only grandchild, and surprisingly enough my adolescent is less impudent when she is around.

Mum arrives after seven in the evening when I'm already getting dressed up. 'Off to the theatre?' she asks.

I shake my head in reply.

'Got a date?'

'Something like that.'

'It's about time too,' Mum says.

'But Mum, I didn't say who I have the date with.'

'I can tell it's with some bloke. Is it serious?'

'I always take everything seriously, Mum.'

'You tell him that, not me,' Mum says, sticking up for the man whose existence she has deduced.

I've no idea what clothes are appropriate to meet people who play at heroes; I've never experienced anything of the sort. Jeans, maybe, but I look better in a skirt. I'll wear the red short-sleeved blouse and a long cotton skirt – as black as my expectations in life. It comes halfway down my calves and at least hides the fact that my legs are already getting thinner. I shouldn't think jewellery is the thing, but I'll wear a thin gold chain so that my neck isn't so bare.

I open the drawer where I hide my valuables; the chain should be lying in a wristwatch box, but it isn't there. I open the other few jewellery cases I own but the chain isn't there either. And in the process I discover that the gold ring I inherited from Grannie Marie is missing. I grow agitated. I'm careful with my things and don't misplace a hankie or a sock, let alone a piece of gold jewellery. Even so I open all the other drawers and rummage in them.

'Looking for something?' Mum wants to know.

'No, not really.'

If a thief had got into the flat, he would definitely have taken something else as well, and we'd certainly have noticed there had been an intruder.

I go into Jana's room, tell her to turn down the racket and ask her whether she didn't borrow some of my jewellery.

I sense a momentary hesitation. 'But Mum, I'd never wear anything like that,' she says, trying to adopt a disdainful tone.

'And how about one of your pals?'

'Mum, what do you take them for?' She knows nothing about my jewellery. 'I'll lend you something if you like,' she suggests.

But I don't want any of her chains or rings.

The thought that my daughter might be capable of stealing from me appals me so much that I prefer not to go into it further.

I go to say goodbye to Mum.

'You're all in a tizzy,' she says, and wishes me a good time.

I'll have a good time, provided I manage to forget that my daughter's probably stealing from me.

Jan is waiting for me outside the Hradčanská metro station. He kisses me and says my outfit suits me. He's glad we'll be together the whole evening. He leads me through the villas of Bubeneč and tries to explain to me the sense of hero games. They are a bit childish, but he thinks that playing games is definitely better than gawking at the television screen, where rival gangs shoot it out, or at the computer screen, where you can make two other gangs shoot at each other. Here you can take part in everything in person; you can encounter dwarves, dragons, vampires, monsters; you can travel wherever you fancy, or go back in time and meet Edison, Jan Žižka or even Napoleon. Most of his friends prefer to be make-believe characters, such as medieval knights or princes, or fight with monsters.

As we're climbing the stairs in the house he has brought me to, he tells me I don't have to join in. I can just watch if I like and ask questions as a way of getting to know the rules, of which there aren't too many anyway.

I don't understand the game, even after it has started; there are too many distractions. It is a large room and the walls are covered in big pictures from which the faces of monsters from comics leer down at me. Quiet, meditational music is heard from hidden speakers. The light shines through a green filter so that we all look as if we are drowned. Apart from Jan and me there are also two girls, some youngster and a large-bellied young man who is introduced to me as Jirka, whom I possibly know by his voice, as he works for radio news. Unfortunately I only listen to Classic FM. One of the girls, who has a visionary gaze, squirrel teeth and long legs, is called Věra. She can't be more than twenty. I don't manage to catch the name of the other girl; recently I've been finding it increasingly difficult to remember people's names. But names aren't important. Anyway nobody here remains the person they are; instead they become someone they possibly want to be. It ought to appeal to me: I've always wanted to live a different life from the one I lived. Karel Čapek wrote a novel about it. People live only one of many possible lives and usually it is one that they are least happy with. The trouble is that the lives they offer me here don't attract me.

Jan recaps the situation that they are all supposed to accept. 'It's 1437,' he says, maybe on my behalf too. 'Sion Castle is under siege. Jirka – Jan Roháč – has already been resisting the troops of Hynek Ptáček for four months.' The youngster, who has apparently been reincarnated as the leader of the besiegers, stands and bows. 'Master Roháč is unaware,' Jan continues his explanation, 'that Ptáček's people are digging an underground passage in order to penetrate the castle. Eliška,' he says, indicating the long-legged girl, 'whose brother is in the castle, manages to ingratiate herself with Master Ptáček and discover his plans. Last time she was given the task of finding a way to get into the castle with this important information.'

'I've one question,' the fat one says. 'What's the water situation in the castle? Could I fill the moat?'

Jan declares that something like that is out of the question. There is scarcely enough water to drink. But the moat is deep and steep enough to offer sufficient protection, he assures his tubby companion.

From what I can see, it's clear that my lover is the game's director or whatever, whose job is to set the scene for the other participants and describe the period they are about to enter. He offers them roles and skilfully asks them questions about how they'd behave in certain situations, and on the basis of that he determines how well they have fared. That's most likely the reason he brought me here, so that I should see how he holds sway and so that he can demonstrate his knowledge. I'm touched. But the game is very slow to get off the ground, and while the leggy creature tries to think up ways of getting into the besieged castle, my mind wanders back to our flat and I try to work out whether my own daughter stole from me or whether she simply enabled some of her pals to do it.

They offer me some refreshments but I decline; I don't feel like food. I let them pour me some wine although just lately wine tends to depress me. The fact is I'm out of place here. All the people here are very young, so young, in fact, that I'm scarcely aware of anything but my age and not belonging here. They are all young enough to be my children, including my lover. They enjoy playing games. They can take delight in being part of an imaginary world; so far nothing in real life is a real burden on them, and even if it is, they still have strength enough to put up with it.

I watch the long-legged visionary, who is supposed to deliver the important message. I'm not interested in what she'll do, I'm noticing how adoringly she gazes at my lover, while looking at me out of the corner of her eye. I don't appeal to her, I don't belong here; I don't even belong to the one who brought me here. She is more likely to belong to him than I am, of course. And most likely on the way out she tries to ingratiate herself with him, to nestle up to him in the gloomy passageway and thrust herself into his arms. And why shouldn't he take her in his arms and kiss her, when she lets him, when she asks for it?

If anything, my life is now headed for the finishing line whereas his is only just picking up speed. I fight for breath when I'm climbing stairs, he just soars through the air, waving invisible wings as he hovers above me. Other times he just leaps ahead and in a single leap covers ten miles.

These are unwarranted imaginings. He loves me; he wouldn't have brought me here if he were interested in some lanky she-wolf, either here or anywhere else. After all he's surrounded by loads of girls that I know nothing about, such as the secretaries he's bound to have at hand. I've noticed that he almost never mentions his work, as if wanting or having to conceal it from me.

He tells me I'm precious to him. Maybe I'm precious precisely because I'm not a little girl any more.

Johannes Brahms's mother was seventeen years older than her husband. And the same number of years separated Isadora Duncan from Yesenin. When they first met, she was forty-three and he was twenty-six. They actually got married. According to their biographies, she married him. She asked for his hand. After all, she was older and more famous. She died at fifty, while he killed himself aged thirty. Before he hanged himself in that Petrograd hotel he wrote his last poem in the blood from his severed veins. I can remember the lines because they seemed to me plaintively wise:

> *Goodbye: no handshake to endure.*
> *Let's have no sadness — furrowed brow.*
> *There's nothing new in dying now*
> *Though living is no newer.*

They say he went mad. Or had he arrived at the truth? If he hadn't killed himself he'd have been killed by the murderer who ruled his country and who died the day I was born.

But I'm no Isadora Duncan. I'm not famous, I'm simply as old as she was and know how to fix people's teeth. My lover is no poet and I'm sure he won't kill himself; he enjoys life and enjoys playing games. For him life is still a game in which he has accepted me as a fellow player for a while until one day he lets me go again.

The hopeless inevitability of it all and my future loneliness bear down on me. I ought to have stayed home with my little girl: she is in danger and therefore needs me. I've neglected her. At the very moment when I should be there with her, I'm sitting here fretting among strangers, whilst she could be drowning, vainly trying to stay afloat, feet groping for the bottom, calling and waving her arms. Nobody hears her, except for some fiend sitting in a boat who hauls her out and has a syringe with poison waiting in his pocket.

I can see her little arm groping for my breast that is full of milk; her fingers that are like a doll's, except that they are warm, gently touch my skin.

Suddenly I see it, that hand encroaching on my jewellery drawer and taking the chain and the ring away to the one in the boat who pretends he's saving her.

What if my sister is right about me living in fear but refusing to see what she saw at first glance?

I can't bear to be here any longer; I get up and tell Jan I have to go home.

He interrupts the game for a moment and goes out with me to the front hall. 'I expect you found it boring.'

I tell him I wasn't bored but that I'm worried about Jana. I ask him not to be cross with me for leaving.

As if he could be cross with me, he says. I am not to be cross with him for not leaving with me; he doesn't want to spoil the game for the others. He accompanies me out to the stairway, switches on the light, leans towards me and whispers that he'd sooner be with me.

Mum is still up and impatiently asks me how I've enjoyed myself.

I tell her that it was interesting.

'And where have you been exactly?'

Mum feels like a chat. So I go and fetch a bottle of Frankovka and pour us some before trying somehow to describe what I've just experienced, although I know it's not what matters. So I tell her who I was there with. And that maybe he's in love with me. I also tell her how much younger he is and that he's an ideal young man: he doesn't smoke or drink apart from sipping a drop of wine from a glass as a favour to me, he doesn't swear and he brings me flowers. I don't tell her that he investigates the crimes of the people that Dad served.

My mother acts as if she hasn't registered the information about his age; she wants to know if I'm love with him.

I feel silly saying yes like a little girl, but I'm not able to disown my young man, so I say, 'But I'm over forty-five, Mum!'

'So am I,' my mother declares, 'and I have been for a long time.'

'But you've had Dad.' I try to remember the time when Mum was forty-five. I was twenty-three. I had two siblings, one of whom was unknown to us: Mum, my sister and me. I was at university, lounging around in pubs, occasionally getting drunk and not caring a damn about home. I can't picture what Mum looked like then. I can't imagine her falling in love with someone, even if Dad hadn't been there. Forty-five, I used to think in those days, was the age when you wake up in the morning and you can already hear the death knell in the distance.

'How's Jana,' I ask, in order to change the subject.

'She's asleep. But she seems odd to me,' Mum says, accepting the new topic. 'Is she ill?'

'Did she complain of anything?'

'No, not at all.'

'So why do you think she might be ill?'

'She told me she was cold,' my mother said. 'She put on a sweater and huddled as if she had a fever. That's not normal in this heat, is it?'

'Did you ask her why she felt cold?'

'She just said, I'm cold. She sat in the armchair and stared in front of her. As if she could see someone who wasn't there. She even mumbled something to herself. Maybe she's exhausted.'

'What from, for heaven's sake?'

'They make awful demands on them now at school. I heard about it on the radio.'

'They may well make demands but that doesn't bother her in the least.'

'It's just as well it'll be the holidays soon,' Mum says, harping on the same note, 'and she'll get a bit of rest. You both need some rest.'

Yes, it will be the holidays. I've saved up for them. We'll go to the seaside. I've already booked a holiday in Croatia. I'll take my little girl a long way from here. I'll take her across the sea to a desert island where no dealer will find her, and if one did find us I'd throttle him and throw him in the sea, even if it meant a life sentence.

3

I searched the entire flat but I couldn't find my jewellery any-where. For a week now I've checked my purse morning and evening. This morning I discovered that three hundred crowns had disappeared from it. Overnight.

Jana comes home only slightly late. She tosses her bag under the coat hanger and is making her way to her bedroom to kick up her usual racket.

'Jana!'

My tone of voice arouses her vigilance. 'Yes, Mum?'

'I need to talk to you seriously.'

'But you always talk to me seriously.'

'Stop playing the fool. You play truant . . .'

'But we had that out ages ago. I've stopped playing truant now.'

'And you steal.'

There is a moment of consternation and then she says, 'That's not true.'

'It is true and you know it.'

'I've never stolen anything from anyone.'

'I don't know about anyone else, but from me you have. You seem to think what's mine is yours.'

'I don't think anything of the sort.'

'And what about my jewellery?'

'I don't know what you're talking about. I expect you mislaid it somewhere.'

'Jana, you know full well what happened to them.'

'Your jewellery is no concern of mine, or any fucking jewellery,' she shouts. She acts so hurt, that I almost waver.

'Last night three hundred crowns disappeared from my purse.'

'I didn't take them.'

'So can you tell me who did, then?'

'You lost them somewhere. Your money's no concern of mine.'

'You forgot to say, your fucking money. It's no concern of yours, you just take it.'

'That's not true!'

'And you lie into the bargain.'

'That's not true!'

'It's obvious to me what you need the money for.'

'I didn't take any money.'

'So I'll take you to the drop-in clinic to have them do a blood test and get some advice about what to do with you.'

'I'm not going to any clinic.'

'You'll go with me where I tell you.'

'I won't.'

'Jana, you don't realize what you're doing. Once you get into it, you'll never get out of it and you'll ruin your life. For good.'

'I haven't got into anything.'

'So what did you need the money for?'

'I didn't take any money. Or anything else.'

'I already know you stole from me. I'll have to find out about the rest.'

'I'm not going anywhere.'

'And you really think I'll just sit back and watch you ruin yourself?'

'You ruin yourself too.'

'Jana, I won't put up with that sort of impudence.'

'Dad always used to say . . .'

'I don't want to hear a single word about your father.'

'I'm not going anywhere with you.'

'So I'll have you taken there.'

'I'll run away instead.' Suddenly she starts to yell hysterically: 'You're vile. You play the cop with me. You phone the fucking school to find out whether I've bunked off. Now you accuse me of taking money. And you're always telling me what I ought to be like and what'll happen if I'm not. It's my life, not yours. You've fucked yours up anyway, so what's mine got to do with you?'

My hackles rise and I go to strike her even though she's already bigger and stronger than I am. But at that moment my knees give way and my hand, which remains firm even when I'm wrestling with a crooked root during tooth extraction, starts to shake like a leaf.

My daughter takes advantage of my momentary weakness, slips past me and a moment later the front door bangs.

I turn and run after her. I just manage to catch sight of her as she disappears round the corner of our street. I know I won't catch up with her, but I keep on running. I tear along the street with cars rushing by me, past people I don't know, who don't know me and don't care that I'm in distress, who don't care that I exist.

But I do exist. And I'm all alone. There's no one I can turn to for advice or help. If I ran to that boy who tells me over and over again that he loves me and plays at preventing the destruction of Castle Sion, he'd most likely be scared that I'm trying to burden him with something that's none of his business. He didn't father the child, and the person who did is the one who'll help me least of all.

I could try calling my pal Lucie; she'd most likely try to cheer me up somehow. But I don't need cheering up, I need to take action.

Tomorrow morning I'll cancel the surgery and take Jana to the drop-in clinic.

That's if she comes home this evening and if I manage to drag her there.

4

My darling daughter came home after the television news. She was in her room with the door locked before I had a chance to say anything. The next morning she emerged and announced curtly that she was going to school. I could fight with her but I'd probably lose. Anyway I can't decide whether or not to drag her to the addiction advice clinic. There is no point in her meeting real drug addicts and coming to the conclusion that compared to them she is as pure as the driven snow. I ought to seek some advice first.

There's only one person I know who might advise me. I didn't talk to him for twenty years and when we happened to meet in that restaurant the other day I wasn't particularly nice to him.

I don't relish the thought of talking to him, but I call him from the surgery none the less.

Surprisingly enough, I get straight through and over the phone it sounds as if he'd be pleased to meet me; he'll readily see me in his office at the Ministry of Health if I like.

It's only a short distance from home to the ministry, but like most of my colleagues I loathe that particular institution and have no yearning to step inside it, so I agree to meet in a pub.

We meet early in the evening. He's bound to think I've been missing him since the day I saw him again. Perhaps he's got wind of how things turned out for me and, knowing I'm on my own, sees an opportunity to worm his way into my favour for a while without committing himself. He once more tells me I'm more beautiful than I was those years ago. And he assures me that out of all the girls he ever knew, I was the most beautiful – in the same way he assured all the others. But I haven't come for flattery, that's another thing I don't miss; I'm here for him to advise me what to do about my daughter.

He listens to me with feigned interest; everything I tell him is as banal as when someone tells me about their aching teeth.

He feels I need reassuring. He recalls our younger days: were we any better? Didn't we rebel against our parents too? It needs calm and patience, he tells me, using the formula he uses to allay the fears of frightened parents.

Then he advises me to find out what my daughter is taking. If it is something really hard we'll have to take immediate action. However, if she is only smoking grass on the odd occasion, he would advise me to go easy. The main thing is for me to find out who she is mixing with. If it's a bad crowd I should try to get her away from them, although that tends to be the most difficult thing of all. Fortunately term ends in a week's time and he would advise me to take Jana off to somewhere a long way away, where I can keep an eye on her all the time.

He also asks how Jana feels at home. Without realizing it, parents often do something that pushes their child in a direction they don't want them to take. Sometimes it is excessive strictness, sometimes it is excessive pampering. He reels off a list of recommendations that he has prepared for the occasion: I must try not to play the schoolmistress with my daughter or harangue her; I must make sure she doesn't spend nights away from home but not make her feel she's in prison. Instead I should give her the feeling of being loved.

While he speaks, his gaze invades my body as it did years ago; maybe it's all that interests him. He couldn't care less about my daughter, naturally. Why should he, seeing that he also rejected the child he conceived with me that time.

Maybe he'd like to hear that I'm sad, neglected and lonely, that I'm unable to cope on my own with what life has in store for me, and my daughter suffers as a result. Then he could offer me his help, which would consist of adding his worries to mine.

He continues for a while longer with his ready-made recommendations. I could probably make them up myself; nevertheless the realization that Jana's case is nothing out of the ordinary is a slight comfort.

I thank him. He invites me to call him and let him know how things work out, and any other time I might need his advice. 'I'm flying to London next week,' he tells me, as we make for the exit. 'Do you fancy coming with me? I'd take care of your ticket.'

I wouldn't go with you even if they paid me, I don't tell him. 'But you know I've got my daughter here.'

'And how about this evening?'

'I have her this evening too.'

I walk home and my anxiety grows as I approach our building.

But my daughter is at home sitting in the armchair with a damp cloth on her head.

'Headache?'

'A little bit. But it'll be OK.'

She seems pale to me. 'Did you have some supper?'

'I wasn't hungry. Because of my head.'

'What about school?'

'The teachers have packed up. We just loaf around now.'

Silence. I mustn't give her cause to feel she's in prison. Give her cause to feel like a queen.

'Your holidays start next week.'

'I know.'

'I'm taking my summer break in July. I've booked us a chalet at Hvar for the last two weeks.'

Silence. 'I don't fancy going to the seaside,' she announces eventually.

'Why not?'

'I don't fancy going anywhere.'

'You don't fancy going anywhere or you don't fancy going with me?'

She hesitates a moment before replying. 'I prefer being at home.'

'You feel like being stuck here the whole summer?'

'Either here or around here.'

'But I don't. I spend the whole year looking forward to some rest.'

'But there's nothing to stop you going to the seaside.'

Her arrogant replies irritate me but I try to stay cool. 'And leaving you at home?'

'Why not?'

'Because I don't intend to leave you here on your own.'

'Mum, you have to realize I'm not a little girl any more.'

'I don't have to do anything. And you just bear in mind that you're not entirely grown-up.'

'I hate lounging around at the seaside. It's a waste of money.'

'The money's not your concern. What would you like to do?'

'Stay here.'

'And come home at midnight every night.'

'Yeah.'

'Stoned out of your mind.'

'I want to spend my holidays with people I like being with.'

'I appreciate that.'

She looks at me in surprise.

'Everyone prefers to be with people they like being with. Do you think I don't?'

'There you go.'

'But you're coming with me because I won't leave you here to wander around at night with a crowd of punks that you think you like being with. Just because they let you do what you like and because they spend their time lazing around like you.'

'Mum, this is pointless. I won't go to the seaside with you anyway.'

'All right, we won't go to the seaside.'

'But I don't want to go anywhere.' Her expression is defiant. This is no longer the little girl who used to come and snuggle up with me in bed on a Sunday morning. I know I'm partly to blame. I ignored for too long the fact that things were going wrong with her. I wanted her childhood to be different from mine; I wanted her to have more freedom.

But what is freedom? The gateway to an unknown space that even adults get lost in, and my little girl isn't sixteen yet. She's lost in a landscape that lures her, but in fact it's a swamp that she'll go on sinking into until one day she'll disappear altogether.

I'm aware of tears falling from my eyes. I quickly wipe my face, but I can't stop myself from crying.

And this creature looks at me for a moment and then all of a sudden she shoves her aching head into my lap. 'Don't cry, Mummy. I didn't mean it. We'll go together if you like.'

5

I invited Kristýna to take part in a game I had thought up. It wasn't too crazy, or childish even. It was a game without monsters. I invited her because I wanted her to meet my friends. No, I wanted to prove to myself that she was mine not only in private but also in front of people. I wanted Věra to see her with me.

But I shouldn't have done it. Kristýna didn't feel right during the game, or rather she disliked it. I should have realized that she's down-to-earth and not the playful type. She made an effort to please me, but I could tell she was uncomfortable. I didn't try to stop her when she decided to leave after two hours.

We went on playing almost the whole night. Věra acted as disdainfully as she was able. When we were saying goodbye she couldn't control herself any longer and asked, 'Wherever did you pick up that old relic?'

'I didn't pick up her, I discovered her in the archives,' I riposted. 'She has royal forebears.'

'I don't know about forebears, but she certainly has a large backside.'

I told her she was pathetic and that I pitied her.

She replied that she didn't know who was more to be pitied, but I was definitely the bigger dupe.

Dawn was breaking when I reached home. I had the feeling something crucial had happened in my life.

When Kristýna left that evening and we went on with the game, I suddenly realized that it no longer gave me any pleasure and I was simply wasting time. As if I saw myself with her eyes: a little boy still playing games instead of completing my studies, for instance.

People can have a passion for gambling, but that's not my case. In hero games you have no hope of a financial reward that would change your life. Pretending to be surrounded by fairytale creatures naturally required a certain amount of imagination but also a childishness that was inappropriate at my age and in my line of employment.

People often play games to escape the tediousness of their jobs. There was nothing tedious about mine. There was nothing boring about investigating one file after another that reflected nobility of spirit, paltriness and wickedness in varying proportions. Sometimes I felt like a voyeur, like a vulture circling above the desert looking for further carrion. Sometimes I would dream at night of people I'd never set eyes on, although their private lives had been tossed to me, and moreover in a distorted form. Compared to that it was a relief to move around in a make-believe world full of spirits, wizards or even vampires and many-headed dragons. There was something magical about entering an artificial world where you could draw up the rules yourself and influence the course of events. Some of the informers whose files I read plainly did what they had pledged to do for the same reason: a yearning to influence the course of events that the rest had no knowledge of. They believed themselves to possess magical powers to hold sway over human destinies, whereas most of them were just tools, mere puppets in the hands of others who believed the same. And so on *ad infinitum*.

What was important for me was that I was able to bring the game to an auspicious or at least acceptable conclusion, which was something I never managed to do in my private life or at work. But it was high time I started to bring affairs in my own life to an acceptable conclusion too. But it looks as if I'm not fated to do so.

Mr Rukavička–Hádek, who had the job of suppressing those who espoused the ideas of Scouting, naturally failed to turn up for questioning. He sent his excuses and included a medical certificate saying that his state of health did not allow him to travel. When he was the interrogator, medical certificates like that were of no help. If he needed someone, his henchmen would haul them out of a hospital bed if need be.

So we went to find him ourselves.

The old people's home at Městec was located in a neo-Gothic mansion surrounded by an extensive English park. A carefree and comfortable place for someone who robbed people of their freedom to finish his days.

The superintendent told us she was happy for us to use her office for a short while for our business. She even made available her ageing typewriter. My superior asked her how satisfied they were with Mr Rukavička, and the superintendent again obligingly replied, saying that he was a pleasant and quiet old man who had brought his canary here with him. The bird was apparently his only pleasure. His wife had already passed away and his children didn't visit him. He didn't have too many friends here, but he behaved in a friendly manner to everyone and the nurses spoke well of him.

One of the nurses then led in the man who in the past had used at least two names. He stood there supported by two crutches: an inconspicuous, plump old man with a wrinkled face and a pale skull showing through his remaining grey hairs. He leant his crutches against the wall, sat down in an armchair and asked what he could do for us.

Ondřej introduced us both and said that we had no intention of keeping him long. Ondřej told him he would like to put a number of questions to him as a witness; no doubt he was aware what it was in connection with.

The old man had no idea, or at least he maintained he hadn't a clue. None the less he lent me his identity card so that I could enter the necessary details in the statement.

'Mr Rukavička, you worked from 1949 under the name of Hádek as an interrogator for the State Security,' my superior opened the interrogation.

The old man assumed an injured expression. There must be some absurd mistake.

'But we have documents to prove it,' Ondřej said, taking an entire folder out of his briefcase. 'We've brought them with us. Would you care to see them?'

Mr Rukavička–Hádek took his glasses case out of his pocket, but then shook his head. Reading tired him and he had no interest in our documents.

'I don't suppose you need me to enlighten you about your rights?'

'I'm always happy to be enlightened,' the old man laughed. 'Especially by such a pleasant pair of young men.'

My superior read out the relevant clauses of the law about witnesses' rights and then asked, 'But you don't deny having been a member of the State Security Corps.'

'I served in it for a while,' he admitted, 'fifty years ago. I trained as a cabinet-maker but they had a recruitment drive when I was in the forces. I thought the work would be more interesting.'

'And so you worked as an interrogator for the State Security under the name of Hádek?'

He explained that he was sometimes required to use a particular name. He really couldn't remember what name it was after fifty years.

'And how about the names of those you interrogated?' Ondřej asked.

'I didn't interrogate anyone.'

'Would you like to see the statements of those you interrogated?'

'People say all sorts of things. I've told you what I think about your papers. They don't interest me.' The old man looked annoyed and reached out for one of his crutches. Maybe he wanted to scare us off, or let us know he could leave at any time he wanted. 'I ought to know best what I did or didn't do.'

'So what did you do?'

'I sat in an office. What else?'

'OK. So what did you do in that office?'

'Lieutenant, do you think you'll remember what you did today fifty years from now? That you came to see an old fellow in an old people's home, for instance, and issued some absurd charges against him?'

'So far we haven't preferred any charges against you. We've simply spoken about your job and the name you used. Do you think that constitutes a charge?'

'You'd never know, these days.'

'I'll read you out a number of names,' my superior said, ignoring his invective, 'and then I'd like you to tell me something about

154

them.' He started to read the names of the Scout officials who were convicted, among them my father's.

The old man shook his head in denial. No, he couldn't recall even one of the names. 'Who are they supposed to be?' he enquired.

Ondřej explained that they had all been convicted on trumped-up charges. Alleged evidence of their illegal activities had been supplied by a Captain Hádek.

'I've no idea,' he said. 'Maybe they'd done something if they were convicted, but I had nothing to do with it. None of those names means anything to me.'

'And what does the name Rubáš mean to you,' I intervened.

He looked at me as if to say, You keep out of it – your job is to write down that I don't remember anything. And then to my surprise he suddenly looked as if he'd remembered. 'I think that someone of that name used to be a trainer at Bohemians.'

'It's interesting that you remember a football coach but you can't remember the names of the people you interrogated.'

'I've told you already: I didn't interrogate anyone.' Then he added, 'A pity I won't be around in fifty years' time to ask if you remember my name after all that time.'

'It'll be harder for us,' I said. 'You had quite a number of names for one man, Mr Rubáš.'

He grinned as if my comment had pleased him. Then he said: 'You're still young. You've no idea what fifty years is. Let alone notching up eighty years. So you'll never understand what went on then. What it was really all about. We wanted to build something, not like today, when people are only after money.'

Ondřej tried to put a few more questions to him, but we both realized that nothing would come of it. The old man hid behind his eighty years and the half-century that had elapsed since the period that interested us; he pretended to remember nothing, no event, none of the names of those he interrogated, not a single name of those who collaborated with him. All he could remember was the name of a football coach. The witnesses who could testify against him were all dead and what we really had against him was long ago covered by the statute of limitations.

There was no point in wasting any more time and giving this man the satisfaction of still managing to win a battle with the class enemy in his eightieth year. The statement I compiled contained not a single fact that might explain anything.

'A nice quiet old man,' I said as we drove back to Prague. 'A pity he didn't show us his parrot.'

'Canary,' Ondřej corrected me. 'Maybe he's really fond of it. Under a normal regime he wouldn't have interrogated anyone or tortured them. He'd have spent his life making tables or coffins. The fact he had no conscience wouldn't matter to anyone; no one would even notice. What will we do with him now? Just recently a message came through from the ministry saying we waste money. I'm beginning to think they're right. We squander time and use up petrol. And on the odd occasion that we put a case together, it never comes to anything. The public prosecutor's office cheerfully returns everything to us, saying that it is insufficient for them to initiate proceedings. They imagine that after fifty years it's possible to find the same sort of witnesses and evidence as in a case about something that happened a month ago.'

'They imagine nothing of the sort,' I objected. 'It just suits them to use that pretence.'

Then the two of us fell silent. I was overcome with despondency. I thought about the fact that this very man had once wielded power over my father; he'd actually beaten him and tortured him for weeks, as well as dozens of others that we'd never find out about and never finish counting. We are powerless to do anything with him because, unlike him, we recognize the presumption of innocence. Because unlike him, we are decent people.

Maybe I'm a decent person, but at that moment it was more of a hindrance. I had the feeling I'd failed yet again; this was something else I hadn't managed to bring to a conclusion; in the name of some higher law I had merely looked on as that beast ridiculed his victims. If only I'd told him what I thought of him!

It looks as if Dad will never receive justice anyway. And what about me?

I felt such a void before me that all of a sudden I didn't even feel like living.

What will I manage to achieve? What am I to set my hopes on?

On the way back I also thought anxiously about Kristýna. I'd lose her too, one day. Love is another area of my life where I'm unable to make the grade.

When I met her the following day I asked her if she knew the precise time of her birth.

'Do you want to make my horoscope?' she said in surprise. 'You'd better not. You might discover something dreadful about me.'

'I just wanted to see what my chances were.'

She told me the hour of her birth, but like most people, she didn't know the precise minute, and yet even a four-minute difference could lead to an error. But I compiled her horoscope as responsibly as I could and investigated the prospects of our relationship. Even though our elements, fire and water, seemed irreconcilable, we'd had hopes of setting up home together. According to ancient astrology we were both subject to Jupiter, who rules the household.

Kristýna is almost certainly highborn. She is like an underground lake. There is hidden within her a passion which, if it erupted, could be life-giving but also destructive. Not for those around her but for herself.

She is kind and caring, and her wish is to ease people's pain, which is why she does what she does, even though life held out many other possibilities to her. She is magnanimous but also anxiety-prone. She longs to marry but fears betrayal. So what hope do I have? I don't know.

We get on well together. I've never experienced with her the sense of emptiness that I've felt with other women. It struck me that she experienced everything to the full, including each of our conversations, in a way I'd never encountered before. For her everything took place on the boundary between joy and grief, delight and suffering. She avoided the idle chatter enjoyed by most of the women I'd known.

Sometimes she would talk to me about her patients and the quirks of fate and reversals of fortune they experienced, but mostly we spoke about the quirks of fate and reversals of fortune of the people whose lives I researched.

I was more categorical in my judgements than she was. I told her about Dad. I also mentioned the encounter with the fellow in the old people's home, who I'm sure was his interrogator. I told her of our powerlessness in the face of criminals who pretended loss of memory. I asserted that nothing had really been done here to evaluate the guilt of those who helped to suppress the freedom of others, and told her I would therefore do everything in my power to ensure that their guilt was still assessed retrospectively and punished if possible.

Kristýna maintained that it would be to nobody's benefit to do so. Who was to judge, when almost everyone was entangled either willingly or otherwise. And in fact we keep on getting entangled. 'In the way that you're maybe getting entangled with me,' she said.

I didn't understand what she meant.

'My dad was a member of the militia and in charge of political screening,' she explained. 'He would have considered your father his enemy.'

'And would you have agreed with him?' I asked.

'I couldn't stand him. I couldn't stand my father,' she repeated. 'As soon as I started to understand anything, I didn't even want to see him or speak to him.'

'You see,' I said. 'You virtually lost your father while he was still alive. So what do you mean by entanglement.'

'In your father's eyes, mine was also unacceptable,' she said, 'and now the two of us are lying here together. Neither of them would have approved. Your mother wouldn't either.'

'It's great we're lying here together, since we love each other,' I said. 'And don't drag our parents into it.'

Later, when I was leaving, I realized that her father was indeed one of those who had persecuted mine. It's not her fault, just as it's not my fault that my father was the persecuted one. Even so, I prefer not to think about our different backgrounds. I ignore them and intend to ignore them, just as I ignore Kristýna's cigarette smoke even though I can even smell it in her hair.

In fact, the only way to exist is by ignoring the things we don't like and the things about people and the world that could disturb us.

6

It's almost 8 p.m. and Jana isn't home from school yet.
Today they received their school reports. My daughter made an effort to temper her insolence with appeasement and announced to me yesterday that she would fail maths and expected at least five Ds and a B for conduct. I made up my mind not to shout at her or reproach her in any way. But she didn't come home.

First I rang Mum, in case she'd gone there, and then Jana's best friend. I managed to catch her in, but she didn't know anything about Jana, or so she maintained, at least.

Shortly afterwards Mum called me and told me to do something.

'I know, but what?'

'You know how it is,' she presses me. 'Children get bad marks and out of bad conscience or fear they run away or even do something to themselves.'

'Who would Jana be afraid of, Mum?'

'You ought to know.'

'Jana isn't a child any more. Maybe she just went somewhere with her pals.'

'But she'd have phoned you, at least, wouldn't she? You ought to report it to the police right away.'

'I'll wait a little while longer.' I smoke one cigarette after another. I also call my ex-husband, even though I know it'll be pointless.

No, he hasn't seen Jana for at least three weeks. It grieves him because he feels lousy and doesn't know how much longer he has to live. He starts to give me a lengthy account of his ailments. He's only interested in himself now. I bring the pointless conversation to an end and light another cigarette. My fingers tremble and I want to cry. I have no one in the whole wide world apart from Mum, and she's already old. No, there is one person who loves me maybe, but how could he help me? He'd most likely think I'm being hysterical. I've told him almost nothing about Jana. I was embarrassed about her being nearer his age than I am.

I'll wait another half-hour and then go to the police. What we all have in the whole wide world is the police. Helplines and the police, who come and take a statement and that's that.

At last the phone rings. But it's only Lucie calling to tell me she's miserable and missing her swarthy lover. She is about to tell me all about it when I interrupt her with my present problem.

'But she'll come home,' my friend tries to reassure me.

When I hang up I'm convinced that Jana won't come home. She's sitting somewhere with her gang drinking – hopefully only drinking – and having a good time. I'm the one shaking with fear; she knows she has nothing to be afraid of. And as for her conscience, it didn't bother her when she stole my jewellery and that money and when she lied to me. So why would she do something desperate on account of a school report?

I shouldn't have let things come to this. The moment she comes in I'll drive her straight to the drug emergency unit at

Bohnice mental hospital! They'll give her a blood test and I'll finally find out what she's up to.

But what if she's had an accident? She could have got drunk or high and run under a car. She could have been attacked.

I really ought to go to the police, but I still hesitate. I don't want them putting her on some list and searching for her as if she was a prisoner on the run.

Jan, the master of the hero games and also someone who's had experience of detection, is my last hope. So I finally call him and share my fears with him, while apologizing for dragging him into my worries.

Without waiting for details, he tells me he'll be right over.

The waiting seems endless, even though he gets here in less than half an hour.

He wants to know what sort of report Jana was expecting, whether she is depressive, whether she drinks, what sort of crowd she hangs out with, and what pubs she goes to.

I dutifully tell him that she hangs out with punks, that I don't know what pubs she goes to – she told me she mostly sits around in the park.

He asks me if I've ever looked for her there.

I never have, because she has always come in earlier than me; three times a week my surgery lasts till six.

My replies surely can't satisfy him; I expect he thinks I'm a careless and irresponsible mother.

He ponders for a moment and then says that the punks often congregate on Kampa island. 'Even if we don't find Jana there, at least we might discover something.'

I'd agree with whatever he suggested, just so long as we're doing something. I take him down to my car, but ask him to drive because I'm too distraught.

At this time of the evening the streets are half-deserted and soon we're driving through Smíchov. He manages to park in one of the side streets and we walk down the steps to Kampa. The sound of guitars already reaches our ears; it is getting dark but I can still make out punk haircuts. These are the ones we're looking for: I recognize my daughter even from behind. I run up to her. 'Jana!'

She turns to me. 'Is that you, Mum? What are you doing here?' She is painted as gaudily as a Papuan beauty queen.

'What are *you* doing here?' But I'm still relieved that I've found her and that she's alive.

'I'm here, that's all. School holidays started today, didn't they?' She acts arrogantly, not wanting to lose face with her friends. They have noticed me, but most of them look unconcerned.

'Why didn't you call me?'

'My card ran out.'

'Didn't it occur to you that I'd be worried about you?'

'Spare us the scene, Mum.'

'OK, I won't say any more. Just get your things, you're coming with me.'

By way of reply, she turns her back on me.

'Jana, get up and come with me!'

She doesn't look at me. She doesn't even budge. However Jan leans over her and says: 'Didn't you hear?'

'Who are you? Did you bring some cop with you, Mum?'

For a moment, my blood runs cold at the thought that the word 'cop' will incite the rest of them and they'll start to attack us.

'No,' he says, 'you're wrong. I just happen to like your mother and won't stand by while you torment her.'

'I don't torment her,' she replies; but she is so dumbfounded by what she has heard that she gets up, turns to the others and says, 'Bye then, see you tomorrow. I have to go with them now.'

'Where's your school report?' I ask, because all she is carrying is a little canvas bag.

'There,' she says, pointing towards the river.

'You threw it away?'

'Yeah. It was disgusting!' And she laughs a strange, alien laugh. I say nothing.

NO SAINTS OR ANGELS

Jan seats the two of us in the back of the car and then turns to my daughter. 'You're high as a kite, aren't you?'

She looks at him. 'It's none of your business.' Then she yells, 'You're not my dad!'

'Jana!'

But she's laughing in that alien voice again. 'I feel great,' she informs us. 'I don't care what you think about it.'

'But I do care what's in your bloodstream and I intend to find out.'

She laughs. Then she starts to yell that she won't let anyone take her blood. She's not going anywhere with us and I'm to let her out of the car right away.

I don't intend to argue with her. I simply tell Jan where he is to drive to.

'You want me locked up with loonies?'

'I just want to find out what's up with you.'

'I won't go with you!' She tries to open the door as we are going along. I grab her, get my arms round her waist and hold her with all my strength. We struggle. She manages to open the window slightly and shout for help. When she realizes no one will hear her she tries to strangle me and lunges at Jan, jolting his seat and yelling that she doesn't care if we all get killed. 'I'll kill you. I hate you. You're vile! I'll kill you!'

I manage to drag her back into the seat. I'm lying on top of my daughter; I can smell her breath, which gives off an odd stench. I'm lying on my little girl, who is scratching me, biting my hand and kneeing me in the stomach. She is younger and stronger, and her brain is addled by some poison or other. I know I won't be able to hold her down, maybe she'll manage to jump out or throw me out of the car; then she'll leap on Jan from behind and wrench the wheel out of his hands. She really will kill us all.

Then suddenly she gives in. She is silent. I notice that her face is covered in blood. I have a moment of panic, but it is only blood from the scratches on my hand.

163

The long wall of the mental hospital looms out of the darkness ahead and Jan pulls up in front of the gates.

'You want to leave me here?' Jana asks me. Then she starts to snivel. 'Mummy, you aren't going to leave me here, are you?'

But the gates are already opening and I know I have to leave her.

7

Everything here is white and horrible: the walls, the beds, the lamps and the people. Except for the black bats that hang from the lights from time to time. The head doctor was completely out of his mind when I first saw him, I thought he was a loony in disguise or a junkie. When they dragged me off to the detox unit, which was the name they gave the clink on the first floor, I fought with them as hard as I could but they were well trained and used hypos instead of manacles and whips. They shot something into me and after that I slept for about a month like Sleeping Beauty. When I woke up I was in a foul mood and told them all to piss off. That loony in disguise told me cheerfully that I had classic withdrawal symptoms. He also told me that my blood had been full of all sorts of crap and I ought to be happy that I'm alive.

I didn't mix them, it was Ruda.

I'm going to do a bunk anyway.

There were nine of us in the detox – horrendous! There were some winos, too. We told each other about our lives. Renata was already twenty-five but she looked more like fifty, she said she'd been at it for eight years. This was her third time here and she said she'd kill herself anyway. She said she'd already tried to lots of times but someone had always spoilt it. The last time she lay down on the tracks, but the train stopped about half a yard from her. Then the engine driver jumped down and picked her up and because he was in a state of shock he thumped her and yelled at her that he'd kill her. So why did the cretin stop, then?

Renata told me I should be grateful to Mum for dragging me here. 'Nobody could ever give a fuck about me, and just look at the state I'm in.'

There was also one pro. Her name was Romana and when she told her stories it was great. She said she'd once had eight guys in a night and earned as much as a government minister did in a month. She said she was born in Sicily where half the inhabitants had actually come from India and when she was born, Kali was reincarnated in her. Kali was the fiercest of the Indian goddesses. She even defeated her husband, who was a god too, and then danced a victory dance on his chest. In Sicily, Romana learned witchcraft and how to destroy men.

She said it took her only two weeks to turn any man into a zombie who believed he couldn't live without her. There was a son of a Catholic priest who wanted to reform her, and in two weeks he had aged a hundred years and not even junk could help him afterwards. Another guy, some businessman, started going round graveyards digging up skeletons and bashing himself on the head with the bones until he clubbed himself to death. Then there was this professor who taught magic at university: after he got to know her he had to climb up to the roof naked every night and sit there in all weathers. She said he sat there until one night he froze to the chimney and firemen had to fetch him down. About a dozen of her lovers jumped out of windows. And she'd beaten up a heavyweight wrestler and tossed him off the balcony straight into an enormous cement mixer.

It was obvious she was bullshitting, either that or had amazing trips, but she was great fun.

The worst thing was that they locked me up with an old bag who was actually the reincarnation of Dad's beanpole. She looked like a human being but she had turned into a vampire ages ago and she went for me. I expect she went for everyone, but I hated it that she was out for my blood. I told the nurse about it – she's a bit like Mum's Eva – and she told me not to be afraid, she'd keep an eye on me when I was asleep. So I could only sleep when she was on duty and even then I was frightened and tied a scarf round my neck when I went to bed.

It was lovely outside – outside the window, I mean, because we weren't allowed out. That's what pissed me off most: the fact that outside it was the holidays and the rest of them were lounging on Kampa and I was rotting in here like a squashed tomato.

I'm going to do a bunk anyway.

And we also had therapy all the time. There was this peroxide blonde in a white coat who came and started to go on at us about how it was really stupid to take drugs, even though the rest of us knew it was great. The cow told us that what she was saying was for our own good and she told us to repeat after her, just like Dad, that it's stupid and we won't do it again. And she also asked us about our circumstances. She was really chuffed about Mum being a dentist. 'A mother like that and there you are causing her distress. But you don't want to distress her any more. So try saying it out loud, or at least to yourself.'

Really horrendous!

I never supposed that Dad was actually giving me therapy.

Mum really pissed me off shoving me in here. After all, she was always going on about everyone being the engineer of their own fate. That was when Dad used to go spare about her getting stoned on those drugs of hers.

I didn't begrudge her them. I was sorry for her more than anything else. She almost always had a downer 'cos she only got stoned on the legal drugs. Then she'd have the shakes in the morning, but she couldn't top it up 'cos she had to go and drill in people's gobs, as she put it. She couldn't even imagine what it's like when you're totally spaced out on a really great trip. So why didn't she leave me alone?

And she's got a bloke. That really knocked me out. Really thin: he looks like a piece of bloated string; I bet he took dope too, but he acted as if butter wouldn't melt in his mouth. Mum's completely nuts about him, I could see it straightaway, even though I was completely zonked at the time. I really wish her well; maybe she won't be so pissed off with life all the time and she'll get me out of here.

She came and visited me for the first time on Sunday, after I was let out of the detox. She brought me a cake, some oranges and a book of stories by Karel Čapek. She baked the cake herself, so it was a bit burnt. If only she'd brought me a box of roofies instead – but I couldn't expect that of her. She told me I definitely wouldn't be in for long but I had to make an effort. And she went on in a really inhuman way about having put me here for my own good, 'cos she loves me and doesn't want me to ruin my life.

I pretended to be taking it all in and promised I'd make a real effort to reform.

I'll make an effort to do a bunk out of here as soon as I can.

But I don't know where I'd make for. If I went home Mum would be bound to bring me back here again. Romana told me not to worry; she'd look after me.

But I'm fucked if I go with her; that's all I'd need: to spend my time sleeping around with some guys I don't even know!

And Gran came to see me too and told me how Mum is fretting on account of me and how she is too, because she knows what a clever girl I am and how she pins all her hopes on me 'cos I'm her only grandchild. And just afterwards that ginger-haired guy looks in, the one that hijacked me here with Mum. He brought me a flower, something purple. I expect it was an iris. That totally wiped me out. First he hauls me to this loony bin and then he rolls up with a flower. To have someone bring me a flower, that's something that's never happened to me before. But otherwise he steered clear of the educational claptrap. For a while he fed me with stories about how he keeps poisonous snakes.

Apparently one was so poisonous that if it had bitten him he'd have been a goner in an hour. I told him I hoped the snake had never bitten anyone. And he laughed so much that his John Lennon specs jumped up and down on his nose. He also told me he'd noticed I've got a drum kit at home and said he used to play an American Indian tom-tom. He'd learnt to send signals with drums, flags and smoke. He was always showing off so I told him that I was good at throwing letters into letterboxes and that I could remember all the phone numbers I need – about four, in other words.

Before he got up he started raving about Mum and how she's totally fantastic, totally nice and unique, and how she loves me.

I didn't argue with him. I don't have anything against Mum. I simply told him that if she's so nice, she ought to take me away from here before the vampire witch sucks me to death. And he laughed again. I like the way he's always laughing.

Yesterday the therapist went bananas again and we all had to repeat, We never want to take drugs again, we'll never take drugs again, we'll never use a syringe again. I said out loud, 'We don't want to be daft thickos, we want to be holy. We want wings to grow out of our bums so we can be angels.' So for a punishment I was booted back upstairs to the detox unit.

It looks as if Romana won't be taking care of me now; she tried to hang herself yesterday with the shower hose. It was horrendous. We were all in a state of shock. When they were carrying her out, I heard that nurse that looks like Eva mutter to herself: 'If Renata had done it . . . But Romana . . . ?'

But it was obvious to me that Romana didn't do it. It was that vampire witch. She sucked her to death and then wound the shower hose round her neck to cover her tracks. It'll be my turn next and if I don't run away, I'll die the same way.

They say they'll manage to save Romana, but if they leave that reincarnated beanpole in here with us she'll do us all in.

I was too frightened to go to sleep last night. I noticed the old witch creep out and soon two bats flew in and hung from the lamp, and the bigger one was her.

I got out of bed and ran to find the nurse, and she was really kind and came back with me. 'Look, there aren't any bats here,' she told me. 'Just take a good look.'

I took a good look and they really weren't hanging there any more – 'cos they'd just flown away, and the lamp was still swaying.

CHAPTER FIVE

1

E verything in my life has seized up somehow. I've cancelled my leave and called off the trip to the seaside. My young man has gone off with his pals for a week to the Slovak Ore Mountains – with a tiny bivouac and a big rucksack. I would have gone with him if I could. I used to love Slovakia. We went there every summer in the years following my only wedding: canoeing, skiing or wandering the hills and valleys like Jan is now, listening to a language that was soft and melodious to my ears.

Czechoslovakia fell apart just before my marriage did. I wept for it, but I couldn't do anything to help it; I couldn't even do anything to help myself.

My Mickey Mouse speaks a bit of Slovak. He says to me: 'You have eyes the colour of *veronika*.' *Veronika* is what the Slovaks call speedwell. I ask him whether he loves Kristýna or some Slovak Veronika?

'I'd love a Slovak Veronika if she had eyes like yours, breasts like yours and a nose like yours. And she'd have to be as wise and gentle and make love as well as you do. But there are none like that in Slovakia or anywhere else in the world.' He lays it on with a trowel, the liar, but he knows I like it.

He invited me to go with him, but I was afraid to leave while Jana is in hospital. What if something happened to her, or if she escaped, even? He also offered to stay in Prague, but I refused to let him hang around here on my account. Before he went he told me he'd still have two weeks of leave left and asked me to go away with him somewhere.

There is a heatwave and the city is half-deserted, like my waiting room. Even Eva has taken leave. I'll cope with the few remaining patients perfectly well without her.

Most of the day I sit in the surgery smoking and drinking mineral water with a drop of wine in it. I have nothing on under my smock but my briefs, and even so I'm hot. But I'm glad I have the surgery to go to, because at home I feel uneasy. The flat is empty. I miss Jana's pandemonium. I miss having someone to care for. I miss Jana's calculating two-faced chumminess. I miss someone close to talk to.

'What makes you think, in fact, that you couldn't have a child?' Jan asked me out of the blue.

'Because I'm too old,' I replied.

'Is that the only reason?'

'It's a good enough reason.'

'You're not so old,' he said. 'One of Mum's friends had a baby when she was forty-seven.'

'I've no time to lose then,' I said, turning away so that he couldn't see the tears well up.

Maybe I could still have a child. Medical science does wonders. It came up with the test-tube baby, it managed to clone the extinct Tasmanian wolf and it won't be long before it manages to artificially inseminate an Egyptian mummy. But it's a matter not just of conceiving and having a baby, but also of rearing it. I don't know whether I'd still have the strength. Not now, but in five or ten years' time.

If only I stopped damaging my health the way I do. I hate to think what I'll be like in ten years. And this boy who claims to love me now, what will happen to him in ten years' time when my face will be full of wrinkles and I might even be hobbling around with a stick? He'll vanish; he'll go and find someone younger and I'll be left alone with my child in a world where the drug dealers will be hawking their wares from rucksacks in school corridors. And ultraviolet rain will fall through the hole in the ozone layer.

And what if I'm not around at all ten years from now – my tar-clogged lungs and the rest of me finally consumed by a tumour. I ought to give up smoking, at least. But if I give up I'll start to get even fatter and I'll end up a hideous ball of fat. That's unless I started to do some exercise as my first and only husband always insisted I should. In those days I used to exercise, but I still had the stamina.

In ten years' time Jana is fairly sure to have left home. At least there'd be someone waiting for me when I hobble home from the surgery. At least I'd have someone to look forward to.

'I'm sorry,' my lover said, when he saw I was about to cry. 'I just wanted to convince you that you're not old at all.'

One's as old as one feels, I didn't tell him, but tried to make fun of him instead.

Maybe I do him a disservice. I still tend to compare him with my ex-husband, even though I know he's different. He is gentle and he doesn't believe in reason alone.

I convince myself that he's different. But all men have a selfish streak, and a restless one too, which prevents them from staying with one woman. That's something I oughtn't to forget.

Father Kostka turns up at the surgery. He needs one of his few remaining teeth extracted. I give him an injection and assure him that it won't hurt. The tooth is so wobbly, I expect it wouldn't hurt even without an injection.

'I've no great fear of pain,' he says. As is his wont, he smiles at me with his eyes, and I feel guilty even though my Communist militiaman father is no longer alive.

He sits in the chair waiting for the injection to work. I make up my mind to tell him about the trouble I've been having with my daughter.

'My dear young lady,' – this is how he usually addresses Eva and me – 'people expect a priest to put everything down to lack of belief. But belief isn't the only important thing. The apostle Paul spoke about faith, hope and love. And the greatest of the three, he said, was love. It's not easy to believe in the Bible message in this day and age, but young people don't just lack a belief – they lack love. I don't particularly have your daughter in mind, but there are a lot of young people who try to escape from a world in which they don't find any of those three things. I'd also add that we lack the will or the skill to come to terms with things. We are full of pride and are therefore unable to reconcile ourselves with our fate or the people around us, let alone recognize our Father in Heaven above us.'

By now his gums are numb and I prepare the instruments. Meanwhile he adds that children are simply mirrors of ourselves. We look into them and see their faults and shortcomings, but in reality they are our own faults and shortcomings.

It only takes me a few seconds to extract his wobbly tooth.

He spits out the blood, rinses his mouth and thanks me. 'But I expect you wanted to hear something quite different from me, young lady. Something specific.'

I tell him that maybe what he said is what I needed to hear. From him, at least. I could find plenty of would-be scientific advice in any old psychology textbook.

When he is gone, it strikes me that I didn't ask him where one is to find hope and how to care for love so that it lasts, how to support my child without pampering her. But that's something I have to discover for myself.

I go straight from the surgery to see Jana at the drug treatment clinic.

They bring her to me. She is pale and looks puffy, somehow. 'Hi, Mum!'

I look at her and feel searing remorse. It's awful that I feel at fault – more than she does, even. I ask her how she is and she understandably starts to reproach me for leaving her here in this 'nick'. However she admits that there was some point in it, as the therapy sessions had opened her eyes to a few things. 'Even though sometimes they're totally moronic,' she adds quickly, not wanting to make too many concessions to me.

Then we go for a walk, but it's not easy to converse on the move, so we sit down on a bench. A short distance from us some schizophrenics or alcoholics are weeding a flowerbed. I unwrap an apricot tart I baked her, and my daughter tucks into it with relish. I ask her about the people she's now living with and she says dismissively that they're all loonies and junkies. She doesn't know what there is to say about them or what she's doing there with them.

'Jana, do you remember what I told you about my grandmother?' I ask her.

'Which one?'

'My mother's mother. The one I didn't even know.'

'Oh, yeah. She died in some concentration camp.'

'They killed her with poison gas.'

'Yeah, so you told me.'

'When I told you about it, you said how awful it must have been. And now here you are slowly poisoning yourself.'

She gives me a pitying look, as if to let me know how little I know about real life. 'But that's something totally different.'

I try to explain to her that the only possible difference is that in those days someone held the lives of other people in contempt, while in her case, she held her own life in contempt.

She shakes her head angrily; this doesn't fit in with the performance she had been preparing for me. She starts trying to persuade me that what I said might be true if she'd ever committed anything like that, but she had never taken any poisons, and I wasn't to leave her there any more, that the conditions were dreadful and they wouldn't cure her anyway, as there was nothing to cure.

'Oh, but there is, Jana. Don't forget I know what they found in your blood.'

'That was a total one-off.'

'You can try that one on someone who knows nothing about it, but it won't wash with me.'

'It was a one-off and I'll never try it again. I've realized it was stupid.'

'Am I supposed to believe you?'

She promises me she'll never do anything of the sort again. She even swears it.

I say nothing. I don't want to make light of her pledge, but I know how little store I can set by her determination.

'Mummy, you can't leave me here! I'll go out of my mind.'

'You're more likely to go out of your mind from what you've pumped into yourself. You'll stay here until you're cured. And that takes more than two or three weeks, I'm afraid.'

'Do you really mean it?'

I nod. She picks up the rest of the tart and hurls it to the ground. Then she stands up and runs off.

I have an urge to run after her, but I know I mustn't.

In the evening my sister Lída calls me long-distance to ask for news of Jana. 'Mum told me you'd put her in the loony bin.'

I reply that she is naturally not locked up with mental patients.

My sister didn't think she was, but even so I hadn't chosen the best place for her.

'It's not the best place for *anyone*,' I say.

'We won't argue about that,' she says. 'But I heard they don't get very good results. You can't risk your daughter falling back into her old ways when she comes out.' Then she proceeds to tell me about the guitarist in her band who underwent treatment in a community near Blatná. They managed to cure him. She knows the therapist who runs the community. He's a great guy, she says, and she could persuade him to take Jana.

I'm not sure. I'm not used to my sister helping me, and certainly not of her own accord. 'But I don't know anything about the place.'

'Well naturally you'd go and see it first!'

'I'll have to think about it.'

'Kristýna,' she says, 'you can think about it, but you won't come up with anything better.' She dictates me the therapist's name and address and urges me to do something about it straightaway. 'You can drop by and pick me up,' she offers. 'I'm free on Wednesday; I'll go down there with you.'

Maybe my sister really is sorry for me, or for Jana at least. I'm afraid to believe it, but even so I'm grateful for her concern. I tell her I'll cancel my Wednesday surgery and drive down.

2

My boyfriend called from Slovakia. He told me it was beautiful there and that they would like to go on to Velký Sokol and Biela Dolina.

I told him I knew how beautiful it was there and said I was glad he was having a good time. But I didn't ask him how could he be having a good time without me, if he loved me as he said he did.

He went on to say that he was sorry he couldn't be with me, but he couldn't wait to see me again.

He wasn't looking forward to me enough to come back, but why shouldn't he climb Velký Sokol just because I'm missing him?

I don't know what to do on Saturday afternoon.

I'll visit Mum, at least. Mum's always been my comforter, not because she says words of comfort but because she's always managed to put my troubles into a proper perspective. Or at least she's always heard me out and consoled me with some story from her own life when she hadn't despaired even when she'd been worse off than me.

She has come to terms with Dad's death, but visits the nearby cemetery at least twice a month and puts fresh flowers in the vase I bought. She also needlessly cleans the untarnished marble head-stone. On the other hand she has started socializing with old pals of hers she didn't have time for before; she even goes to the theatre with them, something she never did in the past.

I offered to buy her a dog, a cat, or at least a parrot, so that she wouldn't have to be totally without any living soul in the flat, but she refused. She doesn't want a live companion; she would find it a burden to have to look after anyone now. On the other hand, she has bought herself loads of indoor plants – cacti and peren-nials – to fill every empty space in her room.

And she's laughing again, usually at herself. She even laughs in situations where other people would get annoyed or lose heart. She loves telling me stories about the absent-minded old codgers and grannies that live around there.

But I'm concerned about her physical state. Sometimes she gets nosebleeds that are hard to stop, and recently I had to take her to hospital. She is supposed to take a heart tonic and something for hypertension but she is always 'forgetting' to take her daily dose. And when I tell her off, she says she doesn't need any medicine; she feels fit and I'm making unnecessary fuss about a few drops of blood.

I have scarcely sat down before she is putting the kettle on for coffee and bringing me a piece of marble cake still hot from the oven. Then she shows me some new purple-flowering plant which she expertly describes as a cycad and wants to know the latest news of Jana.

We chat for a while about my naughty daughter and the prospects for a cure, and my mother surprises me by wanting to accept part of the responsibility or even the blame. 'You never wanted to accept your father's convictions,' she tells me, 'and I had nothing better to offer you.'

'But we're talking about Jana, not me.'

'What you never had, you can't pass on,' Mum instructs me. 'So you just gave her things instead.'

I don't ask her what I was supposed to give her.

'Your grandma still used to go to the synagogue, or so she told me,' Mum starts to recall. In fact she doesn't know whether that murdered grandmother believed in God in accordance with the Jewish faith. But if she did, she can't have been particularly strict because she didn't marry a Jew. Even so, she passed on something she had received from her forebears. But she hadn't finished passing it on before she was killed. All she left was her, my mother; but my mother was no longer able to pass anything on. It seemed to her that everything worth professing, feeling or believing had died in that dreadful war, so she passed nothing on to me.

'But Mum, you gave me the most important thing.'

'And what was that?'

'You loved me.'

'Yes, that's something to be proud of – that I wasn't a heartless mother. But you still lacked something, you know as well as I do.'

'We all lack something. And who goes to the synagogue these days? How many people go to church at all?'

'That's not what I meant.' She explains that she had in mind the chain of continuity that was broken when the Nazis were here and which she didn't try to repair afterwards. Maybe on account of Dad, too. It would have made no sense to him.

She's right on that score. Dad refused to accept things that made no sense to him. And what he didn't accept he considered wrong.

Mum waits for my reaction, but I say nothing. It's true that I lacked something. All I had was defiance. If someone had asked me what I didn't want, I'd have had an answer. But I'd have found it harder to say what I wanted. Not to lie and be lied to, maybe. To be of help to people. To live in love. All fairly trite; no lofty goals.

'I owed it to my mum and all the aunts and uncles and my grandma who all ended the same way,' my mother said with regret.

'What did you owe, Mum?'

'That's what I'm trying to explain to you. I behaved as if what had happened was a terrible misfortune, but what did I do apart from the fact that I stopped talking to my own father?'

She tells me that she failed to maintain the continuity; she broke all ties with everything she ought to have had some connection with. She no longer wanted to have anything in common with those who had come to such a dreadful end. She worked off her life, but otherwise all she did was let things go by on the nod so that my father didn't lose his temper too often. And she let us grow up without any connections either; she didn't want us ever to imagine we had anything in common with the ones that were murdered.

'There's no sense in distressing yourself like this, Mum.'

'I'm not distressing myself. I'm just thinking about you, and Jana above all. Maybe she'd be better off if she knew where she belonged.'

The trouble is, where do we really belong? I say to myself. Among six billion people at the very end of the second millennium. In a globalized world. That's the posh name they give to a situation in which hope is on the wane and the only big achievements are hypermarkets.

We belong to a world fourteen billion years after the Big Bang, my ex-husband would say. A world that will last scarcely more than several blinks of God's eye the way things are going on.

But this is just a way to make excuses for myself, to stop myself thinking about what Mum is trying to tell me, or about why so many things in my life have failed.

'I planted some honeywort on your dad's grave,' Mum says, changing the subject. 'Did you notice? No, I don't expect you've been there.'

I tell her that I have so little time these days that I scarcely manage to get to the cemetery. I prefer to visit Jana or her.

'You ought to go there from time to time, though,' she urges me. 'He was your father, after all.'

I promise I'll go sometime and it occurs to me he wasn't just Lída's father and mine. But fortunately Mum doesn't know that.

I go out into the scorching street, which is totally deserted. Everyone who could has left town. I set off in the direction of the cemetery, but I don't go that far. At Flora, I go down into the metro station, where it's cool, at least.

Besides, subconsciously I know where I'm heading. I get off in Karlín. The address of the man named Václav Alois Veselý and who is possibly my brother is already fixed in my memory. I don't know whether I'll take the plunge and pay him a visit. I don't know what I'd say. I can hardly ring the doorbell and ask some strange man, Excuse me, you don't happen to be my brother by any chance?

He might resemble me. If he did, I could immediately give him a hug. Hello brother! This is me, Kristýna, your half-sister.

But it would most likely give him a fright to have some strange woman suddenly putting her arms round him and hugging him.

I don't even have to go in. I can just take a look where he lives. That's if he still lives there.

I turn into the street whose name betrays the proximity of the river. However by now the river is well and truly concealed by factory buildings, ugly warehouses and a maze of walls and garages. I walk along the opposite pavement past dingy apartment houses with lots of little shops tucked in between them. Gypsy children play at the side of the four-lane carriageway.

The house I seek has just two floors. Patches of stone walling show through where the rendering has come away. A TV bellows from an open window. The battered front door is open. I hesitate a moment, but seeing I've come this far I'm hardly going to wait outside.

The passage stinks of mould and sauerkraut. I can't see any list of tenants but there are letterboxes fixed to the wall in the corner behind the door. On one of them I find the name I've attributed to my unknown brother. It is written in large block capitals. The letters lean to the left and their feet are decoratively rounded. They strike me as familiar. I search my memory in disbelief, or rather I hesitate to believe what I've now realized. I wasn't the only one to set out in search of my lost half-sibling. He had come to find me and chosen to leave me threatening letters that he forgot to sign.

So I've found the one I was looking for, the one who didn't invite me. I could turn round and leave but instead I continue along the passage and look for a door with his name.

It's right on the ground floor. I recognize the lettering before I even read the name. I ring the bell and wait.

For a long time there is no answer. And then suddenly the door opens although I have heard no approaching footsteps. Aghast, I stand facing my father in a wheelchair, my father as I remember him from my childhood. Bushy blond eyebrows, hair already going grey, cold, blue eyes and a large prominent chin. He eyes me, a strange woman, with mistrust.

I introduce myself and say, 'I've found you at long last.'

'How do you mean?'

'I always wished for a brother,' I say. 'But I didn't know about you. And now I found a mention of you in the notebooks that Dad left behind. You know he died, don't you?'

'You'd better come in – Kristýna.' He backs away in the wheelchair and instead of turning tail I enter the flat. The living-room door is wide open, I expect it's the only room in the flat. The furniture is of dark wood that predates chipboard. A TV set stands on a low table and a two-ring electric cooker stands on another table in the corner. The walls are hung with paintings in garish colours full of strangely twisted shapes, the distorted bodies of people and animals, as well as tree stumps. They all carry inscriptions written in the same backward-leaning script. Various birds sit motionless in two cages hung from hooks fastened in the ceiling. He follows my gaze: 'They're stuffed. Kristýna, Kristýna,' he then says, 'Mum told me about you.' He wheels himself over to the table, picks up some sheets of paper and crumples them into a ball before tossing them into the waste basket. Perhaps they were letters ready for me. 'I'll make some tea,' he suggests.

I offer to put the kettle on.

'No, no, I'm used to doing everything for myself. But you could fetch some water. The tap's in the passage.'

He hands me a kettle and I go out into the passage for the water. I don't know what I'm still doing here or what I can talk to him about.

'What did Dad die of?' he wants to know on my return.

'He had a tumour.'

'And you're a doctor!'

'Only half a one,' I say, as I usually do when my profession is mentioned.

'I know, Mum told me. I never saw my father,' he adds. 'So don't be offended that I'm not sad about his death. I expect you spent more time with him.'

That's for sure. But it wasn't quite the way he probably imagines. Even so I suddenly feel a sense of guilt towards him.

'I wanted to be a doctor too,' he says, 'but this happened to me.' He indicates the wheelchair. 'So I gave up the idea.'

'How did it happen?'

'I dived into the river and hit a rock.'

'I'm sorry.'

'I've started painting.' He points at the pictures. 'They're all my work.'

'I recognized they were by you. They're . . . they're interesting.'

'I used to design toys for a craft workshop, and textiles too, but I can't get any work these days. It's a shitty awful world. They'd sooner send cripples to the gas chamber! They'd save money and could give the able-bodied a tax cut.'

The kettle whistles. He wheels himself over to it, tips some tea into a strainer and pours the water over it. The mugs he fetches are large and don't look too clean, but why should he have clean mugs here?

'Sugar or rum?'

'I don't take sugar.'

He heads for the dresser and brings out a bottle of rum. He pours some into my tea and then into his own. He treats himself to more rum than tea.

'I'm sorry it happened to you,' I say. 'Do you have anyone to look after you?'

'I look after myself.' I detect in his voice Dad's grim determination. 'Mum used to take care of me before she died. That's a picture of her over there.' He points towards the table, on which a small photograph stands in a frame.

I get up and go over to look at it. The woman in the photo could be about my age, maybe a little younger; the portrait is obviously old, some time from the end of the sixties, to judge by the hairstyle. I stare at the face but find nothing interesting in it. I don't know what I'd say about the woman that Dad secretly loved.

'My girlfriend used to visit me too,' my half-brother tells me. 'But she got married and now she has children. I've got other friends,' he quickly adds, 'they just look in on me and do me the odd favour, but they don't have time to look after me. Dad never came, not even after my accident. He ruined Mum's life and mine. I dived in that water just to show I was somebody, even if I didn't have a dad. Sometimes a single stupid act can decide your whole future.' He has drunk his tea and now pours just rum in his mug.

He depresses me. I sip my tea and think about the fact that this man is my brother. I ought to feel something towards him, but I doubt that I can.

'I imagined you differently,' he suddenly says.

'How did you imagine me?'

'Uglier, I should think,' he says with unexpected bluntness. 'So you have a daughter?'

'Yes.' But I won't tell him anything about her. I don't intend to let him in on my suffering, or my joys, for that matter.

'Bring her to see me some time.'

I remain silent.

'That's if you ever fancy visiting your crippled brother.'

'That's not important – the wheelchair,' I say. 'I'll come any time you want, or if you need anything.'

He doesn't say yes, but he doesn't refuse either. 'How's your work? Plenty of patients?' he asks.

I tell him I have as many as I can cope with.

'And you're earning!'

I tell him it's no great shakes, but enough for us to live on.

'I needed a bridge,' he says, opening his mouth slightly and pointing at it, as if intending to display someone else's dental work, 'and my dentist wanted fifteen thousand to do the job. For a few minutes' work! And I had to save two years to pay for it.'

I tell him I never charge as much as that. If he came to me I'd do him his bridge for free. What I don't tell him is that it would certainly do him a lot more good than writing me threatening letters.

'I didn't know how you'd take me,' he says. 'I wasn't part of your family, was I?'

'We didn't know about you.'

'Listen,' he then says, 'I ought to warn you about me. I'm strange sometimes. I imagine strange things. Such as I'm a powerful dictator. Or a concentration camp commandant. A concentration camp for women. There are loads of women in front of me and I can do what I like with them. Do you know what I mean? Absolutely anything I like: I can tell them to take their clothes off or I can torture them to make them admit to some crime, and then I imagine it.'

'You're saying it to put the wind up me,' I say, and I really do have a feeling of uneasiness, although it's more like revulsion.

'No, they're just things I imagine. I've never hurt a fly. Maybe when I hit my head on the rock that time something happened inside me, like brain damage. For heaven's sake, a concentration camp commandant in a wheelchair, it doesn't make sense.' He laughs briefly. 'But it would make a great gag in some horror serial. Can you imagine it? The commandant in a wheelchair with a red-hot poker in his hand and he comes up to these women who are standing there naked in a great long line and . . .'

'Don't go into any more details,' I request him. 'I don't want to hear.'

'You think I'm crazy or a pervert, don't you?'

I remember Dad's sister Venda. 'Maybe you inherited something,' I say, 'something genetic. It ran in Dad's family.'

'I didn't know that. I thought Dad was normal. Or at least not crazy.'

'No, he wasn't crazy. But he knew how to hurt people. After all, you discovered that for yourself.'

'Yes, I certainly did. Would you like some more tea? Or a drop of this?' He raises the bottle.

'No, no more, thanks. I just wanted to find out if it was really you. There was nothing definite in Dad's diaries.'

'I apparently look like him.'

'You do. A lot.'

'I was afraid I might.'

'I understand.' I get up.

He accompanies me to the door and when I offer him my hand I have the impression that he has tears in his eyes. Maybe he is moved at finding his half-sister after all these years. But he knew about me before; he found me long ago. More likely he regrets losing the image he had of his enemy.

As I say goodbye I cannot bring myself to repeat my invitation for him to call me if he needs anything. He knows my address well enough anyway. If he weren't in a wheelchair I'd say to him, Don't send me any more of those letters! To let him know I knew. But I shouldn't think he'll send any more anyway. He'll find another way of exercising his sadistic fantasies.

I don't go back to the metro, but set off in the opposite direction. I don't feel like being among people. The river bank can't be far away, but between me and it they've built a four-lane carriageway fringed by a fence. I cross the road and quickly make my way along by the fence, even though there is maybe no end to it. Cars rush past me. Above the fence there are billboards with inane advertising slogans and above them all there hangs a bluish haze of hot smog.

So I've found my kid brother, who abused me because I had a dad who never visited him. I expect he imagined me standing naked in his concentration camp while he burnt me with a red-hot poker because I enjoyed his father's affection.

I oughtn't to be angry with him. He has inherited Dad's malevolent soul and on top of that, misfortune has consigned him to a wheelchair.

At last a gap in the fence: a prefabricated concrete road promises to lead me to some cash-and-carry. I set off along it and immediately find myself in a different – silent – world. The road winds between walls, whose decrepitude is masked by ivy. Enormous vehicle tyres, plastic sacks and rusting barrels are scattered over the verges. I'm the only person going this way. The glorified warehouse of a shop is closed, maybe because it's Saturday afternoon, but more likely it's never been open, because no one is likely to wander in here. I press onwards: not a living soul. But in the distance I can hear a riverboat siren; perhaps I'll find a way through to the river, after all. I ought to be scared, but I feel intoxicated, as if I was walking in a dismal dream; I don't get scared in dreams, only when I'm wide awake. The road bends sharply round some tall corrugated-iron hangars and I'm suddenly confronted by something very peculiar. In the middle of a scrapheap, where the road comes to an end, there stands a bizarre structure: two towers that look as if they have been skilfully gnawed away at the top; two towers like two fossilized dinosaurs with intermingled heads. It strikes me that it might be an old fairground tent that was inflated with hot air, or more likely an abandoned film set. But when I come closer I see that it is a concrete ruin with massive walls, most likely the remains of a military bunker built before the war that I don't remember.

The scrapheap stinks and a swarm of flies buzzes above it. I walk round it and finally catch sight of a branch of the Vltava, with its lazy stream of dirty water. I lean against the trunk of an old, half-dead willow and try to light a cigarette. My fingers tremble. Not a soul to be seen. If someone did appear, maybe he'd kill me; death hovers here above the earth and the waters and there isn't a single redeeming feature. I imagine Jana stumbling on this place. I suddenly realize that I understand her; I can understand how she took a fancy to drugs that make the world look different and most likely better or at least more acceptable than it really is.

3

It's Sunday. I could sleep in, but I woke up at five and realized I wouldn't fall asleep again. That meeting with my brother/nonbrother is like a weight on my chest. And it's as if I've only now fully realized the awful thing that happened to Jana. I think about her and go back over the past searching for the moment when my little girl started to fall. If such a moment existed.

Maybe my sister is right in believing that I acted foolishly when I decided to terminate the marriage to my unfaithful husband. If I'd managed to control myself and pretended I saw nothing, or that I saw it but was prepared to wait patiently until his highness, my husband, came to his senses and returned to me, things would have been better for my little girl. Or worse, because he started to

be rude to me even in front of her, and sometimes I was unable to
bear it and started to cry or row with him.

When love goes, contentment goes too. And so does understanding. But why wasn't I able to hold on to that love?

And yet my little girl needed love. When Karel left me, I tried
to give her that love, but it's impossible just to go on giving; well
I wasn't able to, at least. There were moments when my loneliness
weighed heavily on me; the sand scrunched beneath my feet and
I thirsted. I yearned for a loving man; I yearned for him so much
that lovers would come to me in my dreams and whisper tender
words to me, kiss my breasts and enter me, and in my dreams I
would shiver in ecstasy. But I only managed to treat myself to one
real lover and it ended tragically. After that I was afraid of another
disappointment; what else can I expect from men?

And yet I've yielded to temptation yet again; I know I won't
escape disappointment but I try not to think about it, not to think
about the future.

Before I fell asleep last night I imagined the one who tempted
me wandering somewhere in the mountains. He told me it was a
group of men and maybe he was telling the truth. Be mine, my
darling, I begged him. Be mine. Don't abandon me, even if you
stay only to the end of this summer, only a fraction of a divine
blink, don't abandon me.

As Mum said, there is something I lack. A dimension I'm
unable to see into. I'm unable to open the door to it. Dad locked
it against me and my one and only husband added a padlock.
What is behind that door? God? Some love that won't come to
nothing, like love between people? Is it peace in one's heart, the
peace of life, instead of the peace of death that I most often think
of as release when I am feeling low? Is it nobility of spirit that is
capable of rising above all the daily distractions? Is it emptiness that
would enable me to focus on myself and my soul, something I
usually never have the time or the place to do? Or is there the
sound of music? Playing music was what used to help me look

beyond all my suffering and anxieties and fill me with a longing for reconciliation. But I didn't stick with it. I let myself be banished from it and the most I do now is occasionally sing something to myself or listen passively to what others have composed and performed.

What if I went to visit my little girl? She is not guilty for trying to make up for what she's missing in her own way. The trouble is, by pointing at myself, I reassure her she was in the right. She is the one injecting poison into her veins; I'm the one holding the syringe.

Instead, first thing in the morning I set out to visit her father. What I have in mind is reconciliation.

When he opens the door, he shows no surprise at my turning up. 'I dreamt about you last night,' he informs me, after seating me in the armchair.

'How do you feel?'

'A bit better, maybe,' he says. 'I've even put on a little weight.'

'That's good.' I unwrap the rest of the apricot tart and put it on a plate that is unfamiliar to me. Our old plates stayed with me even if he didn't. 'What was in the dream about me?'

'I dreamt that you caught me in the act.'

'Doing what?' As if I didn't know.

'I was with some girl. We were lying in a hotel room with red curtains and a Persian carpet. The hotel lift was out of order and the staircase was blocked off. I thought that if the stairs were blocked off and the lift was out of order you wouldn't be able to reach us. But you climbed the scaffolding.'

'I'm sorry I disturbed you.'

'It's strange how, after all these years, I'm still afraid of you finding me out.'

I don't tell him that there are certain sins that stay with one to the end, but I do inform him that Jana is in therapy.

That takes him aback. The thought of having a daughter undergoing therapy for drug addiction is too much for him, the

athlete and pedagogue, who has always been a shining example
of moderation and opponent of all vices, bar infidelity. 'Was it
necessary?'

'You don't really think I'd have shoved her in there just for the
fun of it, do you? Anyway I don't intend to leave her there. I'm
taking her away from Prague.'

'You take major decisions like that and it doesn't occur to you
to discuss it with me,' he says reproachfully.

I try to explain that I had to act fast. And anyway it's been a
long time since we discussed her together. He lost interest in her;
he had other worries. Besides, I didn't want to upset him just after
his operation.

He gets up and starts to pace up and down the room. It's what
he always used to do when he was getting ready to give me a
telling-off. 'That's just excuses and prejudice against me. Of course
you should have consulted me,' he says. 'I'm still her father, after
all. And I have some understanding of such matters.'

I feel that old sense of uncertainty and fear returning: I've done
something wrong, I've botched something, I'm guilty of something in his stern eyes.

Over recent years, he says, whenever he met Jana he noticed
how she was coming to resemble me more and more. She must
have inherited my genes rather than his. When he first met me, he
recalls, I was just like that. I used to hang around with a crowd in
pubs and get drunk; drugs were still a rarity then. But I lacked any
sense of order or respectability.

I point out that I've changed since then.

But in his view a sense of order is something innate.

'I made a mistake being born at all, then.'

He asks me not to be sarcastic and then launches into a peda-
gogical lecture on the proper upbringing of children. Of course he
names all my failings, of which I'm perfectly well aware: I didn't
like cooking, I skimped on shopping, I was no good at managing
money and spent a lot on clothes for myself, not to mention my

smoking or the many times I spent the evening with some girl-friends and came home in high spirits. What was our little girl to think? What sort of example did I set her?

I know that litany off by heart. How many times did I listen to it contritely while we were still living together. I would stand up for myself and defend my right to a bit of privacy, a little bit of space for myself and those I chose to allow in. I never won though, and always ended up feeling like a whipped cur. I did try to cut down on my smoking, but it didn't last long, maybe because it was one of the few joys I had in life.

And after all, a good example is far more important than any amount of talking, proscriptions or prescriptions, my former husband continues.

I ought to pull myself together. After all I'm in no way subordinate to him any more. I shouldn't let myself be cowed by a man who abandoned me, who ran away from me and our daughter. Let each of us deal with our problems as best we can.

Even so I don't contradict him but simply get up in the middle of his tirade and leave the room.

Once I'm outside in the street it strikes me he was right about one thing: I behaved like Jana. But I forgot to pick up the plate with the apricot tart and smash it on the floor.

4

The building is a farmhouse built of timber, somewhat the worse for wear, which stands alone on the edge of an upland meadow. The track that leads to it is so narrow that if two cars were to meet head on they wouldn't be able to pass. We pull up just by the front door. A little gypsy girl peeps out of it and then disappears inside again. There is a barn next to the farmhouse, and hens and ducks move here and there in the space between them. We can hear the squeal of hungry pigs from a nearby sty.

'It's beautiful, don't you think?' my sister asks.

'The countryside is splendid,' I say cautiously. 'Now in summer, anyway.'

The head therapist receives us in his office which contains nothing but a table, a chair, a filing cabinet and on the wall a picture of Sigmund Freud alongside a coloured print of some saint or other. Freud, the saint and the therapist all sport beards, but the latter also has a shock of black hair and, unlike the saint and Freud, he wears a T-shirt with the inscription CHRISTIAN YOUTH CLUB. He and Lída are on first-name terms. She addresses him as Radek.

He asks me to tell him in detail about Jana. I make an effort to mention all the details, including those I'm ashamed of, namely, that my daughter seemingly not only lied to me but also stole from me.

Then he wants to know if anyone in my family took drugs or was addicted in any other way.

So I admit my smoking and the fact that I drink wine every day albeit in moderation. When I was young I used to get drunk sometimes, but that's really a long time ago. Her father, on the other hand, was exemplary in that respect. Compared to him I damage my health and he used to criticize me for it.

He makes notes on a pad, nodding his head from time to time as if to say, Yes, that's the way it goes. But in fact he says nothing and simply invites me to see over the home.

The house is spacious and austere. Everything looks shabby; the furniture could easily come from some warehouse of dead stock or discarded junk. I notice that some of the windowpanes are smashed or cracked. But otherwise it is clean – the floors are still damp from mopping, and there is no clutter. But I'm less interested in things than in the people Jana would have to mix with. But how much can one tell during a short visit? One lad – he could be twenty – is grinding something in an antique hand-mill, another is wheeling some dung in a wheelbarrow, the little gypsy girl is sawing logs with another young man. For a moment they remind me of target figures in a shooting gallery, except that they all wear jeans and T-shirts.

In the kitchen, two girls are preparing the evening meal. We then visit one of the bedrooms. It contains three beds; on one of them, a young woman with drawn features is sitting smoking; she doesn't seem to register our presence.

'What's up, Monika?' the therapist asks.

'I don't want to go on living,' she says, without looking at him.

'You'll get over it. And we'll talk about it this evening,' he promises.

'She's only been here two weeks,' he informs us when we have left the bedroom, as if to apologize for the fact that there is someone here who doesn't want to go on living. He needn't apologize to me. I've known the feeling so often that sometimes I'm amazed that I'm still alive.

When we return to his office, the therapist tells me that Jana can come here if we like, but the decision must be hers alone. No one will force her to stay here. 'We have a group therapy session with them every day,' he says, 'and everyone must work; it's part of the therapy. When they improve, they can attend school, but it's a fair distance from here and not easy to get to in winter.' He warns me that the routine is strict. 'Drugs are banned, of course, but alcohol and sex aren't allowed either. If they smoke, they may receive cigarettes. At first they have to stay here; during the first month we don't allow either letters or visits. Whoever breaks the rules has to leave the home. If anyone finds the regime too harsh, they may leave. If anyone runs away, they have to leave. And conditions tend to be harsh here, particularly in winter,' he says, once more recalling the winter conditions.

'Winter is quite far off yet,' I say, hoping he'll agree with me.

'Not as far off as you'd think.' And he adds, as if to destroy any false hopes I might have, 'From what you've told me about Jana, I wouldn't think she'd be home before winter. Cured, I mean.

You should definitely arrange for her to interrupt her studies.' He then goes on to say that half of those who manage to complete the entire course of therapy never go back to drugs. Finally he tells me how much I am to contribute each month. There are a lot of other things I'd like to ask about, but he makes his excuses as a group therapy session is due to start in a moment and he cannot invite us to it, unfortunately. But even if I stayed here longer, what else could he tell me? Everything will depend on Jana. I can't imagine her sawing wood or mucking out the pigs; I've spoilt her too much for that.

On the way home, Lída and I stop off at a village pub. She just has bread and cheese, while I have a bowl of goulash soup. I'm famished, not having had anything to eat since morning, but on top of that my stomach is churning at the thought of taking Jana off to some far-flung wilderness where I won't even be able to visit her.

'Don't worry,' my sister tells me. 'He'll help her. He's excellent. He knows how to find the cause, and that's the main thing.' She hesitates a moment before adding, 'He helped me too.'

'You?'

'Are you so surprised?'

'I didn't have a clue.'

'It was eight years ago and I attended him as an outpatient. I didn't tell you, or the old folks for that matter. It was nothing to do with you: it was my business. Mine above all.'

I'd like to ask her what she'd been taking, but I'd feel I was prying. So I simply ask her, 'And what cause did he find?'

'Emptiness. Despondency and emptiness.'

'I would never have thought it.'

'Because you always imagined I was so chuffed with myself. But it was only an act I put on for the rest of you. I travelled around with a band and sang on a couple of CDs, but there are thousands of bands like that, and millions more CDs. It makes no difference whether someone buys yours or not, because in a year's time everyone will have forgotten it anyway. There's nothing worse than taking part in the sort of artistic activity that people couldn't give a monkey's about.' She adds that she envied me my job because it had some meaning – helping ease people's pain – whereas all she did was add to the din that surrounds us on all sides. People applauded her, but they applaud anyone who helps them to stop thinking for a moment about the sort of lives they lead.

'I didn't have a clue,' I say. 'It never occurred to me.'

'We know so very little about each other; we are both engrossed in our own troubles and put on an act for each other.'

'And how did he help you?' it occurs to me to ask.

'He helped me realize what I really feel. And come to terms with reality. To stop looking over the horizon and overestimating my powers.'

'And are you all right now?'

'It depends what you mean. I don't mainline any more. Once in a while I get drunk with my pals and then there are moments, such as after a concert, when instead of being happy I start to cry. I cry my eyes out and then I start to hiccup. And there are other moments when I go and find a boutique and buy myself a pile of useless clothes and end up giving them all away. But apart from that I'm OK.'

I drive my sister home. As we say goodbye we hug each other, for the first time in years.

5

We saw a lynx and in the sky a bird of prey that I identified as a buzzard, but Jirka maintained it was an eagle. Věra sided with me; the rest of them supported Jirka because he's in radio and everyone thinks that radio announcers can't be wrong, although the opposite is true.

I could have argued because Dad and I often observed buzzards, but I didn't feel the need to prove my point in respect of feathered predators.

We have been notching up about twenty kilometres a day. We could have managed more but the route was fairly strenuous: through narrow ravines and sometimes up ladders or steep stone steps, and Jirka had to lug a hundredweight of excess fat in addition to a rucksack and a tent.

I expect it was sweltering at the peak but down here in the gorges the sun reached us only rarely and the nights were actually cold.

I didn't talk with Věra any more than with the rest. Once I helped her with her rucksack when we were having to scale ladders, and I would offer her my hand when we had to jump across a fast-flowing stream. Each time the touch of her hand thrilled me; when we used to sit in the cinema or the theatre we would always hold hands and also when I'd visit her at the student residence, where we were alone together. We would entwine our fingers and I would be aware of the blood pulsing through hers – it was a nice prelude to lovemaking.

I tried not to think about lovemaking or imagine us in a naked embrace when she retired alone to her tent each evening. Maybe she was expecting me to join her. If I'd have gone there, I expect she wouldn't have kicked me out. I tried to think about Kristýna, but she seemed so far away. She dwelt in the other world, the world of work and important issues, the world of directors, department heads, police chiefs and subordinates, not to mention files containing denunciations – and where the rotten so-and-sos who wrote them still walk about with impunity.

Here we followed deserted tracks. When we managed to find our way out of the forest we would sunbathe half-naked on the grass, cook on an open fire, sing songs after the meal and, towards evening, pitch our tents; people are bound together when they share something out of the ordinary. I have come to realize that

197

even suffering or persecution binds people together more than a humdrum existence of peaceful inactivity.

That is something I fear – I'd hate to live that way; I'm excited by everything that appears special or even eccentric. That's why I was attracted to poisonous snakes or the life stories of Hitler and Stalin, for instance. Theirs were destinies like tightened strings. The two of them scaled mountains whose peaks seemed hidden in the clouds, while the foothills were submerged in blood, into which they both eventually plunged.

I don't yearn for peaks reaching up to the sky; the fall from up there is usually fatal. I wouldn't want to stay at the summit for even a moment; it's always a lonely place. They left Stalin lying on the floor in his death agony for hours; they were afraid to climb to the heights where they still saw him, while he was already sprawled on the ground in a pool of his own urine. His greatest rival and also fellow traveller had come a cropper even before he did, falling right into an underground bunker, where in order to escape trial he let himself be shot by his own lackeys. He didn't even get a funeral that some of the millions who had *Sieg Heil*ed him might have attended. *Finis coronat opus.*

The only sort of fate I'd want would be one that raised me above mediocrity and the void from which death winks. The trouble is I don't know what I might do to achieve it. I generally end up indulging in pipe dreams.

Every moment I'm here I feel that I'm getting further and further away from the life I usually lead. These last few days I've had the feeling that my head is cleared somehow; at last I've been able to see in clear outline everything I've ever set eyes on in my life. I've even been able to see in clear outline what is yet to come.

I have come to realize that the work I do is poisoning my soul. It forces me to concern myself with the despicable dealings of the past to such an extent that I end up not seeing anything else. Each of us has some connection with them, either personally or via our fathers or mothers. I got the impression that – like in Sodom – there wouldn't be ten just men to be found in our city.

Before I left Prague I tried to compile the city's horoscope for the next century. It predicted the city's downfall in the year 2006. I tried to work out whether this downfall would be due to war or flood, or to something from on high – although water also comes from above. But now it strikes me that it needn't be the sort of catastrophe that destroys buildings, it could equally be a moral downfall.

When I went to bed in my tent on the fifth day of our wanderings I couldn't get to sleep. I seemed to be seized by an inexplicable agitation, a foreboding that something inevitable was going to happen.

Suddenly my tent flap was lifted and I caught sight of Věra in the dim light of the moon.

'Is that you?' I asked, the way I used to ask her not so long ago when we made love, but now the question took on a new meaning.

'It's me,' she whispered. 'If Mickey Mouse won't come to the mountain, the mountain will have to come to Mickey Mouse.'

'I have plenty of mountains here,' I said. But she quickly slipped out of her tracksuit and lay down next to me.

The moon was shining, so a ray of pallid light fell on us through the fabric of the tent. I could hear the murmur of the stream, and close by, maybe right above us, a bird shrieked. We made love and she moaned more than she had ever done in the past; I don't know if it was due to ecstasy, a sense of victory or sadness.

'Do you love me?' she wanted to know. 'Tell me you still love me.'

But I remained silent.

Suddenly she pushed me away and started to get dressed. I went out of the tent with her. Above us the stars shone and seemed to me unusually bright.

'I'm sorry,' I said. 'But there would be no sense starting again. It wouldn't go anywhere.'

'Who told you I wanted to start something?' she hurled at me. 'I needed to find out if you'd come crawling if I wanted.'

'But I didn't come crawling to you, did I?'

'Oh no? And you dare to say that to my face after what you've just done. You're a vile, disgusting, lying beast.'

Maybe she was right. It struck me that all the time I've been waiting for her to come to me and for us to make love.

At the time when I was striving to become an interpreter of history I once read some medieval legends that dealt with physical abstinence. They decried property, food, drink and also, of course, what is called sexual love – which for their authors was the result of original sin. They went so far in their condemnation of physical desire that the best married couples in their view were those who remained virgins to the end of their days. The hypocrisy of those authors disgusted me. They sneered at the desires of the body without which they themselves would never have been born. But there was one thing I had to grant them: the realization that you have to fix your gaze on something that is above those desires and be responsible for how you behave and the things you do.

I turned away and went back into my tent. I lay down again and tried to think of something nice that had happened to me in the past or something I still looked forward to, but nothing occurred to me.

The next morning we stopped in the town of Rožňava. Soon we split up and we each set off as the fancy took us. I wandered through the sweltering streets and alleyways, where there was little sign of life in the heat of the late morning, apart from the occasional half-naked child running past or a dog with its tongue lolling out. An out-of-the-way sweet shop offered Italian ice-cream but I was more attracted by a nearby shop sign that advertised the services of a fortune-teller.

As I opened the door, I set several bells ringing at once, but the only living creature to appear was a cinnamon-coloured Persian cat. It jumped up on the counter and gazed at me with its yellow, fiendish eyes. A posy of dried herbs hanging from the ceiling filled the shop with a spicy scent.

At last a door at the back of the shop creaked and a smiling woman in a long purple dressing gown appeared. Even if it hadn't been written above the shop, I'd have suspected her of engaging in some kind of witchcraft. 'You wish to have your fortune told, young sir?' she asked.

She had long unkempt black hair and dark Indian eyes, and around her neck she wore a heavy chain that seemed to be gold, as did the bracelets on her brown wrists.

I asked her what she used to tell fortunes, and she told me it was inspiration from God. She could take a look at my palm but it wasn't necessary. Anyway she had to look at my aura first before she could raise the blinds that concealed my future. She gestured me to follow her into an alcove where there stood two faded armchairs and a small table with a few scattered dried flowers on it. Amazingly enough the place was pleasantly cool.

She pointed me to one of the armchairs and sat down opposite. She asked me to place my hands on the table palms upwards, to stop thinking about anything else, and to look in her direction. She took my hand for a moment, but she didn't seem to be concentrating on it. She asked me whether I wanted to know both the good and the bad things about myself and I nodded. She let go of my hand, stared at me and then mumbled something incomprehensible. Then she told me my aura was gradually becoming clearer and I was emerging from it and floating upwards. She could see that I was a good man with many abilities, but I had experienced great pain. She could see me crying over a coffin and snakes winding themselves round my legs, but I wasn't to be afraid as they didn't bite.

'You will have a long life, young sir, and the illnesses you will have won't be any threat to you. I can see sparks flying from your fingertips; you must have touched lots of people with them. Take care, take great care or the sparks from your hands will burn you.'

The cat quietly crept into the room and jumped on to the woman's lap, but the fortune-teller didn't seem to notice, her attention apparently fixed on the images that appeared before her eyes, images that she reported to me. Her concentration impressed me, as well as the fact that she didn't try to baffle me with external aids such as cards or a crystal ball.

In the near future, she continued, she could see many obstacles in my path: they are solid and powerful, but I wouldn't vanquish them, I'd go round them. I would climb into a vehicle that would take me to the royal heights, and no enemies that stood in my way would get the better of me. She told me I had lots of friends, and one friend in particular, who was strong and kind, would stand by me. The disaster that was going to overthrow all the cities around me would pass me by.

I wanted to ask her what disaster she was referring to, but I was afraid of interrupting the flow of her visions.

'I also see a woman,' she went on. 'She is older than you. She is far away and she is waiting for you. But it isn't your mother. Yes, she is looking for you because she is in danger. A great danger that you can save her from. You will be richly rewarded.' She fell silent and raised her hands as if about to give me a blessing. Then she stood up.

I gave her two hundred crowns and went back out into the hot day whose brightness blinded me.

In sudden anxiety I tried to phone Kristýna from the post office but I couldn't get through. When I met up with the others I told them I had to return to Prague by the next train. Věra no doubt thought I was running away from her, but I didn't care what she thought.

In the train my anxiety grew. I knew that someone had been sending Kristýna anonymous threats. Another possibility was that someone who was afraid to attack me directly might attack her as a way of intimidating me. I thought of how delicate Kristýna was, or not delicate so much as vulnerable. Anyone could hurt her. There were people who, as soon as they detected someone's vulnerability, couldn't wait to hurt them.

There was a time when victims were revered as martyrs, these days it is the torturer who tends to be revered.

In Prague I called her immediately from the first call box in front of the station and asked her if everything was OK.

She said it was and was glad I hadn't forgotten about her yet. She would like to see me but she and Jana were just on their way out. She was driving her to another treatment centre a long distance from Prague. She wasn't sure whether she would manage to get back by evening. But she would definitely be home the following day. I could come there and stay with her now that she was on her own.

I asked her if I oughtn't to travel with her. She hesitated for a moment and then said it wouldn't be necessary.

I ought to have made it more obvious that she was in danger and demand that she take me with her. But I don't know whether the danger is immediate or not. As the celebrated Nostradamus put it: *Quod de futuris non est determinata omnio veritas.*

I felt regret that I had come back from my holiday on her account while she seemed in no great hurry to see me, and I told her that I probably wouldn't be able to make it the next day, but that I'd definitely call her.

6

Summer is slowly drawing to a close; the lime trees in the street in front of Mum's house have already finished flowering, and autumnal melancholy has descended on me prematurely, as well as weariness. I drove Jana to that distant spot where I am not to visit her for a whole month and it wouldn't even be a good idea to write to her.

Now I could take a holiday but suddenly I don't feel like going anywhere on my own. Jan talked about us going somewhere together, but we've never even been out for the day. I have the feeling there's something on his mind; he's less communicative. He says he has lots of work on; he wants to go through as many files as possible before they kick him out of his job or he is refused access to top-secret materials. I don't try to talk him round: I'm a bit afraid of us being together all the time; he is full of vigour and I'm a tired middle-aged woman. And besides I've got used to not having a man around full time.

And yet one night it occurs to me to ask him who were the people who went to Slovakia with him and why he has told me so little about them. I ask him in exactly the same way I ask him how he spent the day, what he has read of interest lately or if he knows any new jokes. But I notice that my question doesn't please him. He wants to know why I ask.

'Because I'm interested in you, of course.'

He says he was there with the crowd I'd met at the game he invited me to that time. And he hasn't told me about the trip because he didn't think it made any sense to talk about travelling. It's impossible to describe nature, except in poems, and he is no poet. There is also little point in talking about people I don't know. Where something interesting happened, such as the prophecy at the fortune-teller's, he's told me everything she foretold, and since he's been back the unimportant things have already slipped out of his memory. I recall him once describing to me how people with bad consciences behave when questioned by his colleagues. How they go into lengthy explanations about why they can't remember anything.

I feel a sudden anxiety. 'So that leggy girl – the one you used to go out with – she was there too then?'

He hesitates a moment before replying, as if considering what answer to give me, or even whether I know or suspect something.

Then he replies that she was there too.

It's late and time we were asleep. A little while ago we made love; he was tender to me. I ought to keep quiet and not keep asking questions. But I'm unable to dispel the anxiety that has seized me.

'She didn't even try to seduce you?' I ask.

He remains silent and then replies with a question: 'Why would she try to seduce me? We'd broken it off, hadn't we?' He sits up and gets out of bed.

'Where are you going?'

'I'm thirsty.'

He goes off to the kitchen. I can't bear to wait. I put on my dressing gown and follow him. He is pouring wine into two glasses.

'Are you going to have some wine with me?'

'Yes, I feel like some.'

'But you still haven't answered my question.'

'I don't understand why you want to know now, all of a sudden.'

'Now or some other time.'

'But I asked you at the time whether you'd like to come with me,' he reminds me.

'But I wasn't able to. You wanted me to go with you to protect you from your ex-girlfriend?' It dawns on me.

'I don't need protecting. I love you, don't I. That's why I wanted you to come with me.'

He is still avoiding the question.

'But it was night, everyone around was asleep, and she crept into your tent,' I answer for him.

I can see I have rattled him. 'If she's called you and put ideas in your head, don't believe her.'

'She hasn't called me,' I say. 'Nobody has put ideas in my head. It's how I imagine it. If it didn't happen, you'd have told me long ago that she went with you too.'

He says nothing; he doesn't try to contradict me. He admits nothing and denies nothing. He's not a liar and he doesn't know how to be faithful, just like every other man.

'There you are,' I say. 'I don't need a fortune-teller to tell me what happened and what danger I'm in.'

'I love you,' he tells me. 'I didn't stop loving you for a moment.'

'Not even when the other one was in your arms?'

He says nothing. Then he tries to explain it to me: they were going out for almost two years. He didn't want to hurt her. And anyway he hurt her because he told her he didn't want to have anything to do with her any more.

'Because now you've got me.' I complete his thought. 'You don't need to explain anything to me. I'm glad you have consideration for your old girlfriend. It means I can hope you'll show me the same consideration.'

He repeats that he loves me and has never loved anyone else. He tries to explain to me that there are situations when you do something you didn't intend to, and you are immediately sorry. He asks me to understand that.

I tell him I am able to have understanding for anything – life had taught me that. But that doesn't mean I can accept everything and come to terms with it. I hate betrayal. I once got divorced on account of it and deprived Jana of a home with a father.

He asks me in umbrage whether he ought to kneel down and ask my forgiveness.

I tell him that I don't like fellows who kneel, and I like even less those who ask if they ought to.

I have the feeling my little boy is at a loss – whether to be offended or to burst into tears. He's not a liar and he doesn't know how to be faithful. Most likely he is regretting that he didn't lie. But he'll soon learn how. Maybe I should be pleased that he doesn't yet know how to lie, but at this moment all I feel is disappointment – and weariness.

'Kristýna,' he begs, 'nothing happened, nothing of any importance. Surely you'll forgive me.'

'I don't know what you expect,' I tell him. 'That I'll advise you? Or that I'll go back to bed with you?'

He hesitates. Then he asks if he ought to go.

I tell him I'd appreciate it if he did.

7

My new nick was called Sunnyside and it immediately struck me that Graveside might be a better name, because the nearest thing was an old abandoned graveyard. Though I have to admit that the sun really did beat down all the time – I got quite a tan during the first few days of my nonenforced stay. You see I had to declare that I'd chosen that nick voluntarily. I played up a bit at first but I knew I'd go anywhere to get rid of those vampire witches and where I wouldn't have to listen to the crap from that platinum blonde cow who meant it all for our good. But I said I wasn't going to any loony bin in the middle of a forest; I'd sooner hang myself. Mum tried to persuade me it was for my own good and told me what a fantastic place it was. Dad was born not far from there and lived there at my age, and apparently some of his great-great-great-aunts still live around there somewhere, though I couldn't have given a toss. Mum went on to tell me I wouldn't be there long and it wasn't the end of the world because they had electricity there. I told her that was really something: electricity – I was trembling all over in anticipation. And I asked Mum if they had any fantastic things such as electric chairs, or whether they gave themselves electric shocks after breakfast for fun. Mum got pissed off and said there was no talking to me and told me if I wanted to stay where I was, I could. I started to panic that she might just leave me in that nuthouse and so I told her OK she could send me by rocket to the moon for my own good if she liked.

There were eight of us detoxers at the Graveside by my reck-oning – that's including me. Some of them had already been stuck there for six months. Monika was the only one who was just starting her second month and she was planning to split. She told me that before she came there, she'd worked in a hospital. It had been heaven, she said: there were drugs everywhere you looked. They used to nick Rohypnol, for instance, and give the sick old ladies a placebo instead, and then they'd have great trips. From time to time they even managed to get hold of morphine; that was super because then they didn't have to buy expensive muck from Arab dealers. She was screwing some married doctor that she was in love with, but when it got out, the nerd packed her in and all she had left was the dope. She's come to realize that life without drugs has no point anyway and that people are vile by nature.

So I expect we'll do a bunk together.

Pavel, who has already done his military service and astounded us with card tricks and by making tea disappear from a cup in front of our very eyes, says this place is just like the sort of hassle they got in the army: fatigue duty, kitchen rota, pigs and goats. And the punishments are the same: most often being confined to barracks. I wasn't allowed a leave pass yet anyway, so they couldn't take it away from me. Whenever our dear Radek, who was helping us to be normal people again, found that the floor wasn't completely clean, it had to be washed again. In the first week alone I had to scrub our bedroom floor three times. I was also put in charge of our four hens and a duck with some ducklings. They were always running away from me, especially the little ones, and last week a pine marten got one of them. Radek said it was fate and told me not to be too upset; pine martens were God's creatures too. I wasn't upset at all: I was glad I had one little bugger less to keep an eye on. I called the pigs 'sausage dogs' 'cos they were so tiny, and when they were hungry, which was all the time, they squealed and set all the dogs around barking.

Apart from that, Radek is great, and he's cool in a way. He's got about eighteen children of his own and he still finds time to visit us in the evening. Sometimes he tells us about his life. He wasn't allowed to study 'cos he went to church – he was in a secret church or something, so he had to work for a living and has done almost every possible kind of job: roofing, laying pavements, doing deliveries, and working in a dry-cleaner's where they used to boil up clothes in some acid; when it evaporated it was more narcotic than regular dope. Sometimes his life was a bit like in an action movie 'cos he was always doing stuff with that church. Once, the Communist cops picked him up and tried to make out he'd got drunk and run over some kid. He told them he couldn't have run anyone over 'cos he didn't have a car and had never driven and those creeps said that was even more suspicious so they were arresting him. They told him they were taking him to the nick for interrogation and on the way they talked about how they'd say he'd been shot trying to escape. He didn't really believe them, 'cos if they'd been meaning to shoot him they wouldn't talk about it in front of him, but even so when they got there he refused to get out and they had to carry him. And that really happened: they carried him out and chucked him in some cell and left him there all night in the total cold without food and then they let him go the next evening. And he told us as well that he never even lost his rag over those cops 'cos according to him they didn't know what they were doing, and they were just totally demented due to the training they'd been given and also because of TV.

The thing is that Radek really knows how to take people apart. That allows them to form an attitude about themselves. He doesn't rabbit on about drug-taking being dreadful, he just helps us to think positively and realize why we needed to take dope and others didn't. I've already realized that I took dope to spite Dad because he thought that after they discovered the Big Bang it was all right to do your own thing and not give a damn about others. And that's what he did. Radek had the feeling that what I'd wanted to be was different from him, and different from Mum too.

I get the feeling that I now know almost everything there is to know about me, as well as about Mum and Dad. It's really crucial to have an attitude to yourself and to people around you.

I really enjoy it when we sit and talk about each of us. Pavel, for instance, told us seriously that once when he was on a trip he wanted to bonk his own mum, and she was in such a state of shock she kept saying, Pavel, you must have mistaken me for someone; it's me, your mum – simply horrendous.

Last week when I was on kitchen rota I forgot to order the spaghetti that was supposed to be for lunch and as a punishment I was put on kitchen rota again the next day and in the evening I had to muck out the animals. I felt like dumping the shit under Radek's window, but it wouldn't have done me any good 'cos I'd have had to clear it up and then wash the lawn with a rag. So at least I broke two plates instead and then pretended to be all upset and said they'd slipped out of my hands by accident because they were wet.

The boys here are fairly ace and I think they fancy me. The other day Pavel picked me some daisies and swept the kitchen for me. And Lojza, who's due to go home soon, offered to help me with maths. But I told him I hadn't yet reached the stage where I could do any swotting. For the time being I have to concentrate my efforts on fighting with myself and beating my bad habits. Another time he told me he was sure I'd get over it; he told me I needed to believe in myself. I don't know whether I'll get *over* it; what I want is to get *out* of here. But apart from that I believe in myself.

One little crud who came here right after me did a runner two weeks later. I was curious what Radek would say about it, but all he said was if someone didn't want to stay here he was welcome to go.

The day before yesterday I got my first letter from Mum. She says she's missing me and has talked to Radek on the phone; he says he's fairly pleased with me. Would you believe it: after me forgetting to order the spaghetti and smashing those plates. He knew very well they didn't just slip out of my fingers and that I was putting it all on. Mum also sent me two hundred crowns for when I get a leave pass, and she said she'd drive down and was looking forward to seeing me. Not a word about that ginger bloke of hers; she didn't even give him the letter to sign. Maybe he's already chucked her over like Dad; I'd be really sorry for her if he did. And I've started to miss her a lot too and Ruda – I remembered what a great time we had, but most of all I miss my little room where no one came poking their nose in and no one yelled 'Wakey wakey!' at me at six in the morning.

Yesterday when Monika went shopping she swigged a bottle of beer in the supermarket and one of the cows that works there grassed on her to Radek. So Monika was immediately 'confined to barracks' and on top of that she had to wipe all the passages and stairs. Horrendous! She told me in the evening that she'd had enough of being hassled. She was going to do a runner and asked me if I wanted to come too. I told her I'd been thinking about it since the first day and if she was going I'd go with her, except I didn't know where I'd make for.

She suggested an aunt of hers near Písek. She wouldn't kick us out and we could even help her on the farm until we decide what next. I've got an aunt in Tábor, but she knows Radek so I expect she'd tell us to get lost.

Radek happened to be at some therapists' meeting or something so the only person in charge was Madla, a girl not much older than us who was only starting her training. She used to prat around with us in the evenings and sing songs and play the guitar. Then we'd have to wake her up in the morning. I was a bit sorry for her that she'd be in the shit on account of us, but Radek wasn't that sort. He'll say it was fate and if someone doesn't want to stay in his heavenly Sunny Graveside they are welcome to leave.

So in the afternoon when we were all supposed to go somewhere to the forest for firewood I pretended I had a terrible headache. Monika was on kitchen rota and had to do the washing-up. As soon as the rest of them were gone we packed our rucksacks and left too, but in the opposite direction.

It was a glorious day and neither of us could understand how we'd managed to put up with it for so long: feeding the goat, mucking out, licking the lino and having to rabbit on about ourselves. When we got out of the forest we managed to thumb down a Trabant with some local dumbo at the wheel who was taking his wife to the dentist's in Blatná.

That's a coincidence, I said, my mum's a dentist too, but in Prague.

They were tickled pink that my mum was a dentist too and wanted to know whether we were going back to Prague and where from. I told them we were on a tour because it's so beautiful round here we can hardly get over it.

They were really chuffed and told us to help ourselves to the apples they were bringing with them.

I started on about Sunnyside, saying I'd heard there was some farm up in the woods where there were junkies. Had they heard about it? They said they had and that it was really dreadful how many young people have got hooked on that stuff and the ones up there are the worst of all: they nick things, get drunk and they were all shacked up there together.

'That really must be awful for all the people round there,' I said. 'Luckily we didn't go anywhere near there, otherwise we'd have spoilt all the happy memories we have from the rest of our trip.'

They dropped us in Blatná in front of the castle and even told us how happy they were to have met such nice young girls and how nice it was that there were still some young people who appreciated natural beauty.

Afterwards Monika told me I was a gas. As she knew about the money I got from Mum she dragged me into the nearest supermarket and we bought a bottle of vodka, though I'm not much into booze. But we didn't have enough money for anything we could really trip out on.

CHAPTER SIX

1

I miss Jana. When I'm finished at the surgery, I don't even feel like going back to the empty flat. Jan called me a few times. I talk to him but I don't feel like seeing him. Or so I tell him and myself. But then when I hang up I feel so wretched and lonely that I burst into tears.

Sometimes I get together with Lucie, and almost every day I drop in on Mum. I also visit my ex-husband. I get him something from the shops and cook him an evening meal, the way I did years ago. But he eats almost nothing. He is quickly going to seed: he's already an old man.

Life is sad. Almost everyone ends up on their own. Maybe in the past people still had God with them, but he wasn't really with them, at most they had him in their mind.

I don't mind being on my own, what I mind is that I've failed in my life and the people around me failed too. I reproach myself for handing my daughter over to the care of strangers, for not being able to cope with her on my own. I'm annoyed with myself that when she needed me most I squandered the little time I had left for her on a vain and conceited love affair.

Maybe I understand teeth, but I've never managed to understand the hearts of even those who are closest to me.

The waiting room has been full since morning but I've an urge to get away from here and be alone in the forest, the thickest one possible. The trouble is I won't escape myself anyway.

I work in silence. I don't even talk to Eva. And it would be just the day when I have one serious case after another. Periostitis and three extractions, and to cap it all the last one was a number eight. And as if out of spite the phone hasn't stopped ringing.

I even cope with the number eight. I dictate the details to Eva for the patient's record and the phone is already ringing again. I can hear Eva saying, 'I'm afraid Mrs Pilná can't come to the phone now; she is in the middle of an extraction.' Then she listens for a moment and tells me, 'Apparently it's important. It's to do with Jana.'

'Rinse out, please.' I take the receiver and some girl's voice informs me that Jana is lost. She has run away with Monika. Who's Monika? Oh, yes, now I remember. The new one who didn't want to go on living. 'If she doesn't return by evening,' the girl informs me, 'we'll have to ask the police to look for her. Should she turn up at home, please call us.'

'Do you think she'll come home?'

'Probably not.'

'So what am I supposed to do?'

'I don't know,' the voice says. 'I'm new to this and Radek doesn't get back until the early evening.' She promises they'll call me if Jana turns up.

'She's run away?' Eva cottons on.

I nod.

'What are you going to do? Shall we call it a day here?'

I call Mum and let her know what has happened and ask her to go over to the flat and stay there until I get home. There's no point in sending patients away when they have appointments – anyway I don't know what I could do at home except wait. And being stuck at home would be even more intolerable.

'She's bound to turn up.' Eva tries to cheer me up. 'They'll call you soon, you'll see.'

But nobody calls and so I go on working. My fingers go through the routine motions, inserting the correct drill and using the right pressure. I even talk: asking things and giving orders, and all the while I imagine some dimly lit den full of junkies, a car driven by some pervert or a pimp, all of them taking my little girl away from me.

'That doesn't hurt?'

'No, doctor. You really have a way with your hands.'

I have a way with my hands, but nothing has ever turned out right for me.

'That's the lot,' Eva suddenly announces and leaves the door to the waiting room open. 'Shall I ring around all the people who have appointments for tomorrow to let them know you won't be here?'

I shrug. I've no idea what I'll be doing tomorrow or whether they'll find Jana by then. 'No, don't call anyone.'

2

Back home, Mum wants to hear some details, but I don't know anything. 'What if Jana came,' it strikes me, 'and instead of coming here went to your place?'

But Mum had already thought of that and pinned a note to her door saying where she was. 'You shouldn't have sent her so far away,' she reproaches me. 'She's not used to that way of life.'

'Was I supposed to let her lead the sort of life she was getting used to?' I don't know how I'll get through the rest of the day. I smoke one cigarette after another. I can't even stay sitting down. I dash about the flat tidying things. I have to do something. I call Sunnyside again. The girl's voice tells me they still have no news of the runaways, but the boys of the community have decided to go and look for them.

'Do you think they'll find them?'

'They're the only ones who have any real chance. They already know them and know where they might find them.'

I try calling girlfriends of Jana's that I know but I get no reply anywhere. No one's home. Naturally, it's still the holidays.

I ask Mum to stay in my flat while I go and look for Jana.

'Where?'

'I don't know. Everywhere.'

'When will you get back?'

'I don't know that either.'

'But it's pointless, isn't it?'

What isn't pointless? I don't ask her. Instead I tell her I'd go round the bend just sitting here doing nothing.

'Have some sense, Kristýna, and stop panicking,' she urges me. 'There's no way you'll find her. Instead you'll probably do yourself a mischief. Look how uptight you are.'

'I'm not a little kid any more, Mummy.'

First I drive to Kampa, but in the place where we found her last time there are just a few dogs running around.

I run over to the old millstream on the edge of the park as if intent on fishing Jana out of the water. There is a couple snogging on one of the benches, but they don't notice me.

You don't happen to have seen my Jana – fifteen years old, blue eyes, a high forehead, long legs, a punk hairstyle . . . ? – I don't ask them. I dash back to the car and set off in a southerly direction, upstream, out of the city. I push the poor old banger to such limits that it whines. The countryside flashes past me as splashes of colour.

Where are you heading, Kristýna? You haven't the foggiest idea where you're going, have you?

I'm going to find my little girl.

How do you think you're going to find her in this wide world? And what will you do if you don't find her? How will you go on living?

I turn off the motorway, drive through Příbram and all of a

sudden, here it is: the cemetery wall and the Church of the Exaltation of the Holy Cross.

I pull up and get out of the car. My legs barely support me and there is a flickering in front of my eyes.

It's still daylight. I don't know why I stopped here. After all, Jana is hardly going to visit any of her father's relatives; she doesn't know them anyway. And even if she came this way, why would she hang around here?

I stopped here because I'm afraid to drive to the place she ran away from. I stopped here on my own account. Because of the grave of Jan Jakub Ryba who wrote the Christmas Mass that always makes me want to weep for joy when I hear it, even though I don't believe in a God who lay as a baby in a manger. Because of the composer who decided one morning that he couldn't go on living. He was then only slightly older than I am now, but he was at the end of his tether. And he had a faithful wife and good children.

So he put a razor in his pocket and set off for the wood known as The Crevice. There, they say, he sat down on a boulder, and when there wasn't even a crevice to let through a ray of hope, he slit his throat. That's how my ex-husband related it anyway.

I don't have a razor in my pocket, yet I'm not sure I want to go on living. I have yet to find a faithful man and my only child is on the run.

Women don't generally use a razor; it's usually pills or the gas oven. There's a bottle of analgesics in my handbag that would definitely put an end to my pain and disappointment for good. The wood known as The Crevice still stands, only the trees have changed. They erected a stone monument on the spot where the composer ended his life. My first and only husband took Jana and me to see it while we were still together.

We are not together now; we have fallen apart.

I oughtn't to waste time. I must drive on in search of my little girl. But now that third one has crept up behind me: the eternal

---

infant, God's messenger, and she's whispering to me that she's my little girl too and I can find her at any moment and she'll hug me and stay with me for ever and we'll be happy together and all the fear and pain will disappear.

The little girl promises to lead me to the wood, and she's so considerate that she even fans me from behind with a little breeze. You'll sit down on a stone, she coaxes me, swallow what you brought, then lie down on the moss and you'll feel fine: no one will ever run away from you again, no one will hurt you or let you down; no one will betray you, no one will want anything from you, not even me; I'll just gently fan you as long as you like, on your journey to that peace that lasts forever.

The little girl has a gentle, enticing voice, and when she waves her hand, mist will surround me and it'll be easier for us, it strikes me.

All right, I'll go with her.

At that moment, the organ starts to play in the church behind me and I recognize the familiar notes. Who could be playing a Christmas Mass at the height of summer? Maybe the dead composer himself chose from the thousand works he composed the very one that refreshes the soul most.

'This is where I was born, on the edge of Rožmitál,' my ex-husband pointed out to us. 'And here I went to school. Can you hear that choir? I used to sing in it: *Master, hey! Rise I say! Look out at the sky – splendour shines on high.* What are you smirking for, Jana?'

'That you used to go to school too, Daddy. You must have been teensy-weensy.'

My poor little girl, your mother's a head case; she's a sad, desperate individual and she's destroying herself like you. She's teetering over the pit. When she tumbles howling into it, what will become of you?

I go back to the church and stand listening, recalling the time when we all still lived together in love. The little messenger, that little girl, has lost patience and quietly disappears without hanging around for me.

I make for the church door, intending to go in and thank the organist, but the door is locked. Goodness knows how long it is since someone passed through it. The organ has fallen silent too.

Only now do I notice that there is a telephone box not far from the church.

Yes, my Jana and Monika have already been found. The girls ran away and got drunk. They will be penalized, unless the others decide to expel them altogether.

'Do you think I could drive over? I'm not far away.'

3

It is dusk when I reach Sunnyside.

They won't allow me to be alone with Jana.

'Heavens, Mum! What are you doing here?' she exclaims when they bring her. 'It's great you came. I'm bound to be banned visitors. And maybe they'll shave my head too.'

My little girl only thinks about herself. It won't occur to her to ask what I felt when they told me she'd run away, or what I've been going through all the time she has been torturing me like this.

'What came over you to run away like that?'

'We didn't run away, we just went for a bit of a walk.'

'And so you took rucksacks with you,' comments one of the boys who is apparently also here as a client.

'We took things in case it rained, you dumbo,' Jana explained.

'A lot of things in case of rain,' Radek chimes in. 'And anyway you weren't supposed to be going for walks, as well you know.'

'Well OK,' Jana concedes, 'but we really did have second thoughts. It will be up to the community,' she continues, turning back to me, 'whether they shave my head, expel me or just make me muck out for a month.'

The psychotherapist adopts a conciliatory expression. 'They won't expel you, you'll see,' he says. 'You're good at making soup and playing the guitar. We'd miss you.'

I'd like to ask her whether she realizes that if she doesn't make the grade here, there's nowhere she'll find help, but Radek sends her away. 'We'll sort it all out with her,' he explains and leads me to his office.

He sits me down directly opposite the portrait of the great Freud. Only now do I realize that I almost succumbed to the temptation of eternal peace because I felt that life by now had nothing good to offer me anyway. I can feel the tears running from my eyes and I can't stop them.

'Don't upset yourself,' the psychotherapist says, coming over to me and stroking my hair. 'They almost all try to escape and we always let them off the first time. Some of them abscond for a month, for instance, and then come and ask us to take them back. There are some, of course, who run away and we never see them again.'

I nod to show I understand. I'd like to ask him how satisfied he is with Jana otherwise, but what could he say, seeing that she tried to escape this very day. 'I'm really sorry that Jana has added to your worries,' is all I say.

'Not at all. That's what we're here for. You see, everybody thinks there should be something to show after a week or two, but mostly it takes months. We've no right to be impatient. None of us are saints or angels.'

'I know.'

'Your sister and Jana herself told me you suffer from depressions.'

I nod and say that I can't see the importance.

'Oh, but it is important for Jana.'

'I've always tried to conceal it from her.'

'She sensed it anyway. Maybe she couldn't identify it or explain it. But when a mother isn't sure whether she's happy to be alive, the child's world loses one of its mainstays and the child then tries to escape it. What we want here is for them to learn to identify and understand what they feel and why they feel it. That's the first step before they eventually stop looking for false means of escape.'

I nod. I realize that this is an indictment of me and I try to stop the tears streaming from my eyes.

'I'm not blaming you for anything,' he says, as if reading my thoughts. 'That insecurity is something deeper and more generalized and involves us all. They,' he adds, pointing to the figures I can glimpse moving about outside the window, 'had no security. They had no idea what direction to take when everything around them seemed to lack any direction. They could have all sorts of possessions but possessions only increased that feeling of emptiness. They are aware of it. They aren't riffraff as those who have learnt to conform and put up with everything think. They are simply sensitive to that emptiness which we close our eyes to. Unless we are able to fill that emptiness we won't cure them.'

I am aware that his words apply to me too. I am also surrounded by an emptiness that I try in vain to fill.

'Of course we engage in therapy,' Radek adds, 'but there is also an effort to ensure that each of them learns to realize their responsibility: to themselves and to life in general. The fact that they look after a goat, pigs and chickens is not in order to save a bit on the food bill but in order to incorporate them into some natural order. It's to remind them that the purpose of what they do is not gratification but the benefit that accrues from the preservation of life. – But most of all we teach them patience. Sometimes you discover in a single lucid moment what you could have been looking for in vain for years. The point is not to destroy ourselves before that moment arrives.'

4

The mornings are already cool and misty and the air stinks. People become more prone to illness – and to toothache. The waiting room is packed all day and Eva and I don't even have time to grab a meal. It's tiring, but at least it's better than being alone at home.

I am unable to put my mind to anything. I don't open a book; I do put on music, but after a while I realize that I'm not listening to it. It feels as if I'm lost in a maze and don't have the strength to find my way out.

I visit my ex-husband almost every other day. He is on his own too and he's a lot lonelier than I am. And he knows he's slowly dying. Now that he knows, he has stopped asking me anxious questions, but I can tell that he is being overtaken by fear. Who wouldn't be afraid? I'm afraid too, although death often seems to me like redemption.

I do his shopping and cook him some tasteless diet meals of which he only eats a few mouthfuls. I peel him an orange and divide it into segments as if he were a child. I make sure he takes his tablets. When I can see that he is totally seized by anxiety, I take his skeletal hand and talk to him. I tell him about the senate elections that he couldn't care less about any more, or about the floods in eastern Bohemia that he will never visit again, or I read him out loud a letter from Jana that he doesn't even take in.

'It's odd to think,' he said last time, 'that the world will continue but I won't see it any more. But where will it continue to?'

I didn't know what to reply. I just looked into his sunken eyes and said nothing.

He remained silent too. Then after a few moments he said that he found it impossible to think that people would still be around in a thousand years, let alone a hundred thousand years. It had nothing to do with the fact that he was reaching the end and that the world would mean nothing to him any more. It seemed to him that people would be unable to survive the tempo they had set. They would destroy either the earth or themselves. Time would move forward and so would the universe but there would be no one here to perceive it, and that seemed sad to him.

He closed his eyes. He'd exhausted himself with that speech. He apologized for those pointless reflections of a dying man.

When I got home I felt a weariness unlike the weariness I used to feel from time to time. It was as if all the burdens I'd ever borne, all the disappointments I'd suffered, all the wine I'd ever drunk, all the cigarettes I'd ever smoked and all the sleepless nights all fused together. I woke up in the night feeling so tense that I couldn't get back to sleep. I got up and went to the window. I stood there smoking as I stared into the empty street. I tried to think of something pleasant, but instead all I saw were skeletal children begging for food on the pavement; I saw fellows with my father's face roaming the city in wheelchairs brandishing red-hot pokers. In the darkness the red-hot metal shone like a torch. I saw my grandmother standing in some enormous tiled room under a shower from which came the hiss of gas. Grandmother cried out and collapsed. There were people all around her. They cried out and collapsed. I saw a ghostly car and someone inside was throwing tiny white bags and syringes out of its window. I could see my recent boyfriend lying naked in the arms of that leggy whore and hear their cries of ecstasy. I saw thieves leaping walls and quietly scaling the walls of houses. I recalled how my own daughter had stolen jewellery and money from me. The images crowded in on me and I started to suffo-cate. I could hear the tramp of militiamen and see my father gripping the butt of his rifle and staring at me as if I were an enemy.

Maybe I do him an injustice; we simply had an awkward relationship.

In the last of his diaries I read how he made Jana a present for her fifth birthday.

I made her a little turbine. When you run water on it, it turns a bike dynamo and makes a little bulb light up. It took me more than a month to make it but I didn't get the impression that Jana was very pleased with it and Kristýna even said crossly, That's not very sensible is it, Dad? It's a toy for a little boy, not for a girl. In the eyes of my educated daughter I will always be a fool, and she's bringing up Jana to think it too. It made me feel miserable.

Dad wanted to give my little girl some pleasure, and maybe me too. He made a toy himself instead of buying one and I scorned him.

I wasn't good at being humble. I didn't know how to make peace with Dad or with my husband after he betrayed me, in the same way that I can't come to terms with my lover's peccadillo. I didn't manage to make it up with Dad even when he was dying. I couldn't make it up with him, just as I couldn't see my heavenly Father above me.

My head aches and I feel sick. I have a migraine on the way. I take a tablet but immediately throw it up.

The next day I had a date with Lucie. It was an effort to reach out for a friend: give me your hand; speak to me!

She has a new boyfriend. Apparently he's a tall young man who is deaf and dumb. When they are sitting together in a wine bar he writes messages to her on a little blackboard saying how happy he is, how he enjoys the wine and how he'd like to kiss her. He's living at her place now, although she told him to keep on his bedsitter so as to have somewhere to go back to. But so far he's still with her. She says he makes love with a passion she's never known and when he cries out you wouldn't even know he was deaf and dumb.

'And aren't you afraid of hurting him?' I asked her.

'Him? But he's happy with me.'

'And what about when he won't be with you any more?'

She laughed. She asked about Jan. 'Why don't the two of you live together if you love each other? Or is it all over?'

I didn't know what to reply. Lucie would regard one accidental – and admitted – infidelity as an inconsequential trifle. I just told her I was tired. Jana was at a drug treatment centre, my ex-husband was dying, and my Mum's health wasn't good, although she put on a cheerful face.

'But I was asking about you.'

'I haven't enough energy for anything, let alone trying to live with someone.'

She couldn't understand. When she falls in love she has more energy than before.

I told her everyone was different. Maybe I wasn't in love any more. I was just disappointed.

'And what does he want? Does he love you?'

'I don't know what he wants. But he'll leave me one day anyway, even though he says he won't.'

'You're crazy. Why do you think about what might happen one day?'

'Because it will concern me. It already concerns me.'

'Kristýna, you need to take things easier. We're alive now, we don't know if we'll still be alive tomorrow.'

I go for a drink of water but I vomit it again.

5

I don't know what to do.

I can't concentrate properly or think about anything apart from how to win Kristýna back. At work I stare at the screen or sit and look at one piece of paper after another without registering what's written on them.

I cancelled the evening when we were supposed to continue the game. Maybe partly because I didn't feel like meeting Věra but mostly because games are the last things on my mind at present.

Jirka is the only person I've confided in about what happened. He said to me, 'I never thought you'd do anything so stupid. Why did you blurt out to her something she couldn't have even an inkling of?'

I explained to him that I was afraid Věra would ring her and spill the beans.

Jirka doubted she'd ever do anything like that. 'That job of yours is making you paranoid. Everyone's a potential informer. And even if she did, you could always deny it. After all, that's what you spend all your day thinking about, and when you're playing games. You know very well that you should never admit anything, even if they torture you.'

I told him that this wasn't like any old interrogation. I thought it dishonourable to lie to Kristýna precisely because I love her.

'There are other ways to demonstrate your love, you idiot.'

So I'm an idiot and I don't know what to do.

I dreamed one night that I went to Kristýna and begged her to love me again.

She said, 'But you let me down.'

I promised I'd never let her down again. I'd do anything she asked.

'OK,' she agreed. 'Delete both of them then.'

I understood that she wanted me to find the files of her father and her ex-husband and destroy them. Her request gave me a scare, because in the dream we were both very important agents and destruction of my files could have wide-ranging consequences. But I yearned for her so much that I promised to do as she asked. 'Now can you love me again?' I asked.

She nodded and started to strip in a brazenly lewd fashion, like a porn star. Then we made frenzied love.

When I awoke I felt sad. As if one could win someone's love by deleting a few data from a computer's memory.

That morning I rang Kristýna and asked how she was.

Her answers were curt and cold. Jana was fine, she was feeling tired. She'd been reading an American novel in which a girl took Prozac. For politeness' sake, she asked how I was. I told her I was missing her. I suggested we might meet but she made excuses, saying she wasn't in the mood and anyway she'd told me how overworked and tired she was.

Mum has asked me several times about Věra. I don't like her asking questions about my private life, but in a weak moment I told Mum we'd split up.

'You're going out with someone else?'

I nodded. I was ashamed to admit I wasn't going out with anyone at the moment.

Mum asked me to bring the new one home some time. She'd like to meet her.

I promised nothing. I couldn't anyway. When Mum tried to get more out of me I started to shout at her that I couldn't stand it when she interfered in my life.

Mum went into a huff and she's not talking to me at the moment.

At work there's a loud rumour going round that they're either going to close us down altogether or they'll find a way to make it impossible for us to operate. Only a few dyed-in-the-wool idealists are interested in the exposure of old crimes. And they are at best figures of fun for the rest. Ondřej told me he has decided to quit as our work seems pointless to him. It almost felt to me like betrayal. I don't know who they could replace him with, but I know I won't feel like working under someone I don't know.

The day before yesterday I was alone all day at work and spent the entire time doing my horoscope on the computer. Surprisingly enough I didn't turn up anything earth-shattering. As far as work was concerned, it made sense. I feel something similar to Ondřej and know I'm bound to leave sooner or later. But how am I to explain the calm constellation in respect of Kristýna? Either she'll come back to me and things will continue, or our relationship wasn't the cataclysmic event I took it to be. It started and came to an end in order to make way for what is yet to come.

Yesterday I bought a large bouquet of red roses and waited for Kristýna outside her surgery.

She was taken aback when she caught sight of me. I had the

feeling she'd sooner turn round and find somewhere to hide. But she came up to me and said hello. She refused the flowers and also refused to go and sit somewhere with me. So we walked a little way along the street together, with me holding a bouquet of flowers like a jilted suitor.

I tried to explain that I had had no intention of being unfaithful to her; it had just happened. Věra had come looking for me and I didn't have the strength at that moment to send her away. I'd never pretended to be a saint or a monk, I had simply succumbed to the moment. I agreed that I'd acted spinelessly; my father would have behaved much better in my place, but I promised I'd never behave that way again.

She told me I was maybe stupid or naïve, but she didn't like spineless people, even though she knew from her own experience that most men would have acted the same way. And one certainly couldn't trust the promises of spineless individuals, of most men, in other words. She knew she'd never be able to trust me again, and what was the point of love if it wasn't based on trust?

I asked her if she would have loved me if I'd denied everything.

'I'd have been able to tell anyway,' she said. 'And then I'd have regarded you as a liar on top of everything else.'

I'm not a liar, I'm a idiot. So now I'm on my own.

6

Whenever the phone rings I get a stabbing pain next to my heart. I'm frightened to breathe until the caller speaks.

On the way home from surgery I see children running out of school and I try not to think about the fact that my daughter isn't studying and I don't even know whether she'll return to school or whether she'll even manage to return to normal life. But so far she hasn't tried to run away again. On the contrary, she wrote me two letters in which she sounded repentant and preached to me about how we did things all wrong in the past. *You were terribly impatient with yourself, Mum, so you were unsatisfied with yourself and you couldn't love yourself.* I hear the therapist's voice in what she writes. But maybe she's right. Maybe they're both right. I ought to be more patient with other people and myself.

Towards evening the phone rings and an unfamiliar female voice comes on the line. The name she gives means nothing to me either. But it isn't someone from the drug treatment centre. It turns out to be my ex-husband's neighbour. She apologizes and informs me that the postwoman tried unsuccessfully to deliver a registered letter to him. 'Your husband doesn't happen to be in hospital again, does he?'

It's a long time since my husband was my husband, I don't tell her, and I don't know whether he might have been taken to hospital. But if he was, I wouldn't necessarily know about it; nobody would inform me.

'But someone in the house would have been sure to see an ambulance if they'd taken him away,' the neighbour assures me. 'I just wondered if you could take the trouble to come over and unlock the flat in case something has happened to him.'

'But I don't have any keys.'

'You don't? But I thought . . .'

'You should have called his last wife. She'd be more likely than me to have them.'

'I don't know her. I've never heard about her. He only spoke about you. And I've also seen you here.'

So my ex-husband was talking to neighbours about me. Whatever could he have told them?

'So what am I to do, if you don't have any keys?'

'I don't know whether anyone else has a set. I've never asked him.' I've never wanted the keys to his flat, even though he offered me a set a long time ago.

'Oughtn't we to call the police? After all, he has been very ill, as you know.'

I promise to call the hospital where he was last treated. And if he's not there, I'll let her know.

'But maybe if you could come over, doctor. You are a doctor and probably the person who is nearest . . .'

My ex-husband isn't in the hospital and they have no news of him.

I dropped by to see him three days ago. He was very weak. He drank a little sweetened tea, but refused to eat anything. 'I won't be around much longer,' he announced. 'I know it, but I don't have the strength to fight for my life any more. And in fact it's all the same if one dies now or in a few days' time.'

I felt sorry for him. I knew how much he liked life and winning. I sat down by him, took his gaunt hand and stroked it.

He burst into tears. Then he said he was sorry for how he'd treated us. 'I was a selfish fool. I left you both in the lurch, but now I've paid for it.'

'Don't distress yourself. There is nothing that can be done to change it now anyway.'

'Do you think you could forgive me?'

I told him that the pain had already gone away and that I was grateful to him for all the nice times we had had together. And I was also grateful to him for Jana. And it was not for me to forgive anything. Only God could forgive.

'God! I've been thinking about him,' he said, 'these past few days. God isn't what people thought him to be. God is time, or time is God. He created the sun, the earth and life. He is eternal, infinite and incomprehensible.'

I walk up to his flat and try ringing the bell. But there is no sound from inside. The neighbour who phoned me opens her door. 'Do you think he's inside, doctor?'

As if I knew.

'Maybe he's just had a turn and isn't able to come to the door. He's not been going out at all lately.'

I tell her that the best thing would be to call the police.

'You mean I should?'

'You're his neighbour. You know more about him than I do.'

She asks me to accompany her and stay there with her. I am a doctor after all, and the mother of that lovely little girl.

So I sit here in a stranger's flat while the neighbour calls the police. I sit here and know that it would be wrong to get up and leave now. The woman makes me a coffee and when I ask if I may smoke, she brings me an ashtray. There's nothing we could have a conversation about so instead she tells me about my ex-husband, how he took care of the grass in front of the building, how he once helped her change a tyre on her car, and while he was still fit, he would always help her upstairs with her shopping.

He never helped me up the stairs with the shopping. He didn't want to have a spoiled wife.

There is no sign of the police. The neighbour rings again and they tell her they have no one available at the moment because they have had to go and deal with a case of mugging. We are to be patient.

Even the police are asking me to be patient now.

We drink another coffee. The neighbour offers me a pastry, but I'm not hungry. She asks me whether I mind if she puts the television on.

I don't mind moving pictures, even though I don't watch them at home.

I'm only half a doctor, as I always say, but even if I didn't know the first thing about medicine, I'd know that the man in the flat next door will never come to the door again.

Eventually two policemen turn up, and they have a locksmith with them. They want to know who we are and if we're sure there's someone inside.

We're not sure but it is safe to assume there is.

It's a safety lock, so it will have to be drilled out. The locksmith wants to know who will pay him for the job.

The neighbour looks at me – after all I am his former wife – and I nod.

The older of the policemen has another try at ringing the bell, and lets it ring with bureaucratic perseverance. Then he lets the locksmith take over.

It only takes a few minutes to drill out the lock and then the door opens and I catch sight of the famous certificates hanging on the wall of the front hall. No one feels like going in.

'Maybe you ought to, doctor,' the older of the policemen suggests.

I open the sitting-room door and I see him straightaway. He is half-lying, half-sitting, supported by one of the couch cushions. He looks like a wax cast of himself. My first, only and now forever erstwhile husband. His dead eyes seem to look straight at me. I really didn't think I'd be the one to close his eyelids.

7

Luckily I didn't get my head shaved, they only shaved Monika because she led me on. I had to chop a whole wagonload of wood and I could forget any leave passes. And even so they all acted as if they were showing us mercy by letting us go on rotting here. Monika cried over her lovely black hair every evening when she took off her headscarf and saw how they'd turned her into a skinhead.

'We were stupid cows to have stopped in the stupid pub,' she kept on saying over and over again. 'If only we'd gone straight to my aunt's where we could already be by now.'

'Or in clink,' I told her. 'If the cops had nabbed us God knows where they'd have shoved us.' And in spite of the wood-chopping it's quite cool here sometimes.

Anyway the boys didn't let me do it all, particularly Pavel. When he was going past he gawped at me for a moment and then said, 'Give it here,' and he took the axe off me. He had hands like a bear, if a bear had hands, and he chopped more in a minute than

I would have in a fortnight. I expect he was a bit in love with me, because he was totally nice to me and when we were doing mutual assessment in the group, he kept saying how great I was 'cos I was cool and I made fantastic potato soup and 'cos I was a gas. When I was feeding the sausage dogs in the sty the other day he came up behind me and put his arms round me and wanted to kiss me. But I was scared because sex is strictly banned here, the same as every kind of dope. I would have quite liked him; he's a quiet sort of guy, not one of those bigmouths that are always rabbiting on, and when he started doing magic tricks he had one of those David Copperfield smiles. He made me take a card and he guessed it was the king of hearts. 'He deliberately planted it for you, you daft cow,' Monika said, 'because the king of hearts means love.'

The other day this little guy came that Radek had asked to give us a talk – 'for a change'. The little guy didn't talk to us about dope but about fertilizers and all the stuff that the rain washes into the rivers and then we drink the toxins or use them to make soup. He was also big into dry latrines and thought they were the future of mankind. I asked him how it was supposed to work in an eighteen-storey tower block, but he didn't bat an eyelid and said that the tower blocks would all fall down soon and anyway dry latrines can be built anywhere, all it needed was to arrange for our shit to be carted away: he called it 'excrement'. When he left we were completely gobsmacked the whole evening. We hadn't had such a gas in ages. Radek was pissed off 'cos we didn't take it serious enough and said that if we realized all the things that go into our water we'd be crying and we ought to give a thought to where we're all heading.

Mum sent me a letter in which she writes that she and Gran were missing me and she hoped I'd stick at it and not run away again. She also says she's found out something that she isn't sure she should even tell me, but she did anyway. Apparently she's discovered she's got a half-brother – which makes him my half-uncle,

I suppose – and he's in a wheelchair because he dived in the river and banged his head on a rock or something. It was a real shock for me. She'd read about it in some old letters of Granddad's; she didn't have a clue about it before then and Gran still hasn't and Mum says I'm not to mention it in front of her. She says the reason she's telling me is so I should realize how marvellous it is that I can run around and that I'm totally fit, and it's up to me what I make of myself and all the tosh about how I mustn't destroy myself. I found that rich coming from her, who is systematically destroying herself, as Dad used to say.

That letter fairly knocked me out. It made me realize that people are vile by nature, as Monika says. I remembered how Dad ran off to live with some fucking beanpole and then she left him and then Mum finds some half-brother of hers in a wheelchair. Maybe one day I'll discover some crippled half-brother that they didn't tell me about, except that I won't find out for another hundred years. And I'm vile too: I didn't tell Mum that I nicked her chain and that ring, or that I was shagging boys.

And I also realized I haven't the foggiest idea what I'll do when I finally get out of here, because I flunked at school and now I'd even fail in the subjects I just squeezed by in because anything that accidentally got stuck in my memory has been well and truly dislodged since I've been here. Life is simply horrendous.

I was suddenly in a crisis and I had this immense urge for a fix or to at least get drunk, even though getting drunk never really appealed to me. I told Radek about it and he said my crisis was natural and was an obvious sign that I wasn't completely cured yet. He said it would be amazing if I didn't have cravings like that from time to time. And he praised me for not being afraid to talk about it even though he doesn't usually praise anyone, at most he makes a little grin. He also told me to be patient; patience was the important thing and also looking around me and discovering the nice things in life. That didn't do much to cheer me up, because when I looked around me I couldn't see anything that was particularly nice.

But then that evening, out of the blue, Radek came to me and told me to come outside with him for a moment. So I went. We just climbed a little way above the farm from where there's a fantastic view of the entire landscape, with Blatná on one side and those hills that are almost mountains above it and on the other side the Temelín nuclear power station. The moon happened to be shining and I imagined that those towers were like space rockets ready to fly to it. But Radek wasn't looking at the scenery, he was looking up at the sky and he said, 'That's a lot of stars, isn't it?'

'Yeah,' I said. 'You can see them fantastically from here.'

Radek said there are billions of billions of them, but most likely they are all without life. Life is the biggest miracle and it doesn't matter whether you believe God created it or whether it just evolved, it's still the biggest miracle that has ever happened. And if you don't have respect for that miracle inside you, you can't have respect for the life around you, and the tragedy is, he said, that people don't have respect for themselves and destroy themselves and everything around them. Our job is to carry that miracle of life forward.

At that moment I remembered Dad showing me Saturn and its rings and telling me about the Big Bang. But Dad talked to me about the stars so that I would learn about them and he looked at me sternly and I was afraid he'd want me to repeat after him how narrow the rings are. I realized that Radek wasn't talking about the stars at all, but about me. It struck me that it was a shame he wasn't my dad, but then he said, 'Your mum called a little while ago to say that your dad died.' And he stroked my hair and told me to be brave.

We stood there a bit longer. I couldn't say anything. Then I ran down the hill but at one point I tripped and fell into the grass. I didn't know what to do and I started to pull the grass up by the roots and stuff it in my mouth until I almost suffocated.

CHAPTER SEVEN

1

I am driving Jana home so that she can attend the funeral. She has got over her dad's death and I'm afraid she quite welcomed an excuse to get a break from the centre's military-style discipline for a little while at least. She's so besotted with herself that she hasn't the time to think about anyone else.

In the course of her psychotherapy sessions she has learnt to think and talk about herself without qualms. She tells me how terrible she used to be. She informs me that she first tried smoking cigarettes when she was twelve and grass when she was thirteen, and for almost the whole of last year she was injecting or sniffing everything there was. She also slept with boys and she can't even remember them all because they didn't mean anything to her.

'You really slept with them?'

'Of course, Mum.'

'Since when?'

'I don't recall any more.'

I feel a stab of pain in my head and then the pain spreads to my whole body. Everything ahead of me starts to wobble and the road becomes a blur. There goes my little girl; there she is lying and squirming. Just a little girl, not fourteen yet.

I pull up in front of some country pub in case I ran over my little girl.

We get out.

'Mum, you're white as a sheet. Are you all right?'

'It'll pass,' I say. I feel like screaming and demanding the names of those bastards, then I'd get hold of a pistol and shoot the lot! And I'd save the last bullet for myself for being such a rotten mother.

We are sitting in a bar-room that is already full of smoke at this time of the morning and drinking lousy coffee. I'd like her to give me a moment to get my breath back, but she is unstoppable.

'In the end nothing else mattered to me,' she says about her drug-taking. 'I was even prepared to steal. We systematically stole everything we could: from shops, from the market. I stole stuff from you too, but you know about that. And then I couldn't care less about anything, whether I went to school or whether they caught me and locked me up. I didn't think about anything that was going to happen on a particular day, just about getting my fix.'

I know about it from hearsay and films, and I've read about it, but the thought that my little girl went through all that and that I lived alongside her and suspected nothing and refused to entertain the possibility, that I even left her on her own so that I could be with my lover, hurts me as if someone were driving nails into me. I'm still the same as I always was. I wait here motionless and unprepared until someone places the nail against my chest, raises the hammer and strikes. In exactly the same way I refused to accept that my former – and as of now, late – husband was unfaithful to me. I tried to convince myself that nothing like that could happen to me, that such misfortunes only happen to other people.

My little girl goes on to describe to me the horrors of abstinence and how she was ready to run away the whole time. 'But now I can appreciate,' she says, using a word that is out of character for her, 'that I was only wanting to run away from life and escape everything that was bothering me. At home and at school. Everything. And also I'm beginning to understand Dad and you. I'll tell you both about it some time.'

240

'You won't be able to tell Dad any more.'

'But I can tell you. I'll analyse you. You're the person who matters most to me. When you appreciate what you're doing wrong and understand your weak points, you can live differently and be happy,' she says, repeating the lecture she has just heard.

When we arrive home she rushes into her bedroom, leaps on to the divan and shouts, 'My old bed, my old Bimba, my old drum kit – I've really missed you!'

'The times you could have been here,' I tell her, 'you couldn't leave the house fast enough.'

'Because I was unhappy here,' she explains.

I hug her. I hold her tight. My little girl, what made you do it all; I loved you so much, after all; I didn't have anyone else; I don't have anyone else but you.

While we're getting changed she assures me that only now will she be able to appreciate me for what I am and appreciate being at home. She talks quickly, as is her wont, and with the same earnestness as when she asked a moment ago whether she should take a red ribbon instead of a black one.

We call in for my mother on the way. She notices that my eyes are red from weeping and comments that the man isn't worth my tears after ruining my life.

We ruined our own lives, I don't say to her.

At the crematorium the master of ceremonies sits the three of us in the first row of benches. Alongside the coffin, which I chose, there lie three wreaths. One is on Jana's behalf and one was sent by his old school. The label on the third one has curled up and I can't read it. Maybe someone loved him after all towards the end of his life and sent him a wreath.

The principal of the school, where my former husband, now in a coffin, taught until recently, steps up to the lectern. He makes a bow to the catafalque and then with fervour starts to declaim about a man who loved his profession and sacrificed his spare time to his pupils, who was always reliable and never harmed anyone.

My mind goes back to the last conversation I had with the man I once loved and admired and who strangely is now lying in a coffin that I chose; now he knows nothing about those of us who have been left here a divine blink longer – out of the kindness of passing time.

Did he discover something important at the end of his life that he wanted to share with me, something I could even tell our daughter? Time in place of God, Time that is eternal, infinite and incomprehensible. Does that mean we ought to pray to Time?

Except that time is indifferent to our fate. Time is awful but it is also the only just thing in the world. It lets us reach places like this where we are finally levelled. But before we end up here we can experience something and do something with our lives and it leaves it up to us what we do. It lets us ruin what we like. Time or God, it makes no difference what we call it.

The organist now plays the opening passage of Ryba's Christmas Mass – I had to bring a copy of it, because it's not in the usual funeral repertoire. I close my eyes and lean against the white wall of the Rožmitál cemetery. My one and only husband is standing next to me, alive and smiling at me: 'Why so sad, Kristýna?'

I'm not sad, I'm just dreadfully tired.

2

I'm already in bed when the phone rings.

Mum asks with a frail voice whether she's woken me up.

'Are you all right, Mum?'

'I don't know,' Mum says. 'I've got one of those heavy nose-bleeds again and it won't stop.'

I panic and tell her I'll be right over and in the same frail voice Mum apologizes for bothering me.

Blood is waiting for me as I open the door. It is on the front hall floor and on the carpet in the bedroom where Mum is sitting on her bed, deathly pale.

One oughtn't to treat one's relatives. I place some ice on the nape of her neck and tell her I'm taking her to hospital. Mum tells me she's not going to any hospital; if she's going to die, she'd sooner die at home.

'What are you talking about, Mum? People don't die from nosebleeds.'

'You can die from anything.'

'If you have a mind to.'

She tells me she doesn't have a mind to and says she's feeling better already. The nosebleed came on when she was asleep and she just panicked a bit when she saw all the blood around her. She is sorry she bothered me.

I know it would be hard to persuade her and anyway it really does look as if the bleeding is stopping. So I go and make her a cup of tea at least, and stir in a few spoonfuls of honey. Then I wipe the blood off the floor, change Mum's bed linen and help her into a clean nightdress.

'I'm not keeping you, am I?' she frets.

'No, don't worry, I didn't have any other plans.' I sit down by her and take her hand.

'Not even a date?'

'Not even a date.'

'But I expect you're wanting to get on with some work.'

'I've had enough work during the day. Now I'm going to stay here with you.'

'You don't have to. I'm better now.'

'I'd be on my own at home anyway.'

'I know,' Mum says. 'But what sort of company am I for you?'

'The best, Mum.'

'You don't have to pretend anything to me. But you oughtn't to be on your own all the time. Not now that Karel's gone.'

'Mum, you've forgotten that we've been apart for years.'

'I haven't forgotten. But you waited for him all the same.'

I don't feel like talking about it. I don't feel like talking about anything.

'It's a long time since I did.'

'Exactly. You've been on your own too long. Everything's on your shoulders and it's wearing you out.'

'I'd sooner be on my own than have someone hanging round my neck.'

'Do you mean that young man you told me about?'

'I didn't mean anyone in particular.'

'And what about him? Does he love you?'

'I don't know.'

'Can't you tell?'

'I think he still loves me, or at least he fancies he does, but he doesn't always act as if he did,' I say. 'But, Mum, you should be getting some rest and not worrying about me.'

'I have to worry now. I don't know how long I'll be around, do I?'

'You'll be around for a long time yet.' I go over and plump up her duvet. 'Lie down now and don't think about anything. Rest, you've lost lots of blood.'

'No, wait a minute. But you don't want to get married, do you?'

'Mum, marriage is the last thing on my mind. It's enough that one bloke left me.'

'You can't get that man out of your mind. But someone else wouldn't leave you, or if he did, he'd come back again, like your father.'

'What do you mean, like Dad?'

'Before he died he asked me to forgive him all his mistresses.'

'He told you he'd had mistresses?'

'I knew anyway. I even knew about that son of his. People came and told me about it.'

I remain silent. I don't know what to say. Then I ask her, 'Why didn't you tell us about it?'

'It was his business to tell you. Maybe it's just as well you didn't know, seeing that he stayed with us and didn't leave the home.'

'Maybe *you* should have left home.'

'I thought about it, but I was afraid to. Dad was a powerful man; I thought he would protect me.'

'Who from?'

'In case the Germans came back again.'

'Mum! The Germans weren't a threat any more. It was the Russians who came.'

'I wasn't scared of them.'

'And that's why you didn't leave?'

'And because of the two of you. Besides, I loved him. He could be nice.'

It strikes me that my mother has never known a nice man. Have I? Maybe nice men are figments of our imagination.

'Besides, I didn't want a divorce after what happened to my mother.'

'But they were different times.'

'I know. But people ought to stay together. Anyway it was your grannie who suggested the divorce. Or at least that's how my father told it. She knew what his business meant to him. She only pretended to move out; she stayed with us.' Mum starts to reminisce: 'I remember at home how they used to make beautiful flowers out of leather, cloth and wire. I used to sit there with Mum and she would talk to me and tell me Bible stories, for instance. She guessed we wouldn't be together much longer. After all, she'd studied law, so she must have known about those Nuremberg Laws.'

I'm aware that Mum has never talked about her mother's life, only about Grandma's awful death.

'And she also talked to me about the Jewish festivals, such as the Day of Atonement. People are supposed to forgive even those who have done them wrong. You see, I can remember it after all these years. But I wasn't able to forgive my father as long as he was alive. Then I had a bad conscience about it. You have to take people the way they are, with all their faults and their selfishness. If you don't you get left outside.'

'Outside what?' I ask, although I know what she means.

Maybe she doesn't even hear me; she's tired. We both are. She closes her eyes and says nothing for a while. I am still holding her hand. 'So I forgave your dad,' she adds, 'and you should too. You'll feel much better, you'll see.'

3

On the way home from Mum's I find myself in front of Čapek's villa, although I wasn't conscious of taking that route. It is quiet and locked up as usual, but there are a few cars parked on the little square; drops of rain are starting to drum on their bonnets.

It crosses my mind that in a few weeks' time it will already be the sixtieth anniversary of my favourite author's death. He was a brave man and he suffered from ill health. When he was my age, he had less than four years left to live. When he was my age he wrote: *People have a piece of crystal inside them, something smooth, pure and hard, that won't mix with anything and will allow everything to slide over it.*

I'd love to have a piece of hard crystal inside me and let all my pain, my disappointments, my despair and my loneliness slide over it.

When I get home there is no one waiting for me. And no one will ever be waiting to take me in his arms and caress me. And if Jana comes home, how long will she stay? And what about my first and only husband? For all those years I subconsciously waited for him to ring the doorbell and say, Sorry, Kristýna, I've done you wrong, but I've found out that it is hard to live without you! But my first and only husband will never ring the doorbell now. And what about Jan, who says he loves me, but was unfaithful to me the first opportunity he had? Should I make it up with him

and simply accept that life is like that: betrayal, desertion and forgiveness, and those that don't accept it, suffer?

I pour myself some wine and put on Tchaikovsky's *Pathétique*.
Let the music weep instead of me. Even though I'm on my own,
I'm not the only one who found life hard to live.

I oughtn't to drink. It's ages since wine gave me a boost or
improved my mood. It adds to my weariness, more likely. Instead
of wine I ought to take Nortriptylin or some other antidepressant.
It's just that I don't like the idea of Prozac euphoria.

I sit in the armchair and sleep overcomes me: now I'm lying in
a meadow in tall, dry grass; above me there are clouds and beneath
them a wisp of smoke, too late I catch sight of a flaming figure
tearing towards me. And behind it there are flames. I won't escape
them. The end at last. I feel no fear. I am paralysed, so totally
alone, the way you feel at the moment when flames start to engulf
you and you haven't the strength to run away.

The doorbell.

The ghost of that crazy incinerated aunt has come back to take
me with her.

I'm afraid to answer the door and ask, 'Who's there?'

But it's Jan; he is standing outside with water streaming from his
soaking hair. He is carrying a suitcase.

'What are you doing here?'

'Don't send me away,' he begs. 'I have to tell you something.'

'Is it still raining out?' I ask stupidly.

'I expect so,' he says. 'I didn't notice.'

'So what do you want to tell me?'

'I've moved out of Mum's place.'

He has moved out. His mother noticed that he was down in
the dumps and in the end she managed to get out of him that he
is in love with me and that all is not well between us. He also told
her about Jana, and his mother made a scene and started to shout
at him that he had no sense, so he packed a few things and walked
out. He just wanted to let me know.

I don't know what to reply. He's had a row and tomorrow he'll regret it, but I don't want to send him out into the rain at midnight. I go and make some tea and tell him to take off his wet clothes. I even offer him my sweater, but he has his own clothes in the suitcase. I'm sorry for him. I'm touched. Maybe he really does love me and he won't repeat what he did. And I almost certainly love him still.

I make him up a bed in Jana's room. He looks disappointed but accepts it meekly.

I'm unable to get to sleep. I ought to think about the fact that I have my ex-lover in the flat. And whether 'ex' is still appropriate. All I need to do is give him a hug. Get up and join him in his bed – like his other 'ex' did. I ought to think about why he came and whether it isn't just another of his well-choreographed games – a way of finding his way in here. I ought to think about what I'll do when we get up in the morning. Instead I am simply aware of my weariness and helplessness, and my fear of betrayal.

I fall asleep towards morning. I dream that I'm at Grannie Marie's farm at Lipová. She has given me a cup of milk and some bread and butter to take to Auntie Venda. I took them to her, but when I wanted to leave I discovered that in place of a door, there was just a narrow opening in the wall. I realized I wouldn't be able to squeeze through it. I'd be stuck for ever in this room with my mad aunt, and she'll set light to herself and me. And I tried desperately to squeeze through the crack.

That dream is generally interpreted as a memory of one's own birth, but it was more a dream about my situation. I'm shut inside my solitude and I'd like to break out, but I've shrunk the exit and can't. And maybe it's an image of myself, I'm no longer as slim or supple as I used to be. I'm getting fat; I can't get into clothes I used to wear two years ago. How could anyone still enjoy looking at me, let alone make love to me?

In the morning Jan and I have breakfast together. He has to leave for work even before me.

'You don't want me here, do you?' he asks.

I don't know whether I want him here or not. I'm frightened of taking any decision. I'm afraid of the disappointment that might result. I wasn't able to hold on to a man who was a divine blink older than I was and with whom I had a child. However could I hold on to this young fellow with whom I haven't conceived a child – and won't now?

He waits for my reply, so I tell him he ought to go back home. I don't want us to regret in a few days' time that we acted hastily.

He points out that he isn't acting in haste. He knows he loves me and he believed, still believes that he can convince me of it, if I manage to forgive him.

I say nothing and he says he'll move in with a friend for the time being.

He picks up his case and as he is going out the door I give him a kiss after all.

Maybe he won't come back again. In any case, the day would come when he wouldn't come back, even if I told him I forgave him. Everything comes to an end one day, including life itself.

I briefly collapse into an armchair. From where I am sitting I can't see into the street; all I can see are the roofs of the houses opposite and the sky which is beginning to cloud over again. The clouds are splendid, like dolphins hurling themselves up out of grey water. Rain is on the way.

If it starts to rain, that boy and his suitcase will get soaked again.

4

At night I have oppressive dreams. In them I'm searching for Jana, who has run away somewhere in the middle of a blizzard. I am looking for her on skis and getting hopelessly lost in snowdrifts. I know I'll freeze to death but I don't care; the only thing that terrifies me is that I won't find my daughter. I dream about my late husband; in the dream he is alive and in love with me; he holds me in his arms and assures me that he'd die without me, he loves me so much. In the dream, I'm happy to hear him say it, although I wake up feeling wretched. I'm even visited by the grandmother that I only know from photos, the one who was gassed: she is amazed that I don't recognize her. 'Just imagine,' she says, 'they took pity on me and let me come back again.'

Back again means back to life. I can understand that.

But the little messenger never lets anyone come back to life.

And where am I, in fact?

I've aged five years in the past six months.

I'm intolerant and don't like myself. I started snapping at Eva in the surgery because I had the feeling she was taking her time every time I needed something from her.

I feel like my ex-husband when he was stricken with a terminal illness. Maybe my soul is being eaten away by a tumour.

Maybe I'm my own illness.

I baked Jana some heart-shaped biscuits; I borrowed the mould from Mum and wrote my daughter a long letter in which I told her I was sure things would be fine between us when she came home. We have to discover together why it's good to be alive.

She called me two days later: 'Hi Mum, it's me.'

'I can tell.'

'How are you?'

'Not bad. And how about you?'

'Thanks for the biscuits, Mum. They took a rise out of me, saying they were better for me than purple hearts. But they were great, and they weren't even slightly burnt. We've already scoffed the lot.'

'I'm glad you liked them.'

'We shared them out. Slávek said you must be great. Most of the people here have parents who couldn't give a damn about them.'

'Thanks for the appreciation. What news do you have for me otherwise?'

'I'm fairly used to it here now, Mum. Sometimes we even have great fun. Really. There's something rather special about looking after a goat, for instance, and drinking its milk, even though it tastes horrible. And Radek said he was pleased with me too and said you could already come on a visit.' She talks a little while more about the merits of life at Sunnyside and then gets alarmed that her call has already cost a lot of money; so she quickly wishes me all the best and asks me again to come and visit her, and to my amazement suggests I bring 'that ginger man' of mine along.

I promise to come and ignore the reference to my ginger man.

I've also had a phone call from the man I had discovered to be my half-brother. He asked me whether he could come and see me; he had something for me. I told him he could and asked if I should drive over for him.

No, he would get here under his own steam. All he needed to know was what floor I live on and whether there is a lift in the building.

'I live on the third floor and there's a lift which works most of the time.'

So he turned up on Saturday afternoon. Some elderly lady brought him; I asked her in but she said she had something to attend to in the meantime.

My brother cruised around the flat as if he'd been doing it for years. 'You've got a nice place,' he said. 'Plenty of room. I like the rubber plant. I can tell you look after it. I expect the drum kit belongs to your girl, doesn't it?' He peeped into Jana's room. 'Where are you hiding her?' he asks.

'She's out of Prague.'

'A pity, I'd like to meet her. After all, she's my niece, isn't she? I don't have any relatives on my mother's side. I haven't met your sister yet either. When it comes down to it, I've never known what it is to have a family. Mum was almost always out and she scarcely said anything when she was home.'

I offered him some wine, but he said he'd sooner have tea with a drop of rum, or preferably a hot toddy.

I went into the kitchen to make the toddy and he followed me in. 'I've brought you something,' he announced. He rummaged in his wheelchair and drew out quite a large object wrapped in paper. 'I painted you a picture,' he explained. 'When you came to see me, I said some stupid things; I'm a bit strange sometimes. But I didn't want you thinking I'm like that all the time. Aren't you going to open it?'

The painting is a portrait of me; I can't tell what sort of a likeness it is; I'm not used to lip-reading my image in the language of colours. What caught my attention most was that in the picture I am surrounded by flames.

'You've committed me to the flames like a witch.'

'No,' he said, 'not at all. Those flames signify passion. You seemed passionate to me – full of energy that could burn up everything around you.'

Good gracious, I thought, this weary old woman?

I thanked him for the painting and told him it was interesting. I poured the hot water on the rum and then told him about the aunt who burnt herself to death. After all, she was his aunt too.

Afterwards he talked to me about his youth and how his mother was indomitable and went on loving my father and never lived with anyone else. My half-brother was once in love too. She was a student nurse. Then came his fateful dive. She used to visit him in hospital and afterwards, when he was back home. She stood by him for several years until eventually he told her not to waste her life.

My half-brother told me in a faltering voice the story of his accident, no doubt for the hundredth time: all about the single dive that changed his life for ever. Then he asked me if I had some photos of his father; his mother had just one, and it had been taken forty years ago.

I took out the box of photographs and selected some with Dad on them, both alone and with us. Dad as a young man and in old age; Dad in a blue shirt and red scarf wielding a pickaxe on some socialist labour brigade; Dad at the rostrum; Dad at some celebration where the Comrade President pinned on him a medal for services to the Communists' betrayal; Dad just before his death.

I gazed at him, Dad's unacknowledged son, as he examined these static faces and I waited for some movement from his thin, severe lips. But my brother said nothing and returned me the final photo.

'So that's what he looked like,' I said. 'You needn't regret not knowing him. Life with him wasn't easy.'

'I can well imagine.'

'He left his mark on all of us. And lots of others too. You're not the only one he wronged.'

My brother finished his toddy and nodded. 'He hurt my mother most of all. But that's the way it goes: people hurt each other; that's something I discovered. It's a sort of chain reaction. You hurt me, so I'll hurt you back,' he said, sharing his personal philosophy with me. 'The people who don't are the ones who get hurt most.'

I recalled how he'd tried to hurt me, but since the day I visited him he hadn't sent me any threatening letters. It's easiest to hurt those we've never seen, although we most often hurt those who are nearest to us. But it isn't a chain reaction of tit for tat, simply the result of our selfishness, an expression of our bewilderment in the face of life.

The lady who brought my brother rang the downstairs bell. She refused to come up and asked me to wheel my brother into the lift; she'd be waiting for him downstairs.

I thanked him once more for the painting and for paying me a visit. When I opened the lift door for him, I leaned over and kissed him on the lips. His breath smelled of rum, but even so it reminded me of Dad's, although I couldn't recall when my father last kissed me.

5

I went back home to Mum's last week. Mum behaved triumphantly although she had no reason to. I hadn't come to eat humble pie, I simply had nowhere else to live. I had moved a few of my things to Jirka's and slept there for almost a month, but I knew it was no solution. I had hoped against hope that Kristýna would forgive me and I would move into her place, but when I saw how hesitant she was, I realized that that was no solution either. And I don't earn enough to rent a flat of my own.

Kristýna and I have met a few times and had dinner together: once it was a cold supper at her place, and on about three other occasions I invited her out to restaurants. Since the night I admitted to her that Věra came into my tent we haven't made love. I don't think it's just on account of my one stupid moment of vacillation. Kristýna seems to have changed; she seems to have lost the enthusiasm she once showed for everything, and which attracted me to her in the first place. She keeps on repeating that she is tired. I told her she needed to take it easy and take a holiday, but she said it was world-weariness and no holiday would rid her of it.

She ought to realize that it is weariness due to the sort of life she leads.

Not long ago we were walking up some stairs together and I noticed how breathless she was. 'Don't be surprised,' she told me. 'My lungs are full of tar.' She also drinks more than she should. When I was still sleeping at her place from time to time, she would pour herself a glass of wine first thing in the morning. No wonder she's tired.

I still pine for her, but our occasional meetings haven't seemed to be getting anywhere; they have lacked any climax: we don't embrace; we talk but we no longer touch each other, not even verbally. We are becoming cooler to each other, or at least I am, although I regret it.

Today was Friday the thirteenth; I went to work fearing the worst. My fears were vindicated. First thing this morning our new director called me in and told me they would have to dispense with my services. He had received an order to reduce staff levels and I was the youngest. I wouldn't be the only one anyway, so it would be a good idea to come to a gentleman's agreement before he drew up a dismissal notice.

As if youth could be a reason for dismissal anyway. We both know the real reason, of course. I had tried too hard to do my job properly and unravel what could be unravelled.

I told him I'd have to think it over, but I don't think I feel like resigning voluntarily and going quietly. As I was saying it to him, I knew that on principle I wouldn't give in, even though I have no longing to spend the rest of my life in the place.

As soon as I left the director's office I got on the phone to Jirka at the radio.

He promised to send one of his female colleagues over to see me. She is apparently the most astute member of their political staff.

She called me straight after lunch.

We arranged to meet at five o'clock this evening at a restaurant near the radio building.

She was younger than she had sounded on the phone and her face seemed slightly familiar. I told her so as soon as we sat down in the restaurant and asked her whether she didn't also appear on television.

'No,' she said, 'you know me from somewhere else. If you remember, that time in November, nine years ago, we were both sent to Ostrava to win over the miners.'

Of course I remembered. But there were quite a few of us in the group, so we didn't really notice each other. I started to apologize for not recognizing her.

'But it's ages ago. I also have different-coloured hair, a different hairstyle, and I'm fatter and older.'

I told her the colour of her hair suited her, that she wasn't at all fat and she didn't look a day over twenty.

'You're a real gentleman,' she said and smiled at me as if I were an old friend from the good old days.

I was glad we had previously met under those circumstances; I felt I could be more open with her than if they had sent any old member of staff.

I tried to fill her in briefly on the job I am doing and explain that there must be a lot of people who would sooner I stopped delving into their pasts and revealing their past crimes.

She took notes and told me they would definitely invite me to the studio next week to take part in a interview about this business, although she was doubtful that it would help me keep my job. The opposite most likely.

'I'm not worried about my job. I always enjoy a change.'

'So do I,' she said. 'Life would be boring otherwise.'

So we started to chat about our lives since. She was surprised I was still single; she had already managed to get married and divorced.

Our conversation started to stray beyond the usual bounds of discretion. She complained about her bad experiences with men, whom she found selfish and boorish, while I spoke about the anxiety I feel about emptiness, which undermines my ability to get really close to people. I didn't mention Kristýna.

For the first time in ages I could hear the rumble of tom-toms in the distance and it set my blood racing. Several times during our conversation my hand touched hers and she didn't move hers away.

It occurred to me to ask her if there might be a job for me in the radio, in case I really was dismissed; I told her I wasn't an absolute beginner and had earned extra cash by writing articles on the side.

She was sure I'd find something there: she told me the radio was an enormous funnel for collecting people. It wasn't hard to get in but it was hard to find a niche. She added that it would be nice if we were to become colleagues. She stood up; she unfortunately had a rendezvous to go to.

The mention of a rendezvous aroused an almost jealous curiosity in me, but all I said was that we would definitely see each other soon.

She asked for my telephone number and gave me hers, at work and also at home, in case I didn't catch her at the radio. She told me she was looking forward to meeting me again, so it was fine that we'd see each other the following week.

Most likely she says something similar to everyone she is about to make a programme with, but I was sure she also expected something more from our coming meeting than just an interview, so her comment thrilled me as if we'd just made a date.

In the evening I phoned Kristýna.

I expect she was afraid I wanted to pay her a visit because she started to complain about her tiredness.

I asked her what her plans were for tomorrow.

She said she was driving down to see Jana.

'It's good that you'll get out.'

'You can come with me if you like,' she said to my amazement.

I wasn't sure I wanted to, but the fact is we've never been anywhere together and I'll have a chance to tell her what happened to me at work. It also occurred to me that she might be letting me know that we belong together after all, even though I'm beginning to think that we'll never belong together.

6

I am driving fast, as is my wont. Jan is sitting next to me and looking pleased. I don't know what came over me to invite him to come with me. I am afraid he'll misinterpret my invitation. But I'm not entirely sure myself how I intended it. As an act of reconciliation or just as a joint trip to see Jana, since we took her to the detox centre together?

I can't say what I really want. I don't want to be cruel to the boy; I don't want to hurt him; I don't want to set off that chain reaction: you hurt me, now I'll hurt you. I don't want to hurt him, but I can't be sure that he won't hurt me. I don't know how he perceives me at this particular moment. I rather get the impression that he's wandering elsewhere in his thoughts and moving away from me.

We reach Sunnyside before midday.

They tell us that Jana is out in the forest with the rest and will be back in about two hours' time.

We could set off to find her in the forest, but instead we set off in the opposite direction. Half an hour later we come upon a group of isolated homesteads set around a picturesque fishpond and then we make our way up to a hilltop along a field track. There is a break in the mist and the autumn sun actually tries to warm us slightly. To the right of the path there is forest: the larches have already turned yellow and they seem to glow in the sunshine. To our left there is a freshly ploughed field with fragrant upturned soil.

Going uphill is a struggle for me and I find it increasingly hard to catch my breath, but I try not to let it show. Luckily he's in no hurry. He tells me that it looks as though he'll be given notice at work. He asks me whether he ought to fight it or whether he should quit the job now that he is beginning to feel it's a waste of time. One possibility would be to finish his university course, but he would also like to make use of what he found out over the years by writing it up and publishing it. Not on his own account, or not entirely so. He has the feeling that forgetting the past, as most people in this country do, is a dangerous phenomenon. But if he left his job, he probably wouldn't find anything as well paid. He could also try to work as a freelance for the press or the radio; he has some friends there and it is the sort of work that appeals to him.

It strikes me he's telling me this partly because he is still considering living with me and therefore feels a certain responsibility to me. I tell him that if one is given half a chance one should do something one feels like doing and what one regards as useful.

Maybe it suits him that I'm older; I know more about life than he could know; he needs someone to approve his life's decisions. His mother has probably fulfilled that role so far, but men who aren't able to free themselves from their mothers tend to feel humiliated.

You never know what you mean to other people, only they do, but usually even they aren't able to say for sure.

We finally reach the hilltop. A chapel stands a short distance from the footpath. It looks abandoned and the path to it is overgrown with untrodden grass.

We trample the grass slightly. The chapel is empty: in the place of a sacred painting or statue there is simply a mouldy patch on the wall, but on a small, battered table there stand two blue vases.

Two blue vases; I stand and stare at them in amazement, as if someone had deliberately placed them there on my account. What is the point of two empty vases in an empty chapel without even a painting on the wall?

One for blood, the other for tears: I can hear my old lament.

We stand there motionless for a moment. We don't pray; we don't speak; we listen. I don't know what this place says to him, but no doubt something different from what it says to me. I can suddenly hear the voice of my father, clear and hard, as I knew it when I was small and feared him, when I longed for his love. I hear him, but can't make out the words. Most likely he came to ask why I broke the vase that time. Or he came to save these two abandoned ones? But what if he came to let bygones be bygones?

You have to speak more distinctly, Dad.

But he has fallen silent and isn't coming or speaking any more.

I'd like to hear at least the voice of my once and only husband, whose love I also yearned for, but he won't be coming or saying anything any longer.

In fact all you yearn for is to hear that someone loves you, but generally you don't hear it; most likely they were just words intended to deceive you. When you realize that, you either despair or try to find something to bring comfort.

It doesn't, anyway.

So life comes to an end and time closes behind everyone and everything.

My ex-husband understood that and tried to escape by running away from it. I reminded him of time, being younger than he was, so he ran away from me too. Eventually he bowed down before Time as the Creator God. And he didn't even run away from me: I was the one who closed his eyes in the end. I recall how sad and lonely his death was and I feel like weeping over him at this lonely spot.

And I feel like weeping over Dad. It occurs to me that neither of them were happy; they didn't know how to live with what they had; they wanted something other than what life offered them. They lacked humility. I do too: I couldn't be reconciled with them, nor with my life, therefore. One ought to be capable of reconciling oneself with people, even if one can't reconcile oneself with their deeds.

I glance at the young man standing at my side. He came to me at a moment when I no longer expected anyone or anything new in my life, and he told me over and over again that he loved me. He didn't act as if he did, or at least at one moment he didn't; he didn't even try to deny it, but I couldn't reconcile myself with his deed.

I don't know for what fraction of a divine blink he'll stay with me, it doesn't matter. I don't know how long I'll last, how long I'll be capable of loving; maybe my fatigue will defeat me; maybe I'm no longer capable of coming close enough to someone to live with them. But I won't torture myself with it now; I'm grateful for this moment, for the time he'll still stay with me maybe.

I suddenly hug him of my own accord; I kiss him in a chapel where there is nothing but two empty vases. I don't do or say anything else. And we rush away.

'We'll pick up Jana first thing this afternoon.' He looks pleased and looks forward to her going out to dinner with us.

That afternoon, we drive into town and Jana tells us, with an enthusiasm that I'm afraid to believe unreservedly, how she is beginning to understand that she was on the wrong track entirely and how it happened to her. Last week they took part in a discussion session at some school where they told the children what they had been through and how dreadful it was.

'What about the children?'

'They were totally knocked out,' my daughter says proudly. She is thrilled about learning to understand herself and everyone around her. And me too.

'Do you think you understand me?'

'Yes, I'm really beginning to understand you.'

'I wonder.'

'Understanding isn't the same as agreeing.'

'I never thought it was.'

'I'll analyse you and teach you to have an opinion about yourself. You'll be surprised,' she promises and then starts to talk about her friends who, like her, are learning to understand themselves – 'and when they start to analyse themselves they suddenly end up this tiny!' and she indicates how tiny by a gap between the tips of her thumb and forefinger that a ladybird would scarcely squeeze through. Jan laughs at her, but I can recall her disobedience and stubbornness, so I have the feeling that she really is starting to get somewhere. I promise to let her explain to me how to acquire an opinion of myself.

We sit down to dinner in a fairly decent-looking pub. After lengthy consideration, Jana chooses some oriental dish with rice and some disgusting dark liquid in a narrow bottle. We also choose something and so as to show solidarity with the other two, I order fizzy water instead of wine, for the first time in ages. But they don't notice anyway, they are having a great time together. They almost speak the same language. They like the Spice Girls and know some Varusa or Marusya May who plays the electric violin, and agree that Ms — or is it Mr — Björk sings as if she or he had a mouth full of dried snot. They have even seen the same films and both despise television. Jan asks whether they play any games too, and Jana says they play chess, although she doesn't like the game, and they also play draughts and Ludo. Jan promises to come and teach them to play other games.

I look at the two of them and listen to them chatting away. They're relaxed and it's quite a different conversation from any I've ever had with Jan.

When Jan leaves the table for a moment, Jana quickly says, 'Mum, he really suits you.'

'What makes you think so?'

'Well, you sort of complement each other. You're sad and he's cheerful. And you've got blue eyes and he's got brown.'

'I'm also old while he's young.'

'And you're both nuts.'

An unexpected commendation.

7

On Sunday Mum flew in like an early bird almost before it was light and we hadn't even had breakfast yet.

I was surprised she came on her own, but she explained to me that Jan had had to leave the previous evening because he was going to do an interview with the radio about what happened to him. Mum said she was pleased we'd have a bit of time to ourselves. And she went to see Radek — to give me time to have breakfast in peace, she said. I'd love to hear all the guff that Radek gives her about me.

Monika started to yell from the yard that our pig had eaten my hen. The black one. 'Well, for a start, the hen isn't just mine but also ours and why shouldn't it eat it, seeing it's an omnivore,' I yelled back at her. But it was the marten anyway. All that was left of the hen that I had to look after was a few black feathers in the yard. Horrendous.

Then all of a sudden Mum appeared and looked cool so I figured that Radek must have sung my praises.

When she and I came out of our sunny Graveside, I suggested to Mum that we look in at the church.

'Do you people go to church here?'

We didn't go to church much, but the idea just occurred to me, seeing it was Sunday and Mum had come to see me. And Mum says, 'Why not? I haven't been to church for ages.'

So we went to the local church, which was fairly pathetic – almost no pictures, just some angels flying about on the ceiling chucking some poor devils out of heaven. Only heaven was full of rusty patches where water dripped from the leaky roof.

It was packed inside – at least seven old ladies and a gypsy family with a baby. In the church that Eva used to take me to sometimes I liked the singing, the ringing of bells, the incense and the servers, especially one who had great big ears. The servers here were totally normal, but the priest was ever so young and pale and really, really tiny; I bet they took the mickey out of him when he was at school. He was so touched that we'd come to his church he couldn't get over the shock and kept tripping over his words. When the singing started he sang really out of tune, but in the end you couldn't tell 'cos at least six out of the seven pensioners sang out of tune too. I quite liked the priest; I just felt sorry for him being stuck on his own in that empty church and not even being allowed to get married or have kids. And I imagined what he'd do if I came and told him I fancied him, if he'd like me to stay and keep him company.

Then he started preaching about some Saint Francis, saying he'd been really poor and humble and patient and when they wouldn't let him into some pub or monastery when he was cold, wet and hungry he was ecstatic. I wouldn't be ecstatic about it, I was ecstatic from dope, and I'm really curious to know what I'll be ecstatic about when I get out of here, and if I'll actually manage to keep it up.

I hate preaching 'cos it's too clever-clever and a drag. So I just kept thinking about what was going to happen when I leave this place. I imagined rushing to school again every morning even though it doesn't do anything for me, and I couldn't imagine who I'd find to talk to if I never saw Ruda and the others any more, just because they're still on dope.

Then we all said Our Father who art in heaven and at that moment I thought of Dad and wondered if he was in heaven. But he didn't believe in it; he believed in the Big Bang, when there wasn't a heaven or an earth, nothing just that little marble that everything came out of. And how could the poor old guy be in heaven, seeing they'd put him in a furnace and burnt him?

It only hit me the night that Mum drove me back here after the funeral that maybe I behaved badly towards him, because I always thought it was vile the way he left us in the lurch. But maybe he didn't really want to. Sometimes Mum would really make him unhappy when she had her downers and didn't want to talk to anyone; she couldn't even work up a smile; and when she came home from the surgery she'd just sit in an armchair and smoke and drink her wine. He tried to talk it over with her and he'd do everything that needed doing at home. He'd say to her, Give us a little smile, Kristýna, but it was pointless and so in the end he ran away. And I also imagined the flames licking round him when they closed the curtains in the crematorium so we couldn't see, and all of a sudden I was so sorry for him that I started to cry. Monika woke up and when she saw I was crying she says to me, 'What are you bellowing like a cow for, you stupid cow?'

So I tell her my dad had died and they've cremated him and she immediately calms down and says, 'Oh, your old man died. Pity we haven't got a fix.' But we didn't have anything and anyway I've decided it'll be better not to go back on it.

At the group session the next day Radek said it was good that I was sad and cried 'cos it's a way to make things up with Dad and I won't be tempted to do anything silly to spite him. And it also means I've made it up with Mum, because I hated her always thinking about Dad and blaming herself instead of accepting that that's the way life is.

Mum looked touched somehow in that church, even though she didn't sing or cross herself; but when the rest knelt down she did too and bowed her head. Mum's got a lovely head and neck. I'm not surprised that ginger bloke who's been going out with her since the spring is gone on her. I'd fancy her too. And he fancied me when we were chatting together last night; it was cool and from time to time he made eyes at me, but he always made sure Mum didn't notice.

As soon as the Mass was over we scarpered, but Mum said she was glad I'd taken her to church and that she was going to take me somewhere too and show me something. She drove me to the pond: actually it's more like a big dirty puddle and round here we know it as the Stink-hole. A footpath runs from there up a horrible steep hill. Mum must have been in a great mood or she'd have never climbed a hill like that. All the time she looked as if she was about to tell me something important, such as she was going to marry Jan, but she didn't say anything. So I just kept her amused by rabbiting on about what things are like here. Such as last week we had our first fall of snow and when I was already in bed the lads started yelling that they could see the aurora borealis outside and I must come out and see it before it disappears. So I ran out into the snow barefoot and they start taking the mick out of me like mad for falling for their crap about the aurora borealis. And I told Mum how I look after the hens and ducks, and how I'll happily go and work on a farm after Radek says I'm cured or, even better, go and help people in need – people like me, for instance, when I almost ruined my life with dope. I also told her I realize now what a pain I was, but I really did hate school and there was nothing I enjoyed. Even at home it was horrendous sometimes.

Mum asked if I missed Dad that time, and I said I did at first but that she missed him more and for much longer, and that had really pissed me off.

We kept climbing upwards with the forest on our right. Two old lady mushroomers were coming out of it as we passed. There are loads of magic mushrooms around here and I never knew before you could trip on them, but Monika used to get stoned on them and she was so smashed on them that she thought she was a goner.

'Yes, I do admit,' Mum said, 'that I was fed up from time to time, but you have to realize that it's like an illness, sometimes I couldn't help it when I had a depression. And sometimes there was even a good reason.'

So I explained to her that she always saw the bad side of things most of all. Me and Radek talked about it. I said she probably didn't have positive thinking and before I started getting on her nerves, there was Dad and before him my granddad. And his opinion was that that explains lots of things to him, and he said she herself had told him that she was destroying herself, and how she had played up her father the way I'd played up Dad. It's really horrendous the way everything repeats itself, even the totally stupid things.

'You say really nice things about me, the two of you,' Mum says, 'but otherwise your analysis was very good.' She keeps looking as if she wants to tell me a secret, but in the end she just points to some old ruin in front of us and says, 'Do you see that chapel? I want you to see inside.'

When we reached it, the ruin looked even more pathetic. It was completely empty inside, even emptier than the church earlier; there was nothing inside at all except for a little table with crooked legs and on it two vases covered in bird crap or something. There weren't even any flowers in them. I couldn't figure out what Mum wanted to show me there.

'Look,' says Mum. 'There are no saints or angels. Just two vases and nothing else.'

I could see that, but I still couldn't understand why she was showing it to me. Probably because it looked sad to her, all abandoned and ransacked.

But Mum said she was there the day before with Jan, and while she was there she realized that it isn't important what people built around themselves. In that place you could feel more than in some church full of pictures and sculptures. She said she now knew that it's up to people to learn how to hear everything that speaks to them and above all themselves; that was the most important thing. And she also said she knew she'd been awful and yelled at me, but in fact she wasn't yelling at me but at something inside her, because she couldn't come to terms with the fact that life is the way it is and she is the way she is.

That really knocked me out. Plus the fact she looked so cool. I wasn't used to that any more. I just wonder how long it's going to last.

We stood there for a few more moments and I remembered Dad. What would it be like if he was here with us too? Maybe he'd look cool too and be happy that he's here with us and not on his own, the way he was at the end, when he had nothing left, not even the little marble that made all things seen and unseen. It's really strange how people aren't able to stay together and are rotten to each other. I wanted to tell Mum I love her, but when I glanced at her she looked really moved and she was whispering something to herself, as if she was praying, only she never prays. Maybe she was singing something to herself, such as the song about the midge, which wasn't really about a midge at all but about how great it is to be alive. I didn't want to disturb her so I didn't say anything.